Near the ice-cold creek, Lane stopped dead in his tracks, paralyzed with fear. An Indian had burst out of the woods behind his partner and was running toward the man, his tomahawk raised.

Lane tried to yell a warning. It came out an incoherent yelp. His partner looked at him, a querulous look on his bearded face. But then he heard the Indian behind him and whirled. He raised his bloody skinning knife, dropping into a crouch. He dodged the downswing of the axe, ducking under it and planting a shoulder in the redskin's breadbasket. As he heaved the warrior over his shoulder and sent him splashing into the creek, a rifle spoke from the trees. The bearded trapper crumpled, shot in the back.

Lane turned and ran, as bloodcurdling war cries split the clear spring air.

BATTLE OF THE TETON BASIN

① SIGNET

SAGAS OF THE AMERICAN WEST
BY JASON MANNING

☐ **HIGH COUNTRY** A young man in virgin land. A magnificient saga live with the courage, challenge, danger, and adventure of the American past. (176804—$4.50)

☐ **GREEN RIVER RENDEZVOUS** Zach Hannah was a legend of courage, skill, and strength . . . Now he faces the most deadly native tribe in the west and the most brutal brigade of trappers ever to make the high country a killing ground. (177142—$4.50)

☐ **BATTLE OF THE TETON BASIN** Zach Hannah wants to be left alone, high in the mountains, with his Indian bride. But as long as Sean Michael Devlin lives, Zach can find no peace. Zach must track down this man— the former friend who stole his wife and left him to die at the hands of the Blackfeet. Zach and Devlin square off in a final reckoning . . . that only one of them will survive. (178297—$4.50)

*Prices slightly higher in Canada

Buy them at your local bookstore or use this convenient coupon for ordering.

PENGUIN USA
P.O. Box 999 — Dept. #17109
Bergenfield, New Jersey 07621

Please send me the books I have checked above.
I am enclosing $_____ (please add $2.00 to cover postage and handling). Send check or money order (no cash or C.O.D.'s) or charge by Mastercard or VISA (with a $15.00 minimum). Prices and numbers are subject to change without notice.

Card #_____ Exp. Date _____
Signature_____
Name_____
Address_____
City _____ State _____ Zip Code _____

For faster service when ordering by credit card call **1-800-253-6476**

Allow a minimum of 4-6 weeks for delivery. This offer is subject to change without notice.

Battle of the Teton Basin

High Country, Volume 3

by

Jason Manning

A SIGNET BOOK

SIGNET
Published by the Penguin Group
Penguin Books USA Inc., 375 Hudson Street,
New York, New York 10014, U.S.A.
Penguin Books Ltd, 27 Wrights Lane
London W8 5TZ, England
Penguin Books Australia Ltd, Ringwood,
Victoria, Australia
Penguin Books Canada Ltd, 10 Alcorn Avenue,
Toronto, Ontario, Canada M4V 3B2
Penguin Books (N.Z.) Ltd, 182–190 Wairau Road,
Auckland 10, New Zealand

Penguin Books Ltd, Registered Offices:
Harmondsworth, Middlesex, England

First published by Signet, an imprint of Dutton Signet
a division of Penguin Books USA Inc.

First Printing, February, 1994
10 9 8 7 6 5 4 3 2 1

Copyright © Jason Manning, 1994
All rights reserved

Cover art by Robert Hunt

 REGISTERED TRADEMARK—MARCA REGISTRADA

Printed in the United States of America

Without limiting the rights under copyright reserved above, no part of this publica-
tion may be reproduced, stored in or introduced into a retrieval system, or transmitted, in any form, or by any means (electronic, mechanical, photocopying, recording,
or otherwise), without the prior written permission of both the copyright owner and
the above publisher of this book.

BOOKS ARE AVAILABLE AT QUANTITY DISCOUNTS WHEN USED TO PROMOTE PRODUCTS OR
SERVICES. FOR INFORMATION PLEASE WRITE TO PREMIUM MARKETING DIVISION, PEN-
GUIN BOOKS USA INC., 375 HUDSON STREET, NEW YORK 10014.

If you purchased this book without a cover you should be aware that this book is
stolen property. It was reported as "unsold and destroyed" to the publisher and neither the author nor the publisher has received any payment for this "stripped book."

for Jody

ACKNOWLEDGMENTS

The author is indebted to the following works: *Entrepreneurs of the Old West* by David Dary, for descriptions of Fort Union and St. Louis, as well as other aspects of the fur trade; *Life on the Mississippi* by Mark Twain, for information on steamboat travel on the Mississippi River; Josiah Gregg's *Commerce of the Prairies*, written in 1842 by a man who spent nine years on the Santa Fe Trail; *Jim Bridger: Mountain Man* by Stanley Vestal and Frances Fuller Victor's *The River of the West: The Adventures of Joe Meek*, for descriptions of the epic 1832 battle at Pierre's Hole.

Chapter 1

Josey Lane was a trapper. For almost a year he had been employed by the American Fur Company. Having come west the previous summer, he had survived his first winter in the high country and was therefore, by most standards, justified in calling himself a mountain man.

Oh, and what a winter it had been! Lane had never seen the likes back home in the red hills of northern Georgia. It had been so cold that the creeks froze clear to the bottom and bank to bank. Trees cracked in two. Critters floundered in deep snowbanks and died. So cold that the spittle froze on a man's whiskers, and his fingers would freeze to the barrel of his rifle or the blade of his knife were he so greenhorn—careless as to allow that to happen. So cold that at times Lane could have sworn the blood was frozen solid in his veins.

Doc Letcher, the brigade's booshway, had told him something about an invincible summer in the heart. Quoting some Greek poet. Or was it Roman? Lane couldn't rightly remember which. How had Letcher put it? Something like how in the bleakest winter of life a man had to find that invincible

summer down deep inside himself if he wanted to
survive.

Letcher was a puzzlement, mused Josey Lane as
he sat on his heels, rifle cradled in his arms, at the
rim of a cutbank, above a purling creek that danced
down the heavily wooded slope of a mountain in the
Absaroka Range. Letcher talked like a schoolteach-
er, or a politician. Real educated. Used fancy words,
and was always quoting poets and such. Read books,
which, in Lane's opinion, since he could neither read
nor write a lick, was really something.

Yet in spite of all that fancy talk and book larnin',
Doc Letcher was as tough as they came. He'd been
in the mountains for years. He knew it all. They
called him Doc not because he was a medical man,
but because one day, having taken a Crow arrow in
the thigh, he had calmly used balsam sap and a poul-
tice of beaver skin to close up the wound. He still
carried the arrowhead in him. That was the thing
about mountain men. Minor wounds—in other
words, all wounds that were not fatal—were treated
in a cursory manner if not ignored altogether.

Yes, Letcher knew his way around the *pays d'en
haut,* as the French Canadian voyageurs called the
high country. He had tangled with grizzlies. Had tangled with Indians, too. Which was one thing Josey
Lane had not done. Not yet anyway. He figured he
would, though, sooner or later. It was just bound to
happen, did a man stay out here long enough. Lane
dreaded the day and looked forward to it at the same
time. To be an Indian fighter—now that was really
something. Lane's pa had fought the Creek Red
Sticks with Andy Jackson. His pa had also declared

him to be a lazy, no-account shirker, because Josey Lane hated farm drudgery with a holy passion. It was due in large measure to this difference of opinion concerning Josey's worth that had compelled the youngster to head west and engage in the glamorous adventure of fur trapping.

Of course, he had found out there wasn't that much glamour in the business after all. Proof of that was his partner, Doc Letcher's brother, Hampton, wading up to his waist yonder in the creek. The sky was clear blue and the spring day sultry, but this creek was glacier-fed, and the water was bone-biting cold. Hampton was checking their traps. Mountain men always worked in pairs. All sorts of disasters could befall a trapper, and his chances were made a little better if he had company. One man watched while the other toiled. Lane and Hampton took turns, and Lane always preferred keeping an eye peeled to getting his feet wet in some icy stream.

Lane looked off up-creek, where the water came gamboling down the mountain through the towering conifers, cascading over jumbles of smooth rock. A magpie was winging from tree to tree, and the flash of black and white had captured Lane's attention. He yawned. The song of the creek and the soughing of the wind in the boughs of the evergreens, the air as clean and sweet as wine in the lungs, and the sun warm on his back made him drowsy.

"Wagh!"

Lane turned his attention back to Hampton. The latter had found brown gold. He was hauling drowned beaver, trap and all, to the opposite bank, a stone's throw downstream. A full-grown beaver could weigh sixty pounds, and this one looked every bit of that. But Hampton was a burly character. On dry land he commenced to skinning the beaver.

The pelt, bait gland, and tail was all he would retain. The skinned and mutilated carcass would be returned to the creek. The pelt would be scraped by one of the camp-tenders—in this brigade's case, two Flathead squaws—then stretched on a willow hoop and set in the sun for a day or two before being folded with the fur inside. Once eighty or so "hairy banknotes" were collected, a pack was made up, utilizing a scissor-press of wood and rawhide. The castoreum would be extracted from the bait gland, and the rancorous orange-brown fluid stored in a horn vial until needed to bait a trap. The tail would be charred over a fire and then boiled for good eating, or basted with wild goose oil, if such was available. It was the only part of the beaver worth eating, unless you were starving. Beaver meat had to be soaked in water for a short forever, and then heavily seasoned with gunpowder, just to render it barely edible.

Lane stood and stretched the kinks out of his legs. He figured to wander across the creek to see what kind of pelt they had harvested. If it was especially fine—a "plew"—it might bring six or eight dollars, if the market this year was anything like last year's. Of course, the company realized the lion's share of the "take." A mountain man's percentage of the pelts he brought in was enough to pay for powder and shot, some whiskey and tobacco, and maybe some trinkets for his squaw, if he had himself one to warm his blankets and mend his buckskins.

So Lane figured he had a vested interest in the condition of the beaver skin—enough of one anyway to warrant wading that ice-cold creek. He was especially interested in acquiring some trinkets, and with such foofaraw, enticing some young Indian maiden into becoming his squaw. Being young himself, not quite yet eighteen, Josey Lane had never known a woman, and he was ready for the experience.

Then he stopped dead in his tracks, paralyzed with fear.

An Indian had burst out of the woods behind Hampton and was running toward the trapper with his tomahawk raised.

Lane tried to yell a warning. It came out an incoherent yelp. Hampton looked up at him, a querulous look on his bearded face. But then he heard the Indian behind him and whirled. He had set his rifle aside to skin the beaver—all he had in hand was the bloody skinning knife. This he raised, dropping into a crouch. He dodged the down-swung tomahawk, ducking under the swing and planting a shoulder in the redskin's breadbasket. Then he straightened up and heaved the warrior over his shoulder. The brave splashed into the creek. Hampton turned to finish him off. A rifle spoke from the trees. Hampton went rigid, then crumpled, shot in the back.

More Indians emerged from the cover of the woods. The warm, clear spring air rang with their bloodcurdling war cries.

Josey Lane turned and ran.

Chapter 2

They had tethered their horses a hundred yards upstream, having decided to work their way down the creek to check the seven traps set in this particular stretch. The horses were Lane's destination.

He did not even consider using his rifle or the pistol in his belt. Flight alone occupied his thoughts. His skin crawled, as though a thousand invisible graybacks were swarming all over his body. Hampton Letcher was dead. Wasn't he? Lane threw one wild look back. He immediately wished he hadn't, because he looked in time to see one of the Indians bend down and, with a few deft strokes of a knife, lift Hampton's scalp. The brave held his bloody trophy aloft and uttered a horrible, guttural scream of triumph that chilled Lane to the bone marrow. The young trapper made a strangled sound. Completely unnerved, he stumbled on.

Two warriors broke cover upstream, on the same side of the creek. They blocked his escape.

Lane fetched up. The pair of Indians started for him. They were yelping like wolves on the heels of a wounded elk. So were the ones behind him. Lane looked back again. A few of the braves were crossing the creek to get to his side. Most, though, were coming up the other side at a loping run and were about to draw abreast of him. Several more, apparently, were rustling around in the brush to his right. He couldn't see the latter, but he heard them yelping. All he could do was take to the creek. He jumped off the cutbank.

It was his hope to land on his feet, but the current was too swift and swept his legs out from under him. He went under and lost his grip on the rifle. He was slammed against a submerged rock. The impact knocked the the breath out of him. He choked down some water. He was drowning! In a panic he flailed to the surface, gasped for air, but gagged on the water in his gullet. Vision blurred, heart racing, he stumbled forward, fighting the current. He kept thinking about the horses. Once mounted he could escape these fiends. Letting the current sweep him downstream did not even occur to him. My God, how many of them were there? Some lookout he was, letting a whole war party slip up on him and poor Hampton.

The waist-high water conspired against him, and he cursed it, struggling to maintain his footing, striving to make some headway. Suddenly he was out of the main channel. Now the water was only knee-high. Now he could make better progress. They were all around him, those screaming savages. Why didn't they shoot? Lane thought suddenly about the red clay hills of Georgia and sobbed.

Ahead loomed a daunting obstacle—something he had been aware of before the attack, but since had forgotten all about. The creek was flowing over and between a line of boulders that blocked his path. Lane tried to clamber up these water-smoothed rocks. He clawed at the slippery granite, to no avail. He couldn't make it. Wheezing, he turned at bay, his back to one of the boulders. It was deeper here, at the foot of the falls—the water came up to his chest. As an afterthought, he dragged the pistol out of his belt. Of course, it was perfectly useless now. The powder was wet. Why didn't they just kill him and be done with it? With sickening despair, Lane knew he was doomed.

But the Indians were still on the banks of the creek. They were taunting him. Laughing at him.

Josey Lane got mad then.

It was bad enough that he had to die. But by God they didn't have to laugh at him while they killed him!

The fear left him. In its place came a cold and defiant hatred for those red devils. He waded out of the creek. As he approached the bank, the Indians stopped laughing. They watched him warily, weapons raised. Most of them had rifles. Why didn't they use them?

"Go on and shoot!" he yelled, so angry he choked on the words.

Not one of them fired. They weren't sure what to make of him, realized Lane. It was his turn to laugh. Not a very good laugh, but it made him feel a little better. Sloshing out of the creek, he headed for the nearest warrior. Five paces away he stopped and raised the pistol, aiming at the Indian's head.

The warrior, and several others, fired simultaneously.

One of the bullets pierced Lane's heart. He was dead before he hit the ground.

Josey Lane died better than he had done anything else in his tragically brief life.

Through the morning mist they came, on mountain mustangs barely half-tame. There were three of them. Doc Letcher was in the lead, as usual. Leading was something Letcher was accustomed to. He had that self-confidence others looked for in their leaders. He made quick decisions, and they were usually the right ones.

He was a tall, lean man, with eyes as blue as glacier ice and hair black as the ace of spades. Unlike most mountain men, he kept himself clean-shaven. With his sun-darkened complexion and longish raven-black hair and grime-blackened buckskins he looked more Indian that white. Except for those keen blue eyes, which saw everything and moreover understood the true meaning behind what they saw.

Letcher's burnished bronze face was set in grim lines as he reached the creek where the water fell over the row of boulders. His horse snorted, the smell of death invading its flaring nostrils, and performed a nervous dance. With a firm hand Letcher brought the animal under control.

"Jaysus," breathed one of his companions, both of whom had checked their ponies alongside Letcher's.

The man who spoke was named McLeary. A redheaded, red-faced Irishman who, in Letcher's opinion, drank too much and swore too much and talked too much. He wasn't very bright, either. Letcher came across few men out here who were his equal in intellect, and he made an effort not to appear condescending when dealing with his colleagues.

"It's young Lane," said McLeary, staring at the body across the creek.

"Yes," said Letcher curtly. He wanted to tell McLeary he had been blessed with the gift of good eyesight and could tell for himself that it was Joseph Lane. Anger and grief were a violent rising tide within him, but he endeavored to keep his emotions in check. Because he knew at this moment that what he had been dreading since last night, when Hampton and Lane had failed to return to the brigade's camp, was true.

If Lane was dead, his brother was bound to be, as well.

"Injuns," muttered the third trapper, a man named Elias Turner. "They took his topknot."

But they didn't hack him to pieces, mused Letcher, trying to think in a detached, clinical way. They hadn't stripped the corpse and opened it up and scattered the guts all over the place. They hadn't cut off the private parts, or cut off all his fingers, or carved out his eyes with the tip of a knife.

Indians often mutilated corpses in that way, when consumed by blood-craze. But, save for his scalp, Lane had been left untouched. Why? The boy obviously had impressed his foes with his courage. It wasn't easy to earn the respect of Indians. They mutilated what they despised. Lane had earned preferential treatment, then, by dying well. For that, at least, Letcher silently congratulated the lad.

"Where's Hampton?" wondered McLeary. "You figure he's gone beaver? He must . . ."

He stopped abruptly, because Letcher's cold blue eyes were boring holes right through him. The Irishman realized sheepishly—and with a strong dose of fear—that as was so often the case, he had spoken without thinking. A bad habit, which would one day get him killed.

"Come on," rasped Letcher, and took the lead.

He paused a little farther along the creek, dismounting to kneel and study the ground. McLeary and Tucker kept to their saddles. Mounted so, they could see the moccasin prints in the dirt. Indians— but of what variety? Letcher would know. The man knew it all. He could *smell* an Indian a mile off and tell you what tribe the red devil belonged to.

Letcher stood. "Blackfoot," he said bleakly, looking around, scanning the woods.

The other trappers looked around too, their faces twin testaments to the fear that Letcher's grimspoken word had lanced into their hearts.

"Maybe Hampton got away, Doc," offered Turner, but the others could tell by his tone of voice that he didn't believe it possible.

"My brother's dead," said Letcher bluntly.

"The Blackfeet used to be our allies," said McLeary, plaintively. "Hell, Doc, we work for the American Fur Company, don't we? Don't that count for nothin' anymore? Don't we give them guns and firewater and such?"

"It doesn't cut us any slack with the Blackfeet. Not anymore. Not since Sean Devlin delivered the plague to Whirlwind's village up on the Judith River, winter before last."

"You sayin' Devlin's to blame for this?" asked Turner.

"He is, damn his soul," said Letcher through clenched teeth. " 'Murderous, bloody, full of blame.' " As Shakespeare's words left his lips, a cancer of vengeance clawed at his guts. "And he's going to pay for what happened here. Credit where credit is due."

"But he's long gone out of the high country," said Turner.

"No matter. Wherever he is, I'll find him. Letcher climbed back into his saddle. He flexed broad shoulders and took a deep breath. What was done, was done. The dead were dead, and the living kept on living. In Devlin's case, for just a little while longer. "Come on," he told the others, "let's find my brother's mortal remains."

Chapter 3

A fortnight later, Doc Letcher appeared at Fort Union.

As usual, the post was bustling. Back in 1828, Kenneth "Redcoat" McKenzie had expressed his intention of finding "a union at some convenient point" where the American Fur Company could locate a headquarters for the purpose of dominating the trade of the rivers as well as of the mountains. With McKenzie, thought was action. The spot selected was five miles up the Missouri from the confluence of the Yellowstone with that river, where the forlorn ruins of the stockade Major Henry and his Rocky Mountain boys had built back in '23 could still be seen.

The shape of Fort Union as compared to those ruins, mused Letcher, were symbolic of the American Fur Company over the Rocky Mountain Company. The difference, in his opinion, was the fact that the former had the money of John Jacob Astor behind it, and the firm hand of McKenzie on the rudder.

Astor's company had indeed flourished since 1828, and two more posts were planned for this year of '32. Fort Cass would be the first American Fur Company post in Crow Indian territory. The site selected was three miles below the mouth of the Bighorn River on the east bank of the Yellowstone. Fort McKenzie would be raised this spring up above the Marias on the Missouri, closer to the mountains.

When he had first heard of the plans for these new posts, the former, Fort Cass, had most impressed Letcher for what it signified. When the American Fur Company had arrived on the scene, the Absaroka Crows had been hostile to them. There were two reasons for this animosity. One was the established bond between the Crows and the Rocky Mountain Fur Company. The legendary Zach Hannah was in large part responsible for this. The Crows thought highly of him.

This bond had been cemented in turn by the hostility between the Rocky Mountain trappers and the Blackfoot Indians, the arch enemies of the Crows. *The enemy of my enemy is my friend,* thought Letcher.

The other source of Crow distrust for the American Fur Company was a man, a legend of sorts in the high country. Sean Michael Devlin. "Coyote," as the Indian and trapper alike called the notorious Devlin, had slain one of the most popular warriors in the Crow Nation. Rides A Dark Horse. Letcher wasn't certain of the facts behind the slaying. He had heard a number of versions, and knowing how mountain men and redskin both liked to embellish their narratives, Letcher took it all with the proverbial grain of salt.

Devlin had once been employed by the American Fur Company. Back in the days when Vanderburg had run the show for Astor, who sat in his posh New York manor and counted his millions. Vanderburg was gone now—and Letcher thought that was good riddance—and so was Devlin. Now McKenzie ran the field operations. Ran it on his own terms. Not for nothing did they call him the "King of the Missouri."

The Scotsman was impressive. No doubt he was in large measure responsible for the improved relations between the American Fur Company and the Absaroka Crow. It didn't hurt the company in this regard, either, that Devlin was no longer on its rolls. McKenzie could talk the devil out of his pitchfork.

It had been McKenzie, with the assistance of an old trapper named Berger, who had sealed an alliance between the Blackfeet and the company. In McKenzie's opinion, one could not underestimate the importance of that alliance. The Rocky Mountain Fur Company had survived only because of its friendship with the Crows. The American Fur Company could not have lasted long caught between the hostile Crows and the warlike Blackfeet.

Making friends with the Blackfeet had been no easy task. They had declared war to the death against all white interlopers. Some said it was because Lewis and Clark and their bunch of intrepid pathfinders had killed a Piegan horse thief, and the Piegans, like the Bloods, were Blackfoot cousins. Letcher thought it was just Blackfoot nature to war. They warred against the Sioux. They raided the Flatheads and the noble Nez Percé. And they had traded blows with the Crow Nation for generations, long before the arrival of the first "hairface" trapper.

The only time the Blackfeet tolerated anybody else

was when they proved themselves of value to the tribe. This explained the success of the Hudson Bay Company in trading with them. That was before McKenzie and the American Fur Company had come along. The Hudson Bay men had exchanged guns and ammunition with the Blackfeet in return for the furs harvested by the tribe. The fact that the Blackfeet turned around and used those guns on other whites had not deterred the Canadians one bit. All was fair in love and war . . . and business.

Berger had brought a band of Blackfeet to Fort Union last year, for the purpose of patching things up between the tribe and the company. Devlin's lethal gift of plague-infested Nor'west blankets to a Blackfoot village had made an unholy mess of things. McKenzie had treated the Blackfoot envoys like royalty. They had been hesitant to trust his blandishments. Letcher could scarcely blame them. He had been present during the Blackfoot visit, and he had concluded at the beginning that McKenzie would fail.

But he had underestimated the wily Scotsman.

Because McKenzie had conspired with Berger to escort the Blackfeet to the post at a particular time—the week the *Yellowstone* was due to arrive.

The *Yellowstone* was the company's steamboat, built in Louisville in the spring of 1831. It had been McKenzie's suggestion to experiment with steamboat transportation on the wild and woolly Missouri. Many had scoffed. The Missouri would chew up a steamboat, they said. Company officials were dubious. But when the *Yellowstone* chugged resolutely upriver on her maiden voyage as far as the small company outpost called Fort Tecumseh, in the Dakota Sioux country, and returned with a valuable cargo of buffalo robes, furs, and ten thousand pounds of smoked and salted buffalo tongues, the doubters had become ardent believers. Steam had conquered the Missouri—a feat keelboats could never accomplish.

It was while the Blackfoot delegation had been McKenzie's honored guests at Fort Union that the *Yellowstone* had arrived. As McKenzie had hoped they would be, the Indians were much impressed. There was powerful magic in the "Fire Boat" that could walk on water. Then and there they had decided to accept the good offices tendered by McKenzie and treat once more with the American Fur Company. No longer would they trade with the Hudson Bay men down from Canada. The British might as well burn their sleds and turn loose their dogs, because henceforth the Blackfeet would bring their beaver pelts and buffalo robes to McKenzie.

But something, thought the grim Doc Letcher as he rode through the gate of Fort Union, had gone wrong. The Blackfeet, it seemed, had changed their minds. Perhaps, in the tribal councils held during the long winters, when in the snowbound villages of the northern hinterland the warriors had nothing much else to do besides ruminate and debate, McKenzie and his magical Fire Boat had not seemed impressive enough in hindsight to outweigh the terrible tragedy the Blackfeet had suffered at the hands of Coyote.

McKenzie, mused Letcher, would not be pleased

with the news of the Blackfoot attack on an American Fur Company brigade.

Letcher didn't care. Neither did he care if McKenzie sanctioned his mission of vengeance.

In fact, the last thing Letcher expected was a commission from the King of the Missouri to bring back the renegade, Sean Michael Devlin.

Chapter 4

No other post could rival Fort Union in size and importance. The structure was two hundred forty by two hundred twenty feet. The stockade was made of square-hewn logs a foot thick and twenty feet high. At the southwest and northeast corners were two-story blockhouses made of stone, twenty-four feet square and thirty feet high.

As Letcher rode through the gate he could look straight across the compound at McKenzie's house. The Scotsman preferred to live in a style that was incongruously high by frontier standards. His house was a sturdy two-story structure with glass windows and a big stone fireplace. Within, Letcher knew, were fine furnishings brought upriver on the steamboat.

To left and right, around the compound, were barracks, workshops, stables, and a stone powder magazine that could hold fifty thousand pounds of gunpowder. Most of the structures were well constructed of cottonwood timber. In the center of the compound was a flagpole flying the Stars and Stripes. Around this the breeds and "tame" Indians who worked for the company had pitched their tents, since the white trappers were loath to share their quarters with men of their ilk.

Fort Union was totally self-sufficient. The post's complement included blacksmiths, carpenters, coopers, and other craftsmen. To work for McKenzie you had to demonstrate a skill entirely removed from shooting and laying traps. Beyond the palisade were pens holding cattle and pigs. The horses were kept either within the compound or let out to graze under heavy guard. Corn and other vegetables were raised in a large garden. A well had been put in. So the post had food, water, and plenty of ammunition, and Letcher figured it could withstand a sustained siege.

"Letcher," called one of the gate guards, stepping forward. "What brings you? Where's Hampton? The rest of the brigade?"

Letcher decided that there was nothing to be gained by sharing his news with anyone but McKenzie. Besides, McKenzie would prefer being the first to know rather than the last. Other trappers were converging on the gate. They realized that Letcher's presence without the rest of his brigade meant *something* and they were eager to find out what. But Letcher wouldn't accommodate them.

"Where's McKenzie?"

The gate guard tossed a thumb over his shoulder at the big house. His amiable grin faded as he became reconciled to the fact that Letcher was not going to play their game. Letcher nodded curt and silent thanks for the gate guard's information and rode on across the compound.

McKenzie stepped out onto the long gallery of the big house. He was a black-haired, square-faced man, wearing a tailored brown broadcloth suit, a white, ruffled shirt, and hand-tooled boots. He dressed like a dandy, but there was a brawny strength beneath that fine fabric. Iron determination was etched into the firm set of his wide, thin-lipped mouth. His brows were knit in a perpetual scowl. But his voice was smoothly resonant, and his tone was amiable as he addressed Letcher.

"Hello, Doc. Come in. I have just received a case of cognac from St. Louis. Share a glass with me."

"No thanks. I can make many more miles before sundown."

"What news do you bring me? How fares your brigade?"

"My brother is dead. Joseph Lane as well. Killed by Blackfeet."

A muscle in McKenzie's jaw was working now. He did not bother asking Doc Letcher if he was certain of his facts. Letcher would be. Of all his lieutenants, McKenzie regarded Letcher the most reliable.

Letcher dismounted and stepped up onto the gallery, reins in hand. Face-to-face with McKenzie, they could talk privately. All eyes in the compound were on them, but no man would venture near without a sign from "King" McKenzie that he wished them to do so.

"I am truly sorry to hear about your brother," said McKenzie.

"And Josey Lane. He was a brave young man. He had his whole life ahead of him."

"What of the rest of your men?"

"I left Turner in charge. Told him to gather up all the traps and move south. That war party had left the valley, but there is always the chance they might return."

"I see." McKenzie had a standing rule: no booshway was to abandon his brigade under any circumstances. Letcher had by his own admission willfully broken that rule. McKenzie was a stern overlord who showed those employees reckless enough to commit infractions little mercy.

"I appreciate your coming to inform me of these developments," said McKenzie.

"I owed you as much. Maybe more. But you don't have to walk wide around it. I left them to fend for themselves. Broke your law."

"And do you wonder if I might have you thrown into the guardhouse?"

"I wondered if you might *try*."

McKenzie smiled.

"Under the circumstances, I think I will forgo the dubious pleasure." The Scotsman leaned against a porch upright, thumbs hooked under his waistband, and surveyed the activity of the compound with a narrowed, glinting gaze. "Well, I didna truly believe the Blackfeet would keep the peace with us for long. Peace is not in their nature. That's a flamin' shame, too, Doc, because the best beaver country left to us is in Blackfoot country."

"The beaver will be gone in a matter of years. Then what?"

"Buffalo robes, my friend. The market is growing back east, and even more so in England. In a few years, when the beaver hat is out of fashion, the buffalo robe will take its place. Buffalo tongue, too, will be a delicacy offered by all the best restaurants from

Boston to Savannah. But the robes will be the thing. As you know, the creature carries a good coat only a few months out of the year—the winter months. And only the cows and the young bulls provide the truly fine pelts. Those cold wet winters in the Northeast, not to mention in old Albion, will guarantee the market."

"You are a farsighted man, McKenzie."

"One must stay ahead of the game. And the competition. Bill Sublette, late of the Rocky Mountain Fur Company, and a man named Campbell have been treating with the Sioux tribes for buffalo robes. They trade whiskey for them."

"Whiskey! That's against federal law, isn't it?"

"Aye." McKenzie smirked. "But who is there to enforce federal law west of the Mississippi? I've been trading sugar and coffee for robes, but what Indian wouldna prefer a gallon of cheap liquor to four pounds of sugar or two pounds of coffee for a robe? So I've ordered a still. It will arrive within the week on the *Yellowstone*."

"You're buying into grief," said Letcher, who admired and liked McKenzie and did not care to see the man get into hot water. "What if word gets downriver to Fort Leavenworth that you are running a distillery here? The company could lose its trading license."

McKenzie shook his head. "And do you think that John Jacob would let that happen?"

Letcher shrugged. Arguing with McKenzie was futile. Once the man made a decision he stuck with it. On that you could rely.

"The Blackfeet will come down in force this summer," predicted Letcher. "The land will run red with blood. I suppose a federal law against selling whiskey to the Indians will be the least of your worries this year."

"Aye. They'll come, as you say, for blood this year. Every white trapper will be fair game, Rocky Mountain boy or one of our own."

Letcher could sense that McKenzie was dreaming up some scheme in response to these new developments. On the face of it, no doubt, the scheme would appear outlandish. But that was the way the Scotsman's mind worked, leaping ahead of problems and landing square on the solution. More often than not, the solution was the right one.

"So what will you do?"

"It'll be war. We'll do well to ally ourselves with the Crows—and the Rocky Mountain Fur Company. There are yet a few hundred mountain men who swear allegiance to Major Henry's old enterprise."

Letcher was skeptical. "You think they'd go along with that?"

"It's true, there's bad blood between us. Thanks in no small part to that bloody-minded fool Vanderburg."

Letcher nodded. Vanderburg had sent American Fur Company men out to spy on the Rocky Mountain brigades, and then lead Blackfoot war parties to their trapping grounds. By this treachery dozens of Rocky Mountain boys had perished. It had been a dark and bloody business indeed.

"But I'll send a man to see Bridger," continued McKenzie. "I do not believe anything is impossible, and besides, how does one know unless one tries?

Jim Bridger and Broken Hand Fitzgerald are intelligent men. Perhaps they will see the wisdom of joining forces. Letting bygones be bygones."

"Maybe," said Letcher. "At any rate, I wish you luck."

"You'll be wanting no part of the fight, then? The Blackfeet killed your brother, did they not?"

"Sean Devlin killed him. I can't blame the Blackfeet for doing what they've always done. You always know where you stand with them. The same cannot be said for Coyote. He's to blame."

"I follow your reasoning. But do you think you can take him alone? Devlin's a killer. He did for Mike Fink, if you'll remember."

"Yes," said Letcher dryly. "He has a certain reputation. But it won't save him this time. He owes me his life. 'Revenge is a kind of wild justice.' "

"Francis Bacon. But Bacon goes on to say, I believe, that the more man's nature runs to revenge, the more ought law to weed it out."

"A man is his own law out here. And if it's justice he seeks, he'll find it rests in his owns hands." Letcher stepped off the porch and mounted his horse. "I'll be on my way. Good luck with your war, McKenzie."

"Wait."

McKenzie came forward to take hold of the bridle cheekstrap.

"My guess is that Devlin is back on the Mississippi," said the Scotsman. "That's where he came from. He stole his brigade's packs, you know, and left his men to die at the hands of Zach Hannah and his free trappers. So he is bound to have gone east, if only to find a good price for the plews."

"East is the way I'm headed."

"If you find him, Doc, bring him to me. I'll turn him over to the Blackfeet. Perhaps that will buy us one more season before we have to fight this inevitable war. I need time, to mend the breaks between the companies, and to bring all the mountain men together in common cause."

Letcher thought it over. This was an appeal he was hard-pressed to ignore, he wanted to kill Devlin himself.

"If you say you will," continued McKenzie, "I will tell Berger to inform the Blackfeet. At the very least they will spend weeks discussing it in their councils."

"When I find him," said Letcher coldly, "I'll try to do as you say. Good-bye, McKenzie."

McKenzie was pleased. "Bring Coyote back. The Blackfeet will wreak a terrible vengeance upon him, and your brother's blood will be answered for."

Without another word Letcher turned his horse and rode out of Fort Union.

Chapter 5

Zach Hannah awoke from a night's sleep feeling as tired and achy as if he had climbed through the roughest sort of mountain terrain for days on end.

Dawn light crept through the window draped with calico curtains. He lay alone in the rope-slat bed with its thin mattress of folded buffalo robes. Throwing aside another buffalo robe that served as a blanket, he stood, wincing as he stretched sore muscles and rubbed the back of his neck. A long, lean man with yellow hair long enough to brush his shoulders, and a recently trimmed beard of darker hue on his face, he dressed quickly in dun-colored buckskins. Even in late spring it was quite cold up here in the high country.

Morning Sky had arisen before him. That had become commonplace of late. Zach had little to do these days. He found himself idle, with time on his hands, since severing all associations with the Rocky Mountain Fur Company and bringing his wife and son deep into the remote mountain fastness of the Wind River Range. He did some hunting, and some scouting, the latter to ascertain whether Indian war party or white trapper brigade was trespassing upon his seclusion. Nothing of the kind had occurred for a year now. The Wind River Range was virtually trapped out, for one thing, a fact that had entered into Zach's calculations from the very beginning.

He pushed aside the blanket curtain that separated his and Sky's bedroom from the rest of the one-room cabin built by his own hand last summer. There, in the stone fireplace, crackled a spirited fire. Jacob's bed was empty. Yet there was no sign of Sky or the boy.

Dread stabbed at Zach Hannah's heart. He threw open the door and stepped out onto the porch. Morning Sky was drawing nigh the cabin, toting a bucket of water, just fetched from the nearby creek. The snow-fed stream was born five thousand feet above, a hundred rivulets at the base of the snow-field joining forces to rush down the steep rocky shoulder and cascade over the five-hundred-foot palisade of rugged granite at the foot of which stretched the broad and verdant table where Zach had built the cabin. The creek meandered across the table, resting placidly a moment before plunging over the rim and on down through the tree-garbed flanks of the mountain to the floor of the valley several thousand feet below.

"Is something wrong?" asked Sky.

"No. Nothing. Let me carry that."

She surrendered the bucket, and he carried it inside, placing it on the sturdy trestle table he had made—as he had made every other piece of rough-hewn frontier furniture in the cabin.

He turned to find her standing at the threshold framed against the pink-tinged dawn light, and her beauty almost snatched his breath away. Every day she seemed to him more beautiful. The product of a French Canadian father and a Blackfoot mother, Sky had inherited the best features of both bloodlines. Her complexion was like honey, flawless and smooth as silk. In the sun her black hair had a glossy blue sheen. Her figure was willowy, her features aquiline, and her eyes were the most startling shade of violet-blue.

"You did not sleep well last night," she said.

"Bad dreams. Where's Jacob?"

"Hunting." Sky smiled. "He has set out traps for rabbits, as you have shown him, and he carries the slingshot you made for him, in case he comes across a squirrel."

Zach nodded. Jacob was nearly five, and already knew a great deal of woodland lore. He had strict instructions not to stray beyond a carefully enumerated boundary, and Zach was confident he would not. Still, he could not shake that sense of black dread. He wanted to step outside and call Jacob in. But he refrained, knowing that it was the dream that had rendered him so filled with apprehension. A boy needed a certain amount of freedom, in order to develop a degree of self-reliance as well as self-respect.

Sky moved to the fireplace. She had brewed some coffee in a pot and brought him some in a tin cup.

"We are nearly out of coffee," she said, a gentle reminder.

Again Zach nodded. "And running low on sugar and gunpowder, as well. The rendezvous will be in the Teton Basin a couple of moons from now. Pierre's Hole. I'll go pick up some supplies."

"You have done no trapping this year."

"I still have credit with Bridger from last year's plews."

"What did you dream of?"

He considered trying to avoid the matter. But there was no good way of doing it, not without hurting Sky's feelings and leaving her with the impression that he was pushing her away and withholding something from her. That he could not do. He was all she had. She had never once complained of the isolation here, but he sensed that at times she felt as though she were held captive in a prison of snow-draped peaks, an exile in a mountain home, cut off from the rest of the world.

"Wolves," said Zach.

Her violet eyes darkened. "Tell me."

Zach sighed. "I was out in the middle of nowhere. It was the dead of winter. The snow was very deep. I don't know where I was going, or where I had come from. But I saw the wolf pack way off in the distance behind me, on my backtrail, running hard, trying to catch up."

"Were you afraid?"

"Not of them. It's just that . . . well, every time the wolves come I seem to be in some kind of trouble. And I was wondering what kind of trouble I was in this time, in my dream. Whatever it was, I wasn't aware of it. That made it worse. Did it lay just up ahead, in ambush? Were the wolves trying to catch up with me before I walked right into it?"

Sky's heart was racing. She put great stock in dreams. And she was convinced that wolves were her husband's totem. Years ago, when Zach had been caught in a deadly blizzard, his leg broken, a hundred miles from help, wolves had appeared and by their actions saved him. They had killed a horse, and horse meat had sustained him and his companion, Devlin. Then the wolves had come a second time, and Devlin had slain one, and the wolf meat had provided them with enough strength to make it the rest of the way through the frozen wasteland to safety. Meanwhile, a spirit-wolf had appeared to Sky—she knew now that it had come to reassure her, to let her know that Zach would return safe, though at the time she had misconstrued the visitation, believing it a portent of disaster.

Then, when Zach had ventured alone into the mountains, an angry and bitter man, following her abduction by Devlin, he had survived his first winter in a valley not far west from here, and his only company, or so he had told her, was a wolf pack.

And again, when he had been a captive of the Blackfeet, the wolves had come, wreaking havoc among the village's horse herd on the very day that Zach had cheated death. Once more after that they had appeared, to kill a young buffalo, and by so doing providing Zach with meat and a warm robe in the frigid heart of the winter before last.

Were these all coincidences? Sky didn't believe it for a moment.

"In your dream," she said, "what did you do? Did you not wait for the wolves?"

"Well," drawled Zach, reluctant to continue but seeing no alternative. "I knew I ought to, yet for some reason I kept going. Even though with every step I was more and more certain that someone—I mean, something—lay in wait for me. Somehow, in my dream, I could see the running wolves wipe out my tracks in the snow as they followed my trail. I couldn't help myself, couldn't bring myself to stop. Seemed like I was in some great hurry to get somewhere, but exactly where I couldn't tell you. I just kept walking, even as my instincts screamed at me to stop. Felt like I walked forever."

He sipped his coffee, avoiding her gaze.

"What was it?" she asked.

He shook his head. "I don't know. I woke up."

And he sensed immediately that she did not believe him—that she knew there was more. More he wasn't telling.

Jacob burst into the cabin, his still-plump cheeks flush, his blue eyes bright with excitement.

"Riders," he gasped.

"Where?" snapped Zach.

"Down in the valley?"

"Indian?"

"I don't think so, Father."

Zach smiled. Jacob spoke well for his age, and more properly than most raised on the frontier, on account of Zach's habit of buying books for him at rendezvous. Recently he had taken to reading a little himself.

"I'll take a look," said Zach. He put the tin cup down, gathered up his Hawken rifle, powder horn, and shot pouch.

Pausing at the doorway, he glanced at Sky. She was watching him with an unreadable expression. He felt guilty, keeping secrets from her. But he simply could not bring himself to tell her the end of his dream.

No, he could not tell her that he had walked over a rise to find Sean Devlin directly below him, grinning like a coyote as he held aloft a fresh, bloody scalp that Zach knew was Morning Sky's . . .

Chapter 6

Zach went to the rim of the table rock, some two hundred yards from the cabin. He peered down through the tops of the conifers that clung to the steep rocky slope below to spot the riders on the valley floor. Yes, there they were, heading from east to west, three riders and a single packhorse. White men. But too small a party to be a trapping brigade. At this distance, Zach could discern nothing else about them. Were they passing through? Zach thought not. There was no viable pass at the western extremity of this valley. Of course, perhaps these men were unaware of that. Maybe they were exploring.

Decided to at least get a closer look, Zach returned to the corral, near the cabin, where four horses were held. Sky and Jacob came over as he slipped a hackamore onto a dun gelding. The dun was surefooted, and Zach had a long and, in places, difficult descent.

"White men," said Zach. "But who they are and what their business is I can't say."

"Be careful," said Sky, striving to mask her apprehension.

She did not like it when her husband left her. Once he had gone away and nearly perished, that winter of the wolves when he and Devlin had survived a terrible ordeal. Then, when he had left her side to fight in the Arikara Campaign, Devlin had stolen her away, and for years she had been separated from Zach, and despaired of ever seeing again the only man she would ever love. And a third time, he had run afoul of a Blackfoot war party, and the Indians had captured him and hauled him north of the Missouri River, into a country few white men ever came out of alive, and she had come to the tear-stained conclusion that she would never see him again.

Little wonder, then, that it caused her great anxiety to see him go. Every day he left her, if only to hunt or scout, and the fact that a thousand times he had returned failed somehow to mitigate her anxiety. This was a fear she would never conquer.

Zach was in a hurry—in too much of one to bother with a saddle. Yet he paused, for he knew what torment Sky was suffering, and he took the time to lay his hand tenderly against her cheek.

"I'll be back before nightfall," he promised. To Jacob, he said, "Stay close to home, son."

"I will, Father," promised the solemn Jacob.

Zach rode down the mountain. His path took him through tall stands of virgin timber, verdant cathedrals dark and cool and churchyard quiet, and across talus slopes and boulder fields where marmots chattered and darted. The mountains had dressed in their spring regalia. Lichens were like daubs of orange and yellow and black paint on the rocks. Yellow stonecrop and the blue-and-white columbine grew in little pockets of captured soil up here near the timberline.

As he descended, the spruce and Douglas fir gave way to lodgepole pine, aspen, and birch. Here, in lush meadows, the grass grew so luxuriantly and uniformly tall that it brushed the dun's belly. Zach had to keep pulling the animal's head up to keep it from stopping to graze. Here, too, bloomed the yellow sunflower and the scarlet paintbrush and, of course, the ever-present columbine.

Worthy of notice as well, in Zach's opinion, were the plants that, though they did not exhibit the eye-pleasing form and bloom of others, were more useful to the mountain dweller. There was the elk thistle, with its starchy, edible root. Other edible plants included the wild parsley and the mariposa lily, the bulb of the latter considered a delicacy by the Indians. There was, as well, the large boletus mushroom, which Sky liked to simmer in hump and marrow fat—these "buttons" were one of Zach's favorite foods. He liked also the orange chanterelles, which smelled faintly of apricots. These plants had saved many a person from starvation, and Zach's experienced eye took note of their abundant presence.

He noted too the signs of wild animals. There were trees that had been scraped or clawed. Deep parallel gouges in an aspen proved that a bear had recently passed this way. The fresh scars were ten feet off the ground, which meant it had not been just any bear; only a grizzly could reach so high.

Some trees bore the abrasions where elk and deer had rubbed their antlers. Every winter the bull lost its rack and grew a new one in the spring. The growth process could last into the summer and was a painful one, as the new antlers were extremely sensitive, similar to the way in which an infant's new teeth are sensitive. The velvet covering the antlers was full of nerves and blood vessels. Already, some bulls were rubbing their antlers against saplings.

Zach found the sign of a mountain lion, too, a distinctive print in the muck at the rim of a purling stream. He saw rattlesnakes sunning themselves on warm rocks, and heard the warning of a few he could not see.

One thing he did not see was any sign of beaver in the valley, and he experienced a pang of regret. They were completely gone from this valley, and trapped out in dozens more. In less than ten years trappers like himself had made severe inroads into the beaver population. Zach was sorry he had ever taken any part in it. Tens of thousands of animals had been slaughtered, so that gentlemen back east could wear beaverskin hats.

It was all quite ludicrous and, in Zach's opinion, bordered on the criminal. Before long, the beaver would be virtually wiped out. What next? What poor creature would fall prey to the avarice of the white man? Zach had a hunch it would be the buffalo.

He recalled his first buffalo hunt, back in '23, when he and the rest of Major Henry's expedition up the Missouri had been in need of some fresh meat. The awe-inspiring image of that bison herd would remain always vivid in his mind. The Indian and the mountain man killed only what they needed for food and clothing. Now, though, they were beginning to kill the buffalo solely for its hide and its tongue, leaving the rest of the carcass to rot in the sun. At least the Indians used every part of the animal, from horn to hoof, for some purpose.

The bison herds were vast indeed. It was said a traveler might have to set up camp and wait a whole week if a herd happened across his path, before he could proceed on to his destination. Yet Zach figured they would all be exterminated. The avarice of his own race was a bottomless pit. And when the buffalo were gone, what fate would befall the tribes, like his friends the Absaroka Crows, who relied on the bison for food, shelter, and warmth in winter?

Grim reflections, all in all.

Down to the valley floor Zach rode, and two hours after leaving the high mountainside where his cabin stood, he was in the marsh grass and willows. Here, the creek that had been scarcely as wide as a tall man's stride up on the table rock was a roaring, foaming torrent tumbling over a rocky bed. Zach found a shallow ford. He knew right where to look. Venturing out onto the rolling grassland, he cut the trail of the interlopers, just as he knew he would. They were an hour ahead of him. He let the high-spirited dun break into a canter.

He smelled the fire before he saw them, and wondered what kind of greenhorn fools were these to pause for a noonday meal and smoke out here in the open. But when he came over a rise and saw them down in a grassy basin, sitting on their heels around a small fire, reins tied to their wrists and rifles within reach, he recognized them all.

Shadmore, Jim Bridger, and Jubal Wilkes.

Not greenhorns, nary a one of them. Friends and colleagues from a past life.

Zach rode on into camp.

Chapter 7

Zach was not all that surprised to see Shadmore. The old leatherstocking was the only man alive who knew where to find him.

Now Zach wondered if trusting Shad with his whereabouts had been a mistake. A flurry of hot anger swirled within him. He didn't much like his privacy being invaded like this. Shadmore had led Bridger and Wilkes here. But why? And by what right?

The anger quickly ebbed. All things being equal, Zach was happy to see Shadmore. The gray-bearded, squinty-eyed, slightly stooped mountain man had been like a second father to Zach. He had as much as adopted Zach ten years ago, when both had accompanied Major Henry up the wild Missouri on the Rocky Mountain Fur Company's maiden expedition. Raised in the hills of Tennessee, Zach had known a lot of woodcraft, but Shadmore had taken him under his wing and taught him a lot more. Zach was certain he would not have survived all the adventures he had experienced these past years in the high country without the knowledge Shadmore had imparted to him.

This close relationship was the reason Zach had informed Shadmore of his destination, that day Zach had taken his leave of the brigade for the last time. He had not elicited a promise from Shad not to share this information. He hadn't thought such instructions necessary at the time, expecting his old friend and mentor to be the soul of discretion, knowing as he did that all Zach Hannah wanted was to be left alone.

"Wagh!" exclaimed Shadmore as Zach rode into camp. He and Bridger and Wilkes stood. "Glad to see you still got yer hair, hoss."

"Glad to see you're still above snakes, Shad. Hello, Jubal, Old Gabe."

Bridger grinned through his dark beard, friendly gray eyes sparkling. Like Zach, he had come west with Major Henry as a youngster. Born in 1804, the year Lewis and Clark had set out to explore the Louisiana Purchase, Bridger's father had been a Virginia tavern-keeper who had crossed the mountains and the bluegrass country to the new land of Missouri in 1812, settling at Six Mile Prairie, not far from St. Louis.

When Bridger was fourteen, his father, mother, and brother died, leaving Jim to care for his little sister. In this way, too, he and Zach had much in common. Zach's parents had died of cholera, a tragedy that had led to his departure from the Copper Creek area of eastern Tennessee.

Bridger had run a ferry across the Mississippi for a while, and then become apprentice to a St. Louis blacksmith. It was there in that cosmopolitan city, hearing the talk of Indians, Mexican muleteers,

American bullwhackers, army dragoons, and French Canadian voyageurs, that Bridger had decided he had to go west. He had just turned eighteen when Major Henry and his partner, William Ashley, placed an advertisement to *enterprising young men* who were willing to spend a few years in the Shining Mountains trapping "brown gold." Zach had seen and responded to that same advertisement.

Zach had come to like and respect Bridger—old Gabe as men had come to call him, though he was in his mid-twenties. There were others who had been with them in '23—Tom Fitzpatrick, Jim Beckwourth the mulatto, David Jackson, Etienne Provost, Robert Campbell, William Sublette, Antoine Godin, to name but a few. Others had come later: Joe Meek and Jedediah Smith came to mind. Some were dead now. A few had made a name for themselves. Bridger certainly had. He was one of the owners of the Rocky Mountain Fur Company. A few years back, when Ashley and Henry had sold out, Bridger and Fitzpatrick and Milton Sublette and Baptiste Gervais had bought in. The Crow Indians respected Bridger, too. They called him Casapy, Blanket Chief, signifying a man in charge of important things.

"I told Shad you might shoot us if we rode in here like this," said Bridger, only half joking.

Zach slid off the dun gelding's back. It wasn't polite to stay mounted if your intention was to palaver with someone on foot.

"I'm glad to see you," said Zach, with something less than enthusiasm.

Shadmore smirked. "We warn't gonna come any

farther without an invite. That's why the fire. I told
Gabe and Jubal that iffen you didn't come down to
see us we'd turn around and go home. They agreed
to that 'fore I'd bring 'em here."

"It's all right, Shad."

"How's Sky and little Jacob?"

"Doing well."

"I asked Shad to bring us," said Bridger. "And I
wouldn't have done that if it wasn't important."

"What's happened?"

"It's the Blackfeet. They're going to make war on
us this summer. Big war. All the signs point to it,
Zach."

"It's been coming for a spell now."

Bridger nodded. "War parties have hit some of our
brigades this spring. And some of Astor's brigades,
too."

Zach raised an eyebrow. "I thought McKenzie had
a deal with the Blackfeet."

"So did he. But all deals are off. If you're white,
you die, according to the Blackfeet, and the fur company you belong to don't amount to a hill of beans."

"I don't belong to anyone," said Zach, a firm and
not-too-subtle reminder to Bridger that the problems
of the Rocky Mountain Fur Company were no longer
his problems.

"I know. But McKenzie has sent word that he
wants a conference. Me and Broken Hand and Milt
Sublette. He asked us up to Fort Union, to talk over
joinin' forces against the Blackfeet."

Zach's expression darkened.

"You have short memories," he said curtly. "Not
long ago, American Fur Company men led those

Blackfoot war parties straight to our trapping grounds. Twenty good men died on account of it. Friends of yours, Old Gabe, and mine."

"I remember. But that bloody deed was Vanderburg's doing. He's gone now. Kenneth McKenzie had nothing to do with that business."

"You're saying you trust Redcoat McKenzie?"

"I wouldn't go that far. But I'm willing to listen to what he has to say."

Zach shrugged. "Then go and listen. It's not my concern."

Bridger was frowning. He glanced at Shadmore.

"McKenzie asked that you come along, Zach," said the old leatherstocking.

"Me?" Zach was surprised. "Why me?"

"Couple of reasons," said Bridger. "For one thing, you have a lot of pull with the Absaroka Crows."

"So do you. And Beckwourth was adopted by the tribe. He lives with them now."

"Shore," drawled Shadmore. "They like Gabe and Beckwourth well enough. But they've allus been 'specially partial to you. They think you've got big medicine. Now more than ever, since you escaped the Blackfeet."

Zach grimaced. He did not want to discuss his captivity. The memory of that ordeal was a nightmare he knew he would always live with.

"Speakin' of which," said Bridger, "I'm told an American Fur Company man named Bushrod Jones helped you escape. It's come down to this, Zach. Us white men have got to put aside our differences and stand together. If we don't, we haven't got a prayer."

"I still don't see how I can help," said Zach.

"You also know the Blackfeet. You've been in their country and lived among 'em, even though as a prisoner, and you've survived to tell of it."

"I haven't told anybody about it," said Zach. "I'd just as soon forget it."

"The Good Book says 'know thine enemy,'" said Shadmore.

"Have you gone and got religion, old-timer?" asked Bridger, grinning, unable to let pass an opportunity to take a good-natured jab at Shadmore, and hoping at the same time to lighten the mood.

"Wouldn't hurt you none," Shadmore fired back. "You're one of the most sinnin' son of a guns I ever laid eyes on, Jim Bridger."

Bridger turned to Zach. "So what do you say, Zach? Just be for a few weeks. Up to Fort Union and back. Brought Jubal here along to stay with your family while you're away. If you want."

"I'd trust Jubal with my life," said Zach. "But I won't be going. No need to. I want no part of this war. I've done my share of trapping. Killed more than my share of Blackfeet. Now all I want is to be left in peace."

Shadmore and Bridger exchanged grim looks.

"McKenzie said he has word on Coyote, Zach," said Shadmore.

Zach felt as though he had been punched in the guts.

"Seems there's a feller named Letcher on Devlin's trail," continued the old leatherstocking. "Blames Devlin for his brother's death."

"Devlin's to blame for a lot of things," said Zach,

his words as hard as cold steel. "What else did McKenzie say?"

"That was all the letter contained," said Bridger.

He and Shadmore said no more. Just stood there, watching Zach, waiting for his decision.

Zach walked off a little ways. His back to them, he looked up at the towering mountains, in the direction of the table rock where his cabin stood.

And he remembered his dream.

Devlin had to die. Zach realized he could never truly live in peace until he knew for a fact that Coyote had "gone under." If Kenneth McKenzie really knew something about Devlin, then Zach had to know what it was.

With a deep sigh, Zach turned to face Shadmore.

"The hardest part," he said, "will be explaining it to Sky."

Chapter 8

The Missouri was a big river, but not far upstream from its confluence with the Mississippi she "flattened" out as the rivermen would say. She was filled with sandbars and sawyers and every other kind of diabolical obstruction that a river could manufacture to make life difficult for those men so arrogant to dream of using her as a thoroughfare to the fur-trapping country.

The *Yellowstone* had been built for the express purpose of conquering the wild Missouri. And she had succeeded where a dozen other ships had failed. She was nothing much to look at, especially if put side by side with one of those "floating palaces" that plied the mighty Mississippi in all their gaudy, gilded glory. But then she hadn't been built for looks, but rather for the purpose of performing a dangerous and difficult job. She was designed to "shove high" up the Big Muddy, and so she did. By the spring of 1832 she had successfully reached Fort Union several times, hauling provisions as well as trade goods to the American Fur Company post and carrying beaver furs and buffalo robes back down to St. Louis.

On the downriver journey Zach Hannah made on the *Yellowstone,* the stern-wheeler was laden with peltry acquired in trade from a band of Assiniboines who had erected their skin lodges outside the post and lingered for weeks of trading and gambling. As a result, there wasn't much elbow room to be found on board the steamboat. The *Yellowstone* had not been constructed with the comfort of passengers in mind, the skipper, a Captain Teague, reminded Zach. No, she was built to take on the "meanest goldurned river the Good Lord ever made."

At first glance, Zach was skeptical. Many summers had passed since last he had journeyed on the Missouri, but he could well remember her. Some folks swore she was possessed by some malevolent, demoniac force dedicated to the murder of every mortal foolish enough to venture upon her, or at the very least to make them wish they had never been born.

Back in '23 Zach had traveled downriver with Major Henry and a majority of the Rocky Mountain boys in mackinaw boats. Their destination had been the Arikara towns, to teach the Rees a lesson in civility, since the Indians had had the audacity to ambush and murder some of their fellow trappers. The mackinaw boat was a nimble river craft, a flat-bottomed vessel with a sharp prow and a shallow draft, sporting a lateen sail attached to a short, limber mast. They could be propelled by oar as well as sail and could carry fifteen passengers. Going down the Big Muddy was not even half as difficult as going up it, and that journey, though the accommodations had been a bit cramped, had occurred without serious mishap. The river made it a lot easier to leave the high country than to arrive there.

Proof of that had been Zach's first experience with the Missouri, a year prior to the Arikara Campaign. The river had thrown everything in its arsenal at the maiden expedition of the Rocky Mountain Fur Company. Dozens of sandbars, hundreds of snags that had to be laboriously chopped through, not to mention rafts and sawyers in abundance. The former were log jams, put together with an adhesive of mud and sand, natural dams that forced the river into narrow white-water channels. The keelboats used by the company had been hauled by brute force up these spillways. Grappling hooks and capstans had been utilized. The hook—an anchor, really—was thrown out ahead, the stout line secured to a windlass that a half-dozen stout-hearted men worked to warp the keelboat inch by inch against the raging current.

"Sawyers" were fallen trees that attached themselves to the bottom of the river with their roots and limbs, to lurk there, bobbing like a cork, just below the surface. It was a sawyer that had ripped open one of the company's two keelboats and sent its wreckage swirling downstream and half the expedition's supplies to the bottom. Miraculously, no lives had been lost. But the loss of the keelboat had forced the company to winter at the mouth of the Yellowstone, still a good long way from the Shining Mountains that had been its destination.

But Zach had wondered if he didn't owe the Missouri a show of gratitude. Because the Absaroka Crow had come to this winter post on the Yellowstone to give the white trappers the once-over, and with them had come Morning Sky, and Zach sometimes wondered if he and his Indian bride would have met had the keelboat not been wrecked and the company had proceeded on to the Three Forks region of the Missouri, well past Crow country.

This kind of experience with respect to the Missouri River colored Zach's critical assessment of the *Yellowstone*. It did not look much bigger than a keelboat. The paddle wheel was attached to the stern. There was a flimsy-looking wooden shack forward of the wheel, sheltering the engine from the vagaries of high plains weather. The upper, "hurricane" deck held the wheelhouse and a narrow row of cabins behind. The latter were used as quarters for the pilot, captain, mates, and crew. This second deck was supported by wooden pillars. The whole of the lower, or "boiler," deck was open, except for the engine room. It was here that the cargo was stored. Here, too, any and all passengers were accommodated. The boiler was set well forward on this deck. The furnace door opened toward the bow, so that when the steamboat was in motion a natural draft was created.

"We put it forward in case of explosion," the garrulous Captain Teague informed Zach. "That way she'll blow *out*, with any luck, and not break the hull in two. Many a steamboat's been 'killed' by a boiler explosion." He laughed at the expression on the buckskin-clad mountain man's face. "But she's only a wee boiler, as you can see. In fact, she's a locomotive boiler, guaranteed to stand up to sixty pounds pressure. Small yet powerful, she doesn't add much weight to the ship, but she'll produce plenty of power for the times when we require a full head of steam to get through a stretch of alligator water."

Weighing in at a hundred fifty tons burden, the *Yellowstone* sported other features that had been added with the Missouri in mind. The paddle wheel was adjustable. It could be raised and lowered when the vessel passed over sandbars or shoal water. Another special attribute was the "grasshopper," a manually operated crane that could swing out well forward of the ship and drop an anchor. From his keelboat experiences of ten years ago, Zach could comprehend its usefulness. The principle was the same; once the anchor was dropped, the *Yellowstone* was warped up to it. Then, while the little high-pressure boiler labored to keep the ship at least stationary against the powerful current, the anchor was raised, the grasshopper swung out again, and the anchor dropped once more, with the process repeated as often as necessary. Going down the river, the grasshopper would not in all likelihood be used, unless the *Yellowstone* ran aground.

There wasn't much chance of that happening, though, because the *Yellowstone*'s pilot, a man named Jenks, was the best "knight of the tiller" money could buy. At least, that was the gospel according to Teague.

"The river pilot is a special breed," Teague informed Zach. "He can read the river, same way as I imagine a man like you can read the sky and tell what weather the morrow will bring, or a trail and know who or what had passed that way the day before. Now you can't depend on landmarks to tell you where the channel is, for the river—especially this cussed river—is constantly changing on you. No sir, it's the river herself who gives her secret away, if you have the eye to see her telltale markings. And Jenks has the eye. Oh, Lord, yes, he has the eye."

Jenks was a thin, sallow-faced character, laconic and tight-lipped. As far as Zach knew, he said not a dozen words to anyone the entire trip. He was cool as ice water when it came to negotiating the *Yellowstone* through the myriad hazards produced by the malicious Big Muddy. He knew that an innocent-looking mark in the water flagged a bluff reef that could kill a steamboat; that "boils" revealed the presence of a changing channel; that a streak of silver over near the bank betrayed a snag; that circles in slick water meant the river was building a new shoal where once there had been deep water.

But the Missouri was hard-pressed to outfox Jenks. Which was why, Teague said, without a trace of envy, that the pilot earned four hundred dollars for every round-trip the *Yellowstone* made. This was twice what a Mississippi pilot would make on a run all the way from St. Louis to New Orleans and back. The Mississippi was child's play compared to the Missouri, declared the captain, and Jenks was worth every penny. The American Fur Company kept him on the payroll year-round, paying him for two trips a month even in the dead of winter, which the *Yellowstone* idled away in St. Louis, waiting for the ice to break. The Missouri herself did not "ice over" except in her upper reaches, but most of her smaller tributaries did, and when the ice broke, the floes carried downstream posed a real threat to all craft.

Zach found a comfortable berth in among the

stacks of buffalo robes and beaver packs piled high on the boiler deck. There were a few other trappers aboard. Zach did not know what their business was or where they were bound and he did not ask. They made some friendly overtures, inviting him to share a jug or a roll of the dice. But Zach neither drank nor gambled, and apart from that he did not care to make much of an effort to be sociable. The other trappers got the message, and gave him the cold shoulder from then on.

One of the problems was that they were American Fur Company men. During his self-imposed exile the past year, Zach had tried not to think much about the time when Astor's company, then under the direction of Vanderburg and Drips, had allied itself with the Blackfeet—an alliance that was directly responsible for the deaths of dozens of Rock Mountain boys.

Sean Devlin had been one of the American Fur Company's booshways. He had trailed Zach Hannah and his brigade to their trapping grounds, and returned later with a Blackfoot war party. The Blackfeet had killed one of Zach's men and captured Zach himself. Shadmore and Sky and the others had managed to escape. With the Hannah brigade cleared out, Devlin's brigade had moved in, confiscating the furs Zach's bunch had already gathered, and using the traps belonging to Zach's men to add to their haul.

Zach had been taken north into Blackfoot country, to a village where plans were being made to put him to death. Devlin had appeared before the execution date and insisted that Zach tell him where he could find Morning Sky. Of course, Zach had refused to tell him. Shadmore had taken Sky to the safety of the Yellowstone country. It was then that Zach had made a decision, long deferred, that Devlin had to die before he and Sky and little Jacob could get on with their lives.

Escaping the Blackfeet, he had returned to the valley where Devlin and his brigade were trapping to augment the packs stolen from Zach's brigade. His intentions were to recover the packs and kill Devlin, and he had waged a one-man war against the American Fur Company trappers. Unbeknown to him, Shadmore, Jubal Wilkes, and the Spaniard Montez— with the exception of MacGregor, all that remained of Hannah's brigade—had come to the valley with a similar purpose. When the smoke had cleared, Zach was wounded and unable to pursue Devlin, who, like the coward he was, had made off with all the plews while everyone else was busy fighting it out.

Shadmore had dispatched Montez to track Coyote down. That had been two winters ago, and Zach had not seen or heard from the Spaniard since. He had reached the conclusion that Devlin had managed to kill Montez. It wasn't too healthy, mused Zach, belonging to Hannah's brigade. Cleeson, Fletcher, Baptiste, and now Montez—all gone beaver. And Devlin, one way or another, was responsible for all of the deaths.

"He had to go where he could sell those plews he stole from my company," McKenzie had told Zach, back at Fort Union. "And since he's a river rat, it's my guess he has returned to the vicinity of the Mississippi."

"Those plews were stolen from me first," reminded Zach.

"Aye. Have it your way, Hannah. And that's not all he's stolen from you, if what I have heard is true."

"Why send for me? You've got this man Letcher on Devlin's trail."

"Letcher won't bring him back alive. And I need Coyote alive, sir."

"What makes you think I'd bring him back to you alive?"

"Because you are an intelligent man. And you care about the lives of others. Letcher's smart, but he's out for blood, and he doesn't care about anybody else. But if I can get Devlin in time, I am confident of striking a deal with those bloody-minded Blackfeet. I'm almost certain it will buy us another season to prepare for a war which is inevitable. Bridger seems amenable to an alliance between our two companies. But he must speak to his partners, and the booshways of all the Rocky Mountain brigades. I understand that. Mountain men are independent rascals. He can't speak for the rest without first conferring with them and getting their approval. So there will be no deal struck until rendezvous, at the earliest."

"I don't know," said Zach. "Devlin could be anywhere. It's a big world. Why should I waste the rest of my life trying to hunt him down? I have a wife and son back in the high country, Mr. McKenzie. They need me. I'm all they have. And I need them."

"It's for their sake that you are here," replied the canny Scotsman. "We both know that. And surely you can appreciate the poetic justice in my scheme.

Devlin left you to die at the hands of the Blackfeet.
Now you can return the favor. You can be the one to
deliver him up to their mercy—if I may be so cava-
lier with a word which is not found in the Blackfoot
lingo."

In fact, Zach *could* see the poetic justice of which
Kenneth McKenzie spoke. He had considered it,
slept on it, and the next morning agreed to it.
McKenzie had prevailed upon him to take passage
on the *Yellowstone,* which had arrived at Fort Union
the week before and was that day scheduled to em-
bark on its return trip to St. Louis.

"Letcher has a few weeks head start on you," said
McKenzie, "but he went overland. You can gain some
time on him by taking the river."

And so it was that Zach headed east, turning his
back on the high country he loved so well and had
sworn he would never leave. It was in the back of his
mind to give up the search if he found no trace of
Devlin in St. Louis. He wanted to be back with Sky
and little Jacob by the end of summer. Especially if
there was going to be full-scale war. That gave him a
little more than four months. Meanwhile, Shadmore
had promised to join Jubal Wilkes and stay with Sky
until his return. That made Zach feel a little better
about the whole business. But only a little.

Because he could not get the dream—that night-
marish vision of a grinning Devlin holding Sky's
bloody scalp aloft—out of his mind.

Chapter 9

Captain Teague was a well-educated man. He loved the Mississippi River as a patriot loves his country, and he had taken it upon himself to learn everything there was to know about it. He knew its history from one end to the other, having been born on the river, and with every intention of dying on it, his mortal remains consigned to its depths. He called the Missouri the son of the Father of Waters, albeit an unruly and tempestuous son.

Teague's favorite things to do were talk and eat. On several occasions he invited Zach Hannah to his cabin on the hurricane deck to share dinner. Zach didn't know it, but McKenzie had taken Teague aside at Fort Union and made him understand that Hannah was his most important cargo, and that it was Teague's foremost responsibility to get Zach safely to St. Louis. That was all McKenzie had said, and Teague asked no questions, either of him or of Zach, at least directly. But he was curious, and he hoped Zach might open up to him.

The *Yellowstone*'s captain had taken a page from McKenzie's book, in that he ate well and richly. In fact, the food served at his table was far too rich for

Zach's simple palate, accustomed as it was to venison and hump meat. Zach's idea of a great delicacy was what the mountain man called "french dumplings," minced buffalo tenderloin and hump, rolled into balls and covered with flour dough, simmered in marrow and hump fat. Or the uncooked liver of the speckled trout fished from some cold and clear-running mountain stream. Or mushroom "buttons" stuffed with marrow fat and browned over an open fire.

But Teague's delicacies were of an entirely different nature. He had a prodigious appetite for oysters and fish eggs mixed up in some overseasoned paste. He preferred beef steak, cut thick and cooked until all the juices were gone. For dessert he preferred strawberries in a sickly sweet cream, or chocolate cake. It was all entirely too much for Zach. After his first dinner with the captain he had a severe case of indigestion and felt perfectly miserable all the next day. From then on, though he accepted the invitations to dine in the captain's cabin because he liked Teague and hoped to learn something of value from him about what was going on along the river, he was careful not to eat much. Teague was a keen-eyed man, and intuitive, and he was quick to notice that Zach only picked at his food.

"I am a man of great appetites," admitted Teague. "I hope you will not hold that against me. It is the result of a childhood spent in destitution. My father was a keelboat man. My mother and my sisters and I lived in a run-down shack near Hard Times. A more aptly christened community you would be hard-pressed to find, my friend.

"I was raised on poke salad and hominy grits, with an occasional rabbit stew. My father did not provide very well for his family. He was absent for months at a time. Back before the steamboat, the commerce of the river was conducted on broadhorns and keelboats, you understand. A voyage down to New Orleans from St. Louis—from the mouth of the Ohio or the Missouri—and then back again took four to six months. The trip down wasn't so hard, but the craft had to be poled or warped back up against the current. It was a rough, hard career, pursued by rough and hardy men.

"My father's problem—or perhaps it was really my mother's problem—was his propensity for squandering his hard-earned wages on rotgut liquor or a roll of the dice in the Vide Poche dives of St. Louis. He usually came home with his pockets turned out. And seldom tarried long.

"My theory is that he began to feel guilty when surrounded by undeniable evidence of his shortcomings as a provider for those who depended on him. Seeing his wife, old and worn out before she had turned thirty. And his children, barefooted and clad in tattered hand-me-downs and seldom with full bellies."

Teague shook his head, and there was a trace of bitterness behind the amiable smile that split his florid, jowly face with its bushy, flaring side whiskers. He patted his gargantuan belly. "I was always hungry as a child. Now I make it a point always to have a full belly. I will never go hungry again."

The captain went on to tell of the keelboat days, and of the men like his father—rude, uneducated, courageous, hardworking, brawling, profane men. The advent of the steamboat was changing the face of the river entirely, and the complexion of the population of the river valley, as well. Now, with steam power, a craft could beat upriver from New Orleans to St. Louis in five or six days, rather than four to six months. A riverboat departing New Orleans in the morning would churn past Bonne Carre and Plaquemine and be in Baton Rouge before sunset. Before noon the next day it could reach Vicksburg, steaming past Bayou Sara, Natchez, Grand Gulf, and Hard Times in the dark of night. By the afternoon of the third day it could be at Memphis, having swept past Napoleon and Helena, and that night, with a capable pilot who could navigate past Island No. 26 and Dry Bar No. 10 and the Upper Towhead, be in Cairo on the fifth day, with St. Louis less than twenty-four hours distant.

The *Yellowstone*'s captain talked incessantly about the people and the communities along the river, but it was the river herself that preoccupied him.

"She's the largest river in the world, my friend, and it is safe to say the most crooked, too. She draws her water supply from Delaware on the Atlantic Seaboard to the Rocky Mountains in the west—forty-five degrees of longitude. She has fifty tributaries which are navigable to an extent by steamboats, and hundreds more which only flatboats can negotiate.

"Her drainage basin is bigger than England, Wales, Scotland, France, Spain, Portugal, Germany, Austria, Italy, and Turkey all put together. If you count the Missouri as her main branch, she's four thousand miles long. Four thousand miles! I read in a newspaper the other day that she discharges three hundred times the water of that little stream the British are so proud of, the Thames, and she deposits over four hundred million tons of mud and silt into the Gulf of Mexico every year. The scientists say that the river used to empty into the Gulf where Baton Rouge now stands. In other words, the river *made* the two hundred miles from that point to the Crescent City.

"And she is as unpredictable as any human female, Mr. Hannah, I assure you. She will change on you without warning. Down at Hard Times, my hometown, which used to be in Louisiana, the river is two miles west of where it was when I came squawling into this world of woe. Which put Hard Times in the state of Mississippi! The town of Delta used to be a few miles downriver from Vicksburg. Now it's a couple of miles *above* Vicksburg."

Chuckling, Teague shook his head, looking very much like a good-natured father tolerating the antics of a precocious child.

It was only natural that the *Yellowstone*'s captain got around to prying, surreptitiously, into Zach's affairs. He took his time about it, seeking to ingratiate himself upon Zach with his effusive bonhomie. Teague had learned a valuable lesson since signing on with the American Fur Company to skipper the *Yellowstone* back and forth from Fort Union to St. Louis, and this was that mountain men were a prideful, fiercely independent lot, who took strong and oftentimes violent offense when someone tried to meddle in their business. They were not as a rule inclined to answer to anyone, and were generally of the opinion that theirs was a God-given right to go wherever they wanted and do whatever they wished.

Teague, being a discerning fellow, could tell Zach Hannah was every inch a mountain man. He had *mountain man* written all over him. He looked about as wild and mean as any cuss Teague had set eyes on. Zach listened close, watched everything around him, and said precious little. So Teague was more than a little surprised when Zach came right out and told him he was searching for Sean Michael Devlin.

"Heard of him?" asked Zach.

Teague hesitated, contemplating prevarication. But he had the good sense to realize that, for one thing, he was not an accomplished liar—one of his father's strong points that, thank the Lord, he had not inherited—and, for another, that Zach looked to be the kind of man who could smell a lie a mile away.

"Who on the river hasn't?" replied the captain. "He's the man who killed the Child of Calamity."

"Who?"

"Mike Fink, of course. The King of the Keelboat Men. The original iron-jawed, brass-mounted, copper-bellied corpse-maker himself. You a friend of Devlin's?"

"Used to be. Heard of him lately? Know where he can be found?"

Teague rubbed a jaw buried in folds of fat. "I heard a rumor—can't honestly remember where— that he was back on the river. Perhaps down New Orleans way."

"Not St. Louis?"

"No, I'm fairly certain he isn't in St. Louis. But

then I cannot vouch for the authenticity of what amounts to hearsay."

"Who told you?"

"As I said, I don't recall, but if I had to venture a guess I would say another riverboat captain. It is a time-honored custom that when two captains meet they put aside all plans for the remainder of the day and settle down over a jug of whiskey to exchange news. Riverboat captains are the best-informed people on the river, sir. It is our job. We gather news and carry it with us and distribute it all along the way. It is expected of us. We have to know the Mississippi's latest prank, of course, but beyond that we must be aware of what price flour is bringing this year down in the Crescent City, and what sugar is bringing on the market in Cairo. And then of course we have to know what happened in this town or that one."

"I would think, then," remarked Zach, "that a man with Devlin's reputation would be a topic of conversation."

Teague shrugged and took a sip of the cognac he preferred above all other beverages.

"There are many men along the river who desire to keep hidden from the eyes and ears of a prying world, Mr. Hannah. Sometimes they must hide themselves to keep those secrets. Devlin has a very good reason for keeping a low profile."

He gave Zach a hard look, and Zach realized the captain had surmised that his reasons for wanting information concerning Devlin's whereabouts were not friendly ones.

Chapter 10

They reached the confluence of the Missouri and Mississippi rivers without mishap. Jenks's expertise and the surprising power and endurance of the doughty little boiler engine got the *Yellowstone* through more than a few tight spots.

There had been a bad stretch of shoals a day upstream from the joining of the two rivers, but this had not fazed the laconic Jenks in the slightest. Stopping the engines at first sight of alligator water, he sent forth the sounding boat, under the command of the first mate, who ventured out with his oarsmen into the shoals, sounding the depths with a twelve-foot pole. When the mate had located the "best" water he put a buoy over the side and moved on downriver. The men with him raised their oars to the vertical. This was the signal Jenks was looking for.

At the pilot's curt order, the *Yellowstone* surged forward under full steam and slipped handsomely over the reef and into deep water. Not once during the trip did the steamboat "strike and swing" and have to "spar" herself off with the grasshopper.

The Missouri repeatedly tried to conceal her main channel from Jenks, to lure him to disaster. But the

Yellowstone could boast of excellent leadsmen, who worked in tandem on port and starboard sides of the ship, sounding with a marked and weighted line. Zach found the calls of the leadsmen had an almost singsong quality. He became acquainted with their unique jargon. Deep four, quarter less three, half twain, mark twain . . . and with a deft spin of the wheel Jenks would nudge the *Yellowstone* to starboard or port and find the channel again.

Zach had not seen the mighty Mississippi for ten years. Here, not far above St. Louis, she was a mile wide, and her scope and power were truly awe-inspiring. But even more remarkable were the number and variety of ships now plying the river. Back in 1822, relatively few boats were to be seen. The advent of the steamboat had changed all that. Now there were coal fleets and timber rafts, crewed by ex-keelboat men, not to mention steamboats everywhere one looked.

On the west bank of the river, a few miles below the mouth of the Mississippi, a town had sprung up, almost on the exact spot, or so Zach calculated, that he and the rest of Major Henry's Rocky Mountain Fur Company men had pitched camp that first night out of St. Louis. Devlin had been one of six men sent out that night to bring in dinner. Most had returned with a mess of rabbits and quail, but Devlin had appeared with a chicken in each hand. No one had doubted that he'd stolen the birds from some farmer's coop, and Shadmore had then and there been prompted to nickname him Coyote—a name that had stuck.

But now that fine stand of trees beneath which

they had camped ten years ago was gone. The lumber had been transformed into an unattractive clutter of raw-board buildings lining muddy, garbage-fouled streets. There was a wharf boat instead of a dock at the levee, and it was alongside this craft that Jenks drew the *Yellowstone*.

"Why are we stopping here?" Zach asked Teague as the captain descended from the hurricane deck. "We can be in St. Louis in a couple of hours."

"Aye," allowed Teague, "that we could. But it's near on sundown, Mr. Hannah, and the wharves of St. Louis are no place to venture after dark. There will be a hundred boats of every description coming and going, and we have not come this far to risk disaster a stone's throw from our destination. Scarcely a day goes by that a boat is not killed within sight of the town. In fact, for diversion, the good people of St. Louis have been known to bring a picnic lunch to the levee in order to witness the day's disaster.

"When last I was there, two steamboats rammed each other. A boiler exploded. The explosion hurled one of the ship's captains two hundred yards through the air. His corpse landed right in the midst of two young couples out on the levee for a Saturday afternoon picnic. I daresay that ruined their appetites, heh?"

Apart from that, Teague said, they would fare better buying wood for the boiler here than closer to St. Louis. Here, too, Jenks would leave his association report. This was a detailed written account of the trip down from Fort Union, which Jenks would deposit in a box at the local tavern. In the report, a pilot put down everything he could about the stretch of river that he had just negotiated. This was for the benefit of other pilots on their way up or down that same stretch—a courtesy the association required of all its members.

The association, Zach had learned, was much like a trade guild for the "knights of the tiller." Chartered by the Congress of the United States, the association fixed wages, provided pensions for unemployed members, as well as money for the widows of deceased pilots, and even paid the burial bills. All members paid ten percent of their wages to fund the association.

Naturally, steamboat owners had attempted to hire nonassociation pilots at lower wages, but the benefits of the association lured most of the good pilots into the guild, and members refused to work for companies or captains who employed nonmembers. Before long the owners realized they had to deal with the association. The booming steamboat trade demanded it; without association pilots there just weren't enough knights of the tiller to go around.

"It is a good thing, my friend," Teague had told Zach. "These owners are making a fortune on the river trade. They can well afford to pay a decent wage to their pilots. But they wouldn't if they didn't have to. It is a cutthroat business, and a man must look out for his own best interests, as no one else will do it for him. I am hoping that we will soon see a similar guild for captains."

Once the *Yellowstone* was moored to the wharf boat, Zach wasted little time in disembarking. It was a fine feeling to stand on solid ground once more after ten days on the river.

A crowd had gathered on and around the wharf boat. The arrival of a steamboat was always a big event, especially so when the craft was the *Yellowstone*, which had ventured once again into that uncharted wilderness that had captured the imagination of the nation. What incredible tales of adventure would its intrepid crew bear with them this time?

There were numerous children on hand, boys and girls, all barefoot and tan and wide-eyed with wonder. Quite a few adults had gathered, as well, and young and old alike paid particular attention to Zach and the other buckskin-clad mountain men who had taken passage on the *Yellowstone*. Their attention made Zach uncomfortable, and he hastened to escape the press of humanity on the wharf boat. A couple of ragamuffin boys pursued him down the gangplank, tugging on the fringe of his sleeve, pestering him with questions about the buffalo and the Indians.

"You got any scalps, mister?"

Zach drew his hunting knife. "No, but I'm looking to get some," he growled. He tousled the hair of one of the lads. "You have a nice topknot, boy."

They took off running.

Once off the wharf boat, Zach paused to look around. Aside from the hustle and bustle, wagons going hither and riders going yon, and the whole town swarming with people like ants swarm on a disturbed mound, the most remarkable and disturbing aspect of the community was the filth. The levee and the alleys were littered with piles of trash and discarded lumber and freight skids. The stench was particularly offensive to Zach, accustomed as he was to the clean pine-scented air of the mountains. The noise and the people made him claustrophobic. He wondered, and not for the first time, if he had not made an awful mistake leaving his family and his mountains.

"This town's a hairy wart on the face of Mother Nature, ain't it?" came a voice from behind him.

Zach turned, and was surprised to see that it was the pilot, Jenks, who had spoken. It was more words than he had heard Jenks utter since departing Fort Union.

"You were thinking about your mountains, maybe," said Jenks. "Wishing you were back there, far from all this noise and stench. I remember the river when she was pure. Same thing that happened to my river will happen to your mountains. Even the mountains will fall to these people. They keep moving west, mile by mile, and there will be no stopping them. They'll keep rolling on till they get to the Pacific. And the whole country will look and smell and sound like this."

"God, I hope not," said Zach, horrified by the prospect.

Jenks smiled. "You're partly to blame. You and your kind. Me and my kind, too. We're opening up the frontier. We go first, and then everybody else follows. So long."

"Wait," said Zach. "I've been meaning to ask you about . . ."

The pilot's eyes were as blank as a doll's. "I keep to myself mostly. Don't have much to do with people.

Don't like 'em much. Don't get involved in their business. So long."

And he was gone, heading up the middle of the street that cut through the center of town.

Zach decided to follow, at a discreet distance. He figured Jenks was headed for the local tavern to deposit his report in the association box. A tavern would be a good place to start asking questions about Devlin.

The main street ran from the levee west about three hundred yards to the edge of town, there to become a wagon trace winding its serpentine way through more than a half mile of cleared forest, a wasteland of tree stumps, with a few dead trees, spared the lumberjack's ax, standing here and there. Timber crews worked from dawn to dusk in the fast-receding forest beyond, toil punctuated by the crashing of tree after tree. Dozens of wagons filled with cordwood were hauled back to town every day, fuel for the many steamboats that would pause here each week.

So this, mused Zach, was progress. He did not much care for the sights and sounds of it. He wondered if there would be a tree left standing in this country fifty or a hundred years from now. He could envision a barren plain stretching from sea to sea, dotted with ugly, stinking towns like this one.

As he walked along the street, people stared. Dodging a timber wagon driven by a cursing teamster, a drunkard bumped into Zach and belched an apology. A painted lady accosted him, taking his arm in hers and grinding a bony hip against his. She made a lewd proposal that caused Zach's cheeks to

burn with embarrassment. The stench of cheap
smell-pretty on an unwashed body made him nau-
seous. He pulled his arm away and hurried on. Of-
fended by this rejection, she threw a hair-curling
obscenity after him.

Up ahead, Jenks veered off the street into one of
the raw-board buildings. A sign above the door
through which he disappeared confirmed that the establishment was a tavern. Zach strolled on in. The
place was gloomy, insufficiently lighted, and reeked
of bad whiskey, and Zach *heard* the trouble before he
saw it.

"On account of you I got thrown out of the association, Jenks," growled someone in the rear of the
tavern.

"You were drunk when you killed your ship,
Anderson," was the stern reply of the *Yellowstone*'s
pilot. "I was but one of many who testified to that effect."

"Yeah, but you're the one who's here. And me and
my friends are going to teach you a lesson about
meddlin' in other people's affairs."

Zach could see a little better now—well enough to
tell that Jenks was standing among the tables in the
back of the long room, and three rough-looking cus-
tomers were facing him.

Three against one were not fair odds.

Zach took a step forward.

"Look out!" yelled someone. "He's got a knife."

Chapter 11

"Jenks!" yelled Zach. "Get down!"

He brought the Hawken rifle to his shoulder and fired. Jenks was crouching in reaction to Zach's command, thereby leaving Zach with a clear shot at the three men who were his adversaries. The trio scattered like quail, diving for cover behind tables, as Zach's rifle spoke.

Had he wanted to, Zach could have plugged one of them. But killing was not his intent. He fired over their heads. The report of the Hawken in these close confines hammered at his ears. The bullet put a hole clean through the back wall. Several patrons of the tavern, those closest to the door, stampeded out into the street. The bartender vanished behind his counter.

Zach's intention had been to unnerve the three men out to get Jenks, giving the pilot enough time to clear out of the tavern. It worked, but not for long. They were rivermen, and a little gunplay was not sufficient to discourage them altogether.

No sooner had Zach discharged the Hawken than one of the men jumped up and came at him in a headlong charge. He had a knife in his hand. Zach had no time to reload. Stepping into the attack, he struck the man's arm aside with the barrel of the rifle and then slammed the brass-mounted stock into his snarling face. The man crashed to the floor. Dazed, he rolled over slowly, got up on hands and knees, drooling blood. Zach tapped him at the base of the neck with the butt of the Hawken and he sprawled, unconscious.

The other two men were back in the fight now. One of them was pulling a pistol from his broad leather belt. Zach stopped fooling around. The Hawken in his left hand, Zach drew his own pistol, aimed, and fired in the time it took the other man to pull the trigger. The pistols discharged almost simultaneously. The range was scarcely twenty feet. Yet the riverman missed, while Zach hit his mark. The difference was that the man flinched, and Zach didn't. The half-ounce lead ball shattered the man's shoulder. He fell, clutching the shoulder, howling at the pain and writhing in his own blood. In less than a minute he had passed out from the shock.

The third man was coming at Zach now. He knew that Zach's pistol and rifle were both empty, so he thought he had a fair chance of inflicting damage with the evil-looking cane knife that he was wielding like a saber. But before he could reach Zach, Jenks hit him with a chair. The man went down, out cold, in a rain of wood shards as the chair came to pieces.

Jenks stepped over the last man down and took a closer look at the one Zach had shot.

Laconic, as always, Jenks said, "He'll live."

"I reckon," said Zach. "But we'd better get him to a doctor."

"We'd better stay right here," said Jenks. "The law will be along and want an explanation."

"The law," muttered Zach. Suddenly the consequences of what he had done began to sink in. The actions he had taken had been almost reflex. Out where he came from, a man didn't pause to consider consequences when his life was on the line.

Jenks smiled at Zach's expression. "They try to look civilized around here," said the pilot, with more than a trace of sarcasm. "They have a town sheriff and all that. But don't worry. I'm well known in these parts. You shooting this man was a clear case of self-defense. I can vouch for that. So can Eli over there. Can't you, Eli?"

Zach looked around as the bartender, pale and shaken, slowly rose from behind the counter.

"Sure can, Jenks," muttered Eli with a gulp and a nod.

"You just sit down and relax," Jenks told Zach, coming over to put a hand on Zach's shoulder. "This shouldn't take too long."

Zach was sitting at one of the tables, his back to the wall, when the town sheriff arrived, bulling his way through a crowd of spectators that had gathered at the door of the tavern. The sheriff stalked into the room, his flinty eyes flicking from the three men laid out on the floor to Jenks and finally to Zach. The latter was calmly reloading his rifle. The pistol, already primed and loaded, was lying on the table in front of him.

"Who's gonna tell me what happened here?" was the sheriff's gruff query.

"I will," said Jenks.

"Oh, it's you, Jenks." The sheriff's tone turned a shade friendlier. He went to the counter, leaned heavily against it. This seemed to be a signal to Eli. The bartender poured him a glass of whiskey. The sheriff sipped experimentally at first. He grimaced. "Rotgut," he murmured. Then he knocked the shot back. "Okay," he gasped at Jenks. "I'm listening."

Jenks told him the story just as it had happened. At the conclusion of the pilot's narrative, the sheriff glanced across the room at Zach.

"How come you bought in? A man's better off minding his own business."

"I know," said Zach. "But it was three against one, and it didn't look like a fair fight to me."

"He could have killed them," said Jenks, coming to Zach's defense. "The first time, he fired over their heads. Then he just winged that one yonder . . ."

"Talbott's his name," said the sheriff, with the expression of a man who has bitten down on a sour grape. "He's a worthless cuss."

"He was drawing his pistol, intending to shoot Mr. Hannah. They both fired their weapons at the same time."

The sheriff nodded, giving Zach a keen appraisal. "A regular duelist, aren't you? Well." He stirred himself pushing away from the counter. "Guess we'd better get Mr. Talbott over to the doctor's before he bleeds anymore on Eli's floor." He turned to the doorway. "One of you men make yourself useful and help Eli carry this feller over to the doc's office."

As Eli came around the counter, and one of the

spectators volunteered by stepping across the threshold, the sheriff turned once again to Zach.

"Where are you bound, Hannah?"

"St. Louis."

The sheriff nodded. "Good."

As Talbott was carried out, the sheriff roused the other two with whiskey splashed in their faces. He confiscated the knife, pistol, and cane knife, belting the first two weapons and wielding the third in a threatening manner.

"You two fellers are under arrest. Now if you try to run I will catch you. And then I will hamstring you both, and you'll crawl for the rest of your miserable lives. Do I make myself clear on this?"

The two men nodded. The sheriff pointed to the door with the cane knife, and they departed the tavern.

Jenks crossed to Zach's table.

"Thanks for stepping in," said the pilot. "You saved my neck. Anderson used to be a pilot. Ran his ship right into another down in St. Louis. He drank too much then, and still does. The other ship was docked. Anderson's sank to the bottom. A couple folks got hurt, though no one was killed, thank God. I was one of several witnesses. You see, I was the pilot of the other ship at the time. That was before the American Fur Company hired me. Anyway, Anderson got thrown out of the association. Also spent some time in jail."

"He blames you?"

Jenks shrugged. "That's the way some people are. Never own up to their mistakes. Always put the blame on somebody else." He peered at Zach. "I hear you're looking for a man named Devlin."

"That's right."

Jenks pulled out a chair and sat down. "Like I told you before, I make it a point to stay out of other people's business. But I guess I'm lucky you don't have the same rule. Seems to me I owe you."

"You don't owe me anything. I would have done the same for anyone."

"But I'm the one you did it for here today." The pilot drew a long breath. "Why are you looking for this man Devlin?"

Zach thought it over. Then he looked Jenks right in the eye and said, "He's responsible for a lot of good men getting killed. And he kidnapped my wife. He's a cheat and a coward. I intend to take him back to the mountains, where he will be put to death."

Jenks lifted an eyebrow. "By you?"

"I'll kill him if I have to."

"That doesn't answer my question."

Zach sighed. He had a feeling Jenks knew something about Devlin, and he wanted to know what that something was. But Jenks was considering breaking one of his cardinal rules, because he felt as though he owed Zach, and he was asking questions because he wanted Zach to give him a reason *not* to tell.

"I'm going to turn him over to the Blackfoot Indians. Devlin's responsible for a whole village being wiped out."

"How is that?"

Zach's eyes narrowed. "Don't you know anything

about this? How many times have you been up to Fort Union? They know all about this there."

"I know some of it. But what I want is your side of the story."

Zach didn't like being tested, but he swallowed his pride and played Jenks's game.

"Devlin gave them some blankets infected with the plague."

The pilot shook his head. "He didn't know they were infected, did he?"

"No. But that makes no difference to the Blackfeet, believe me."

"What will they do to him?"

Zach shrugged. "Same thing they were going to do to me a while back, I reckon. You see, I was captured by the Blackfeet, thanks to Devlin. I got away."

"What will they do?" repeated Jenks.

"Skin him alive, maybe. Then string him up over a fire."

"Good God."

Zach's expression was bleak, almost cruel. "The Blackfeet have declared war against all the white men. If we give them Devlin it might buy us more time to get ready for that war. You've got two rival fur companies out there, as you know, and there's a lot of bad blood between them. There is some patching up to do, and that takes time. This is McKenzie's idea, you know."

"You're a hard man, Mr. Hannah. It would be more civilized to hunt Devlin down and kill him outright than to haul him back there and give him to the Blackfeet to torture to death."

Zach leaned forward. "We don't live a very civilized

life in the high country, Mr. Jenks." He looked at the blood on the tavern floor. "But then I still think it's a better, cleaner life than folks have here in the *civilized* world."

A ghost of a smile touched the pilot's lips.

"There is a woman named Susannah Cosgrove. She's a widow. Still young and attractive, I'm told. Married a man from Alabama who brought slaves up to Missouri and started a plantation back in '20. She still lives on that plantation—it's called Oak Alley—a few miles out of St. Louis. Making a go of it, which doesn't thrill the Free-Soilers, I can tell you. They spread rumors about her. Say she's a loose woman. That she's been known to bed her field hands. Men come and go from her place. Now, I don't know if any of that talk is true. But folks generally think she ought to have more respect for her departed husband."

"You don't?"

Jenks shrugged. "It's not my place to judge others. But I think she's just lonely. And remember, she's young. A young woman like that still has needs, if you know what I mean. So I wonder, sometimes, what these holier-than-thou people would do were they in her place."

"She has something to do with Devlin?"

"So I've heard. The word is, Devlin visits her on a regular basis. You see, this man you're after has a kind of reputation along the river. He showed up about a year or so back and sold a bunch of plews, made a lot of money. Then he bought himself the best clothes, and ate the best foods, and stayed in the best suites on the floating palaces. And since he'd killed Mike Fink, and claimed to be a great Indian fighter, folks gave him a wide berth."

Zach's heart was pounding in his chest. "Who told you all this?"

"Pilots. Devlin rides the river. Gambles, and does pretty well by himself."

"Can you show me the way to this Cosgrove woman's place?"

"I've never been there. But almost anyone in St. Louis could give you directions to Oak Alley."

"There's no time to waste." Zach started to rise from his chair.

"Settle down, Hannah. I told you, Devlin rides the river. Whenever he passes by St. Louis he stops off to see her. I'm told he brings her a lot of pretty things to keep her happy with him. It might be weeks before he shows up at her door again. If ever."

"Or he might be there right now."

"You'll be in St. Louis by midmorning, and at Oak Alley by noon. If he's there tonight he'll be there come tomorrow."

Zach calmed himself. "I'm obliged for your help, Mr. Jenks."

"Like I said, I feel as though I owed you."

Zach smiled.

"What's funny?" asked the pilot.

"I was just recalling how I met Devlin. It was ten years ago, in St. Louis. He was being chased by four rivermen, hired by a gambler named Tyree."

"Tyree? John Tyree is dead. Killed in a duel years ago."

Zach nodded. "Figured he was dead or long gone. Otherwise, Devlin wouldn't be strutting up and down the river. Anyway, Devlin had stolen some money from Tyree."

"And you stepped in and helped him out, because the fight wasn't a fair one," deduced Jenks.

"Something like that. And now, 'cause I've stepped in to even the odds again, I've found out where he is."

"Life is just one big irony," decided Jenks.

Chapter 12

Doc Letcher checked his horse on the road at the point where a lane branched off and, straight as an arrow, made its way through twin rows of young oak trees to a whitewashed house a hundred yards away. On the other side of the road from the house, also about a hundred yards away, was a levee, blocking the mountain man's view of the Mississippi River. Letcher could see the plumes of black smoke from the twin stacks of a steamboat working its way upstream to nearby St. Louis, but he could not see the craft itself.

A wagon was coming down the road toward Letcher, and he waited for it. Crates of fresh produce were stacked in the bed of the wagon. A pair of mules strained in their traces. A long, thin, lantern-jawed man was on the bench, the leathers threaded through blunt, work-callused fingers. He wore the garb of a dirt farmer. Climbing the reins, he hauled the plodding mules to a stop and gave Letcher a long look, chewing phlegmatically on a wad of tobacco.

"You lost, stranger?"

"Depends," replied Letcher. "Is this Oak Alley?"

The farmer glanced down the lane at the big white

house and then spat a stream of yellowish-brown tobacco juice between the haunches of his mules.

"That's it. You a friend to that Cosgrove woman?"

Letcher surmised from the man's tone of voice that the farmer *wasn't* Susannah Cosgrove's friend.

"Never met her," he said. "But she's the one I'm looking for."

The farmer's sun-faded eyes swept Letcher's lanky frame, clad as it was in fringed and beaded buckskin, blackened in places with grime and long wear. He looked with curiosity, too, at the long rifle in its fringed and beaded buckskin sheath.

"Where you from, mister?" he asked.

Letcher stiffened. "Why? Are you taking a census?"

The farmer scowled. "Just tryin' to be sociable."

"Oh. It came across as prying."

"You'll find the Cosgrove woman in that big house," snapped the farmer indignantly. "If she's got another man in her bed you'll just have to wait your turn, I reckon."

He whipped the mules into motion, glowering at Letcher as the wagon trundled by.

Letcher steered his horse onto the lane and held it to a walk, scanning the house and the surrounding grounds with keen blue eyes that missed nothing. He wondered if Devlin was here now.

He had asked around St. Louis and found some people who knew about Sean Michael Devlin, and one, a storekeeper, who had informed him that gossip connected Devlin with the widow Cosgrove. He wasn't always at Oak Alley, or even often, as he lived on the river, enjoying the high life, making money at the gaming tables and spending it like there was no tomorrow. Whenever he was in the vicinity he spent some time with that Cosgrove woman, or so rumor had it. A sly wink. He wasn't the only man acquainted with her, either. She was a woman of easy virtue. A lecherous grin.

"I wonder," Letcher had said in an offhanded way, "if you would speak so freely of her if you knew I was her brother."

The storekeeper had blanched. He had tried to say something, but stammered so much that his words were garbled past the point of coherency. Letcher had brusquely thanked him for his help and taken his leave.

So here he was, proceeding cautiously down the lane between the young oak trees, hoping he would be fortunate enough to find Devlin here—that this would be the end of the vengeance trail he had sworn over his brother's grave to ride until Coyote had paid for his sins. And he wondered what Devlin's reaction would be upon seeing him. Coyote did not know him personally, but would surely recognize him immediately as a mountain man. Would he run? Or would he fight? Or would he be stupid enough to offer a hand in friendship?

Letcher didn't figure Devlin was stupid. The man had not lived to tell of betraying so many dangerous men by being a fool.

When he found Devlin, Letcher was certain what he himself would do. As certain as he had been the day he had discovered his brother's mutilated corpse. He wasn't going to bother trying to take Devlin alive and deliver him to McKenzie for use as a bargaining chip with the Blackfeet. He didn't think McKenzie's scheme would work, anyway.

Behind the house were cotton fields, with a row of ramshackle slave quarters off to one side, and an assortment of other outbuildings. It came as a surprise to him that individuals were trying to establish the cotton culture up here in Missouri. From talk he had heard during his two days in St. Louis, a number of planters had moved up from the Deep South, lock, stock, barrel, and slave. Prior to Letcher's going west the Compromise of 1820 had been made law, sanctioning slavery in Missouri but restricting its expansion henceforth to territory south of the 36°30′ line of latitude, the southern boundary of Missouri.

Letcher had not thought Missouri conducive to the cultivation of cotton but apparently a handful of men like Susannah Cosgrove's deceased husband had made it work along the Mississippi, where the soil of the flood plain was rich.

Way off in the fields, which were a half-mile wide by a quarter-mile deep, a slave gang was hard at work in the hot sun. But Letcher saw no activity about the house.

The house was a two-story structure with a veranda and upstairs balcony in front, and four plain Doric columns. Two of the louvered, green-painted French windows on the second story were open. As Letcher got closer he could see that the house had been made from big square-cut logs, with vertical notches on them, designed to make them look like masonry. At a distance, with the whitewash, the illusion worked.

Letcher figured the direct approach was best. Besides, it was the one most suited to his temperament. So he rode right up to the front of the house, keeping an eye on all the French windows, especially the ones that were open on the second story, because he had the feeling he was being watched, and he trusted his instincts. A man who remained perpetually alert, he was even more so at this moment, because he had no idea what to expect.

Dismounting, he ground-hitched his horse. Based on past experience, he was confident the mountain mustang would stay put. As always, his rifle was loaded and primed. He did not remove the beaded sheath; he kept the long rifle cradled in the hook of his left arm while sliding his right hand under the sheath, thumb on hammer and forefinger in the trigger guard. Flexing broad shoulders and drawing a deep and calming breath, he stepped up into the cool blue shade of the veranda. He was reaching for the brass door knocker with his left hand when, out of the corner of an eye, he saw a flicker of movement.

Letcher whirled, crouching, bringing the rifle to bear.

A man had come around the corner of the house to stand at the end of the veranda with a double-barreled shotgun leveled at Letcher.

"Don' do it, mistuh," warned the man. "As God is my witness, I'll blow a hole in you big 'nuff to drive a wagon through."

He was a black man. Though his hair was graying, he was wiry and straight and strong in body. He wore somewhat ragged trousers of brown stroud, and a linsey-woolsey shirt mended in several places, and with the sleeves gone. He was barefoot. Somewhere Letcher had heard that most slaves got two pairs of shoes a year, and to make this footwear ration last, they did not often wear them. Letcher did not know much about the institution of slavery. He had been born on a farm in western Pennsylvania, near the headwaters of the Allegheny River. His folks had moved to the banks of the Wabash in Indiana when he was a younker. He could not recall ever seeing a slave in his youth. But this was just one of those bits and pieces of information that he had extracted from conversation overheard or newspaper scanned and that he had filed away in his remarkably retentive mind.

"Jis' drop that there rifle," said the black man.

Letcher knew he stood no chance of fighting it out. Was the man's threat serious? Or just bluff? Letcher thought it was the former. The grim resolve on the man's deeply lined face, and the tone of his rasping voice, convinced Letcher that he would indeed trigger both barrels of the shotgun if he wasn't obeyed.

"I'll lean it up against this wall," said Letcher. "Will that do?"

"Do it slow," advised the other. "Slow as molasses, now."

Letcher moved slowly and leaned the rifle against the wall of the house.

"Step on back," said the black man, stepping up onto the veranda. He jabbed the air in front of him with the shotgun. "Get on back now, like I said."

Letcher took two steps back, keeping his hands well away from his sides, gauging his chances of pulling the flintlock pistol from his belt and getting off a shot if the black man glanced away for even a second. But he found himself reluctant to shoot this man, because he had a gut feeling the man didn't want to shoot him.

"Who are you?" asked the black man. "You got no call to come here."

"I came to see Mrs. Cosgrove."

"Why come?"

"I'll tell her my business, not you."

"If you ever wanna tell anybody anything again, mistuh, you best tell me right now what I wants to know."

"I . . ."

The front door swung open and a woman stepped out. She glanced first at Letcher, then at the black man, and said, "Lucius, what on earth . . . ?"

"Get back inside, missy!" exclaimed Lucius.

But Letcher was already moving, quick as a rattler's strike. He hooked the woman's slender waist with his left arm and yanked the pistol out of his belt. Pulling the woman in front of him as a human shield, he put the pistol to her head.

"No!" yelled Lucius, a strangled cry.

"Drop the shotgun," growled Letcher, "or see her brains splattered all over these pretty white walls."

Lucius didn't even think about it. He let the hammers down and tossed the shotgun into the dust beyond the edge of the veranda.

Letcher had been confident of the man's compliance, having deduced from his reaction to the woman's clearly unanticipated blundering into the line of fire that he held her in high regard.

"Jis' don' hurt her, mistuh," pleaded Lucius. "Kill me if you wanna, but don' hurt her."

The woman wasn't struggling to escape Letcher's rough and rude embrace. Instead, she was quite still, remarkably composed. Yet he could feel her heart fluttering like the delicate wings of a fragile bird beneath the big, callused hand with which he clutched her tiny waist.

"You must be a Free-Soiler," she said, a lilting Southern drawl laced with frosty and high-brow disdain. "Only a cowardly Free-Soiler would hide behind a woman's skirts."

"I'll hide behind the first thing that comes along when a man's pointing a shotgun at me," replied Letcher. "As Shakespeare has told us, discretion is the better part of valor."

"An educated brute," she said wryly. "How interesting."

"You have plenty of spunk," he said admiringly. "So full of brass, with a pistol to your head."

"Oh, you won't shoot. You fooled poor Lucius. You took advantage of his devotion to me."

Letcher took the pistol away from her head and aimed it at Lucius. The black man had been flicking sidelong glances at the shotgun.

"I know what you're thinking," said Letcher. "If you're ready to cross the river, you go ahead and try it."

"Don't act foolishly, Lucius," she said.

"Yes, ma'am."

"If you are not another Free-Soiler come to terrorize me," she said, addressing Letcher, "then just who are you?"

"Letcher's the name. And I'm guessing you must be Susannah Cosgrove. I am looking for a man named Devlin. He and I used to work for the American Fur Company. I'm told you know him."

"I am Susannah Cosgrove. And I do know Sean Devlin. Why are you looking for him?"

Letcher lied by implication. "We go back a long way. Is he here?"

"No. But I expect him any day now. You are welcome to wait for him here, as my guest."

Chapter 13

She was pretty, in a fragile way. Like a china doll, thought Letcher. Pale and breakable. And she had been broken. This he could see. There was tragedy in those gold-flecked hazel eyes, and dark shadows beneath them, as though she had suffered for a long time from some lingering illness that had sapped her strength and wounded her soul.

Her hands were small. The nails were cracked, and Letcher deduced from this that she worked hard at menial tasks. Her lips were full and scarlet, while her complexion was white as alabaster; the effect was that of a red rose floating in a dish of cream. Her auburn hair was parted and flat at the crown, in the fashion of the day, with ringlets falling around the ears to create an impression of winsome negligence, and it was gathered above the nape of the neck into a chignon, decorated with ribbon.

She wore a peach-colored dress of silk taffeta, with a tight bodice, and it flared at the hips over stiffened petticoats. The dress looked new, and Letcher wondered if Devlin had bought it for her. He did not think she could have afforded it herself. For though she lived in a big house on a plantation, there was little evidence of affluence here. On the contrary, what Letcher observed (which was everything) led him to the conclusion that Susannah Cosgrove was finding it difficult to make ends meet.

There was the way the house was furnished, for one thing. She led him into what had once been her husband's library, and left him alone there for a moment while she went to tell the cook to prepare a meal. Waiting for her return, Letcher took a look around. The glass-fronted bookcases were for the most part empty. The horsehair wing chairs and davenport over near the cold black fireplace were worn in places. The rug was threadbare. The candles—in cups, not holders of silver or brass—on the mantelpiece had burned down to almost nothing, yet had not been replaced. There were no paintings on the wall, though Letcher could tell there had been once.

When she returned she moved to a table against one wall, where a few decanters stood on a silver tray. Letcher wondered how long it would take for that tray to end up in the window of some St. Louis shop.

"I have some cognac," she said.

"No thank you."

She sat in one of the wing chairs. "I have had some financial difficulties since my husband passed away. I have been forced to sell some things. His books, the paintings, some furniture. And I must admit the fare at my dinner table will be rather plain."

Letcher forced a smile. It was halfhearted, touching only one side of his mouth. "Plain fare suits me, ma'am. It's what I'm used to."

For a moment an uncomfortable silence reigned. Letcher stood near the fireplace, leaning on his rifle.

"When did your husband die?" he asked.

"Two years ago." She looked away from his very direct gaze.

"My condolences."

"Thank you, but they are not necessary." Her chin came up, a gesture of defiance. "I did not love him. The marriage had been arranged by our families when we were scarcely more than children. At the beginning I honestly tried to manufacture feelings for him, but of course that cannot be done, can it? In time, I could hardly tolerate him. He was an extremely . . . overbearing man. And I was a disappointment to him, as a consequence of my failure to provide him with an heir." She smiled coldly. "One of his several slave mistresses, though, did bear him a son. Does my candor embarrass you, Mr. Letcher?"

"Not at all. I like people to say what they think. It saves time."

'You are better educated than many so-called gentlemen," she observed. "Yet one would not guess that just by looking at you."

"I never got much in the way of formal education. I grew up on a farm, and most days I couldn't be spared to go to school. But there was a circuit-riding preacher of the Methodist persuasion who came by the place on a regular basis, and every time he came he left me some books. The Greek philosophers. Shakespeare, Milton, Chaucer. Beowulf and Caesar. I couldn't get enough of those books. Those words took me to new and wonderful worlds, a long way from the cornfield and the potato patch. And when the preacher came by next he'd pick up the old books and bring me some new ones. One day I just had to pull up roots and see the world I'd been reading about. My brother and I signed on with the American Fur Company and headed west."

"You are not Sean's friend, are you?"

"Do you know him, ma'am? I mean, really know all about him?"

For a moment Letcher thought she was going to cry. Her composure cracked, and her eyes glistened with tears, and he was shocked—but then she pulled herself together, a quick recovery, and he thought, *This woman has a lot of grit.*

"You have no doubt heard some terrible tales about me, Mr. Letcher. That I am a loose woman. That I should still be wearing mourning black, out of respect for my dear, departed husband. That, instead, I sleep with every man, of any color, who comes down the lane. Well, as to the former, I cannot grieve for my husband, for I did not love him, and he did not love me. I remained faithful to him while he lived, which is more than he could say. In fact, he flaunted his affairs in my face. And I have not been free with my favors since his passing. But vicious rumors were started by free-soil men, who detested my husband, and myself, and everything we stand for as Southern-born slaveholders. How ironic it was, that during all those months, filled with all those lonely nights, I was being accused of taking one man after another to my bed just to avoid being lonely."

She paused, studied Letcher's face, looking for

some reaction, but his face was a sun-bronzed mask of impassivity.

"There was one man before Sean," she continued. "I thought I loved him. He swore he loved me. And I so desperately wanted to believe him, you understand. I suppose I was vulnerable, and I paid heed to his smooth lies. I even thought it had been planned, by some benevolent fate, in a way. That my husband had died and then this man came into my life and with one kiss took away the loneliness, and that we would live happily ever after." She tried to laugh it off, afraid that she was giving too much away, trying to lighten the mood and thereby mask her bitterness, but the laugh was strained. "I don't know why I'm telling you all this, sir. After all, a few minutes ago, you were holding a pistol to my head."

"So what happened to this man?" asked Letcher, and by asking, tacitly informed her that he didn't mind listening to her broken heart.

"He left me. A little while later I met Sean Devlin in St. Louis. I had gone into town to meet with a factor named Treffin, who, I suspected, was taking advantage of me in handling the sale of my . . . well, I sold most of my jewelry a few months ago. Treffin agreed to take it on consignment, and I just knew he was keeping a larger percentage of the proceeds for himself than we had previously agreed on. At the time I was desperately in need of the money.

"I found Treffin in a restaurant and demanded an accounting. I became angry. He became abusive. He called me terrible names, and then stood up and made as though to strike me. That is when Sean Devlin appeared. He struck Treffin with his cane.

Treffin fell, tried to get up, and Sean struck him a second time. The constable came. Treffin had to be carried off to a doctor. The constable questioned Sean and I. Sean explained that he would have challenged Treffin to a duel, had Treffin been a gentleman, but he obviously was not that, as a gentleman would never speak to a lady as Treffin had spoken so rudely to me.

"No charges were pressed against Sean. He invited me to have dinner with him, at another restaurant, of course. After what he had done on my behalf I could scarcely refuse. He was, I suppose you could say, my knight in shining armor. He had certainly come to my rescue and slain the dragon, hadn't he?"

"They call him Coyote up in the high country," was Letcher's wry remark. "I see why."

"Coyote?" She smiled wistfully. "Yes, I suppose that does fit him well. He is a charming rogue. I knew that almost from the start. Oh, of course, he would tell me that he loved me. But can you fault me for being a bit cynical? Still, I slept with him. I accepted his gifts. Sometimes I sold them, because I needed cash money. I have twenty slaves, and they must be cared for. And it costs a lot to maintain this place. But I am determined to do so. I guess it is because the Free-Soilers are trying so hard to run me out. I have a stubborn streak.

"Sean never insulted me by giving me cash, even though he knew I sold many of his gifts and why. He just gave me more gifts, and never said a word on the subject. I knew what he was doing. Just as I knew that I was only fooling myself. He paid me in jewels and silk, instead of coin."

"Maybe you're being a little hard on yourself, ma'am."

She looked down at the taffeta dress she was wearing. "I entered into the arrangement of my own free will, Mr. Letcher, with no illusions of happily ever after. No, not this time. And why shouldn't I have entered into it? I was being accused of harlotry, anyway. If you are accused of a crime you may as well commit it, if there is some benefit to be derived."

"Do you love him?"

She thought about it for a moment, looking at her hands, clasped tightly in her lap. "I will miss him." She looked up at Letcher. "Because you never answered my questions. Why are you looking for him? Are you a friend of his? No, I rather doubt that you are a friend of Sean Devlin's. Have you come to kill him?"

"He is responsible for my brother's death."

His words were cold—so cold that they cut right through Susannah Cosgrove, and she shuddered violently. She turned her head and gazed absently out through the open French windows at the cotton fields. Letcher surmised that she was wondering what she would do now—now that the lover who made her nights less lonely, and whose gifts provided her with the means by which she held on to this plantation, was about to be taken away from her forever. Letcher felt genuinely sorry for her. But there was nothing he would, or could, do for her. He would not be swayed.

"Well," she said with an air of resignation. "I cannot say that I am shocked. Sean Devlin is a dangerous man. Of course, I am scarcely in a position to say this, but he has no principles. And no conscience. But I think he would be leaving me soon, anyway. I have had this feeling, of late, that he is getting bored with me." She forced a wan smile and rose from the chair, to look over Letcher's shoulder. "Yes, Lucius. Is dinner ready?"

Letcher turned. Lucius had cat-footed into the room, but Letcher already knew he was there.

"Yessum."

She led Letcher to the dining room. The only furniture was a long table with ten heavy chairs, upholstered in rich burgundy brocade. Letcher could tell by marks on the walls and the floor that paintings had once adorned this room, and china cabinets had stood in the corners, and a large buffet had been placed over there, between the French windows.

Lucius assisted a tall, emaciated black woman in carrying the food in from the kitchen, which was located behind the big house. There were bowls of greens and grits, a platter of brown bread and another with cuts of pork. The flatware was plain crockery, not china. The woman dished the food onto plates, serving tiny portions to Susannah Cosgrove first, and then heaping portions on Letcher's plate. When she placed the plate in front of the mountain man she looked up into his eyes. Her own eyes were sunk deep into their sockets. The flesh was tight against her skull, deeply lined on the sides of her mouth and across her forehead. Her gaze was disconcerting. It seemed to pierce right through to his soul.

"That will be all, Marie," said Susannah Cosgrove.

The woman said nothing, and left the room. Lucius followed her. Letcher watched them go. Then he looked down at his plate.

"I hope the food is to your liking," said Susannah Cosgrove. "It is all I have to offer."

"That you offer it at all kind of surprises me, ma'am."

"You strike me as a decent man, Mr. Letcher. If Sean is responsible for your brother's death, then I cannot fault you for what you intend to do. I owe him nothing. He gave, but so did I. No one who enters my house will go hungry."

Letcher nodded. He hadn't realized, until now, how hungry he was. So he dug in.

He was halfway through his meal when the poison began to take effect.

Chapter 14

It came over him quickly, and he knew he was in trouble. His vision was blurred. His insides felt like they were on fire. Worst of all, he couldn't seem to get a deep breath. Wheezing, he groped for the long rifle, which was leaning against the table beside him. He knocked it down instead. Trying to get up, he kicked his chair over, and fell heavily on hands and knees. Groping for the rifle, he found it, struggled to his feet.

Susannah Cosgrove had come out of her chair.

"Lucius!"

He had been waiting just outside the French windows, and at her call he rushed inside—in time to see Letcher, swaying precariously, bring the rifle up. The black man lunged forward, wrestled the rifle from Letcher's grasp. The mountain man fell again. Lucius raised the rifle and then slammed the butt plate down hard, aiming for Letcher's head, striking instead at the point where neck and shoulder joined. It was enough to knock Letcher out cold.

Susannah Cosgrove walked the length of the table to stand beside Lucius and gaze down at the sprawled form of the buckskin-clad mountain man.

Her face was a pale cold mask. When she spoke, her voice was devoid of emotion.

"Take him away from here," she told Lucius. "Leave him in the brush, somewhere that he won't be found until the crows and the coyotes have picked his bones clean."

"Yessum." Lucius stared at her. There was fear in his expression. He was suddenly, and for the first time in all the years he had known Susannah Cosgrove, deathly afraid of her. A man of strong superstitions, he had a hunch the devil was inside her now, and it made his skin crawl to think of it.

She looked at him, and he looked quickly away, but she saw the revulsion in his eyes, nonetheless, and responded to it.

"He was going to shoot me, Lucius."

" 'Cause he knowed you'd poisoned him, ma'am. Jis' like any wild animal what knows it's dyin', he was strikin' out at the thing that was killin' him."

"I had to do it. He was going to murder Sean. I couldn't let him."

"Mistuh Devlin, he gone, ma'am. An' he weren't no good, anyway."

"He's gone, but he will be back. We will be married, he and I. That is why he went into business with Samuel Groves. Groves has already made a fortune in the Santa Fe trade. Once Sean has made his own fortune we will be married. Together we will make Oak Alley the finest plantation on the river. You'll see, Lucius. You'll see."

"No, ma'am. He ain' comin' back, that one."

She struck him without warning, a backhanded

slap to the face, snapping the old black man's head to one side.

"Don't talk back to me, Lucius," she warned sternly. "Now you do what I say."

Lucius got Letcher up over his shoulder. Despite his years, he was surprisingly strong. He had worked in a Cosgrove field, picking Cosgrove cotton, under the lash of a Cosgrove overseer, all his life. He had gone from half-hand to field hand and then, not too long ago, to a member of the house staff, because he was one of Susannah Cosgrove's favorites, and she had never struck him, until today. The fact that she had done so shocked and hurt him far more than the blow itself. Without another word, he shuffled out of the big house with his burden.

Depositing the mountain man in the bed of a spring wagon, Lucius hurriedly hitched up a brace of mules. Letcher was still alive, but barely. Lucius listened anxiously to every rasping, labored breath and wondered how much longer the man could cling to life. The mules hitched, he slipped off unseen to his shanty and was back a moment later, to leap into the wagon, whip up the mules, and roll down the lane between the twin rows of young oak trees, trailing a plume of red dust.

He drove the wagon far enough down the river road to be out of sight of the big house before stopping the mules. Twirling the leathers around the brake bar, he climbed back into the wagon bed to kneel beside the dying Letcher. He took a small bottle from the pocket of his trousers, pulled the cork with his teeth. Raising Letcher's head, he poured the contents of the bottle down the unconscious man's throat. Letcher gagged, choked, came swimming up out of unconsciousness, wheezed as he tried to suck air into lungs that felt as though they had collapsed, and then rolled over and vomited. Lucius put a comforting hand on his shoulder.

"You'll live, suh. Don't fret, you'll live."

Letcher lashed out blindly with a straight-arm that knocked Lucius backward. Before the black man knew what was happening, the mountain man was on him, hands around his throat, choking him and growling like a wild animal. But his mad strength soon failed him, and he sagged, slipping into unconsciousness again. Lucius squirmed out from under him, gasping for breath—and looked up to see a man on horseback alongside the wagon.

The first thing Lucius noticed was that the rider was clad in buckskins, just like Letcher.

"What's happened here?" asked Zach Hannah. "Is he drunk?"

"Nossuh. He been poisoned. He bad sick."

"Poisoned? Where's the nearest doctor?"

"He don' need no doctor, suh. I done give him a potion."

"What kind of potion?"

"Oh, it's got a lot of things in it, suh. Some tallow, and some snake oil. Some turpentine, mustard, and poke root. Some wild cherry bark. A little of this and a pinch of that."

Zach dismounted, tethered the horse to one of the wagon's wheels, and reached over the side of the wagon to press his fingers against Letcher's neck, in search of a pulse. He found it to be faint, but steady.

"How was he poisoned?"

"I . . ." Lucius clamped his mouth shut. He had resolved to at least try and save Letcher's life with the potion because he believed that what Susannah Cosgrove was doing was very wrong, but he wasn't ready to implicate her. "I . . . dunno, suh."

"You're lying," said Zach. "We need to get him out of this hot sun. Pull this wagon over under those trees yonder."

Lucius climbed back into the box while Zach climbed back aboard the horse he had rented in St. Louis early that morning. A stand of elms and water oaks just up the road offered an expanse of cool shade. Lucius drove the wagon down into the trees and stopped. Zach dismounted and again hitched the horse to the wagon.

"I gots to get this wagon, and myself, back home," said Lucius.

"You're not going anywhere until I get some answers. Who is this man?"

"I believe his name is Letcher."

Zach nodded. "Don't rightly know why, but I had a feeling that was so. Do you know anything about a woman named Susannah Cosgrove?"

Lucius swallowed the lump in his throat.

"Well, do you?"

"Yessuh. She's my mistress."

"What about a man named Devlin?"

Lucius again failed to respond. He considered trying to make a run for it. He was in way over his head, mixed up in some bad business, and he didn't know how he was going to get himself out of it.

"'Come on, man," snapped Zach, exasperated.

"Where is Sean Devlin? I want some answers, quick."

"Yassuh." Lucius sat, slump-shouldered in the wagon box, hands clasped tightly between his knees, head down. He looked, thought Zach, like he was praying. Maybe he was. After a moment's silence, he looked up at Zach—looked him right in the eye and told him the truth.

"I know this man Devlin. He's long gone from here, used to spend time with my mistress. Said he'd be comin' back, after makin' hisself rich down in a place called Santa Fe. He done hooked up with a man named Groves, who takes wagons of things like calico and buckles and tools down the trail. Promised to marry her. But he ain' comin' back, leastways not to her. I tried to tell her." Lucius rubbed his cheek where Susannah Cosgrove had slapped him.

"This man, Letcher, was looking for Devlin, wasn't he?"

Lucius nodded. "He a friend of yours?"

"We've never met."

"You lookin' for Devlin, too?"

"I am. How long ago did he leave?"

"Fortnight ago."

Zach grimaced, glanced at Letcher. "I asked you once before. Who poisoned this man? I want an answer."

"My mistress, she tol' Marie, the cook, to put poison in some of the food. Marie gave Mistuh Letcher the part that was. Marie, she's a witch."

"A witch?"

"Voodoo," said Lucius softly. "She's a bad woman, Marie. I don' have nothin' to do with her. I made up that potion in case she got it in her head to poison me."

"So Susannah Cosgrove had him poisoned. Because she wanted to protect Devlin?"

Again Lucius nodded. "She done fell for his smooth talk. That Devlin, he's a flannel-mouthed talker, sure 'nuff."

"I know," said Zach. "Believe me I know."

"She tol' me to leave him by the side of the road. But I couldn't do it. Not this time."

"This time? Who else has she had poisoned?"

Lucius looked off into the trees, shaking his head slowly, sadly. "She done poisoned Massuh Cosgrove."

"Good God."

"He was a bad man, too. Bad clean through. He was mighty mean to her, mean to his slaves, too. 'Cept the women."

"You didn't try to save him with your potion?"

"Nossuh." Defiance crept into the black man's voice. "I let him die. On account of he took my wife."

"Took her?"

"*Used* her."

Zach looked at the black man's hands. They were clasped so tightly the knuckles were white.

"I reckon you'd better get back," he said. "Just lend me a hand getting Letcher out of the wagon."

After they had gently deposited Letcher on the ground, in the grass that grew lush and fragrant beneath the trees, Lucius climbed into the wagon, threaded the reins between his gnarled, callused fingers—and paused to give Zach a searching look.

"You gonna go to the law, suh?"

"You're not worried about yourself, are you?"

"Nossuh. Not exactly. I'm an old man. I don' care what they do to me."

"You just don't want to see Susannah Cosgrove hang."

"Nossuh. The world done rolled over her. You know what I mean? She been hurt—hurt bad. She didn't use to be like she is now. If you gots to turn somebody in, turn me in. I'll tell 'em I killed Mastuh Cosgrove, and tried to do the same for him." He nodded at Letcher.

"Go home," said Zach. "I'll tell no one. We all have to answer for what we've done to a higher law."

"Yassuh. I know that's right." Lucius was looking past Zach, at Letcher. Zach knew what he was thinking.

"I can't speak for him," said Zach. "But I don't think he'll waste his time around here when Devlin's weeks down the Santa Fe Trail."

"God go with you, suh." Lucius whipped up the mules, got the spring wagon back to the road, and headed for Oak Alley.

Bright silver moonlight was streaming through the trees when Letcher came to. He sat up with a start, staring at Zach Hannah, who sat cross-legged a few feet away.

"Who the hell are you?" croaked Letcher.

"Zach Hannah."

"What are . . . Christ!" Letcher rolled over, clutching his belly, and dry-heaved. In a few minutes he was able to sit up again. "God, I feel like a herd of buffalo just run over me."

"You were poisoned."

"Yeah. How come I'm still above snakes."

"There was an old black man . . ."

"Lucius."

Zach nodded. "Reckon so. He gave you a potion. Reckon it worked."

"That Cosgrove woman," growled Letcher, as it all came flooding back to him. "She tried to kill me."

"Forget about her."

"Easy for you to say."

"Devlin headed down the Santa Fe Trail two weeks ago, Letcher. Now you want to go to the law? Hang around for Susannah Cosgrove's trial? If so, go ahead. I'm going after Devlin."

"Devlin's mine. I aim to kill him."

"I aim to see him dead. But not by you. I'm taking him back to the high country. He'll be handed over to the Blackfeet."

"No."

"Listen," said Zach. "I figure we can hunt Devlin down together or separate. Together makes more sense. The Santa Fe Trail is plenty dangerous. Jedediah Smith lost his scalp to the Comanches somewhere down along the Cimarron, they say."

"And when we catch up with Devlin?"

"We'll worry about that if and when we catch him. What do you say?"

Letcher nodded. "I'll accept your offer. But mark my words, Hannah. I'll watch your back, and you can watch mine, until we find Coyote, but when we do, as Heywood once said, it will be every man for himself, and God help us all."

Chapter 15

The Santa Fe trade had grown from a seed planted by pathfinder Zebulon Pike in 1807, who had suggested commerce with the Spanish, and paved the way with his explorations. But the first few intrepid "Yankee" traders who had ventured to Santa Fe had been thrown in jail as unwelcome interlopers.

Ten years passed. The increasingly high prices of goods imported through Mexico had caused the Santa Feans to experience a change of heart. One William Becknell, an American who had for some time been engaged in a prosperous trade with the Indians, blazed a new route across the daunting Cimarron Desert. By circumventing Raton pass, the new route made it feasible to transport goods by wagon rather than mule train. This in turn meant more goods could be hauled the eight hundred miles from Independence to Missouri. By 1831, over a hundred wagons, loaded with a quarter of a million dollars' worth of merchandise, were rolling down the Santa Fe Trail annually. Traders were realizing profits as high as five hundred percent on their investments.

The goods the Mexicans sought could be purchased cheaply on the Mississippi River: linen, broadcloth, velveteen, and muslin; dry goods, pots and pans, coffee mills, and paper; buckles, needles, scissors, knives, razors, and thread; shovels, hoes, axes, and other tools. Becknell had induced seventeen other men to put up some money to buy such goods, and to put their lives on the line to get those goods safely to Santa Fe. Leaving Arrow Rock, Missouri, in November of 1821, with three heavily laden wagons, Becknell had returned in early 1824, the expedition's pack animals weighed down with rawhide sacks of gold and silver. One investor, who had risked sixty dollars in the venture, received nine hundred dollars in return. Becknell had even sold his wagons in Santa Fe; purchased in Missouri for one hundred fifty dollars each, they had sold for seven hundred fifty dollars.

The thriving town of Independence, west of St. Louis, on the Missouri River, was the starting point for most of the brave souls willing to risk the perils of the Santa Fe Trail for the pot of gold that Becknell, and those who had followed his lead, had proved waited on the other side of the "Prairie Ocean." And so it was to Independence that Zach Hannah and Doc Letcher rode.

It was in the month of May that the majority of caravans set out. To tarry until July or August was to court disaster. The trip took seven to ten weeks, one way, and an early blizzard could catch the latecomer. The Baird expedition, one of the first to follow in Becknell's footsteps, had met this fate. A blue norther had caught them near the Arkansas River and killed every last one of their animals. Caching their trade goods, the Americans had walked three hundred fifty miles to Taos in extremely unpleasant weather. At Taos they had purchased mules and returned to their cache, only to be waylaid by hostile Indians. Baird and his men lost their mules and all of their trade goods, and had been forced to walk those three hundred fifty miles to Taos a second time, their venture a total loss.

Zach and Letcher discovered that there were three expeditions being outfitted for the trail in Independence, and they offered their services to each. Twice they were turned away.

Then they met Choctaw Adams.

Choctaw Adams had made a name for himself by trading with the Indians. He was known as a fair-minded man, although his gruff, loud, profane exterior often put people off, and his wrath was something to fear. A big, barrel-chested man with a square, ruddy face and shamrock-green eyes, he was about to lead his second expedition down the Santa Fe Trail. Zach and Letcher found him at a livery at the edge of town, where he was perusing a passel of mules in a corral.

"I cannot recall ever having seen a sorrier bunch of knock-kneed, flea-bitten, sway-backed knobheads in all my live-long days," he was saying as the two mountain men came within earshot.

A mousy little man, who looked even smaller than he really was when standing next to Adams, was grinning like a fox.

"As poor as they are, though," he replied, "where will you find better in this town?"

Adams growled. But if he meant to intimidate the

little man, he failed. The little man just stood his ground and beamed.

"Some thievin' bastard stole two of my mules," snarled Adams. "And I wouldn't be half surprised to find out you had something to do with that, Schuyler."

Schuyler feigned righteous indignation. "Now why on earth would I stoop to such a low and despicable deed, Choctaw?"

"So's you can charge me an arm and a leg for these half-starved bags of bones you call mules."

Schuyler cast his eyes skyward. "I don't know why I should stand here and listen to such scurrilous abuse from you, sir."

"Because you are a greedy son of a bitch and you know damn good and well you've got me over a barrel."

"Do we need to haggle on the price?"

Adams smirked. He dug into the pocket of his trousers and brandished a small sack bulging with coins. This he tossed—threw, really—at Schuyler.

"Would you like for me to select the team for you, Choctaw?"

"What I'd like is to kick your skinny butt into next week. But I'll settle for you getting out of my sight. Go on, git! And take your ill-gotten gains with you, you two-legged turkey vulture, so's I can get a breath of fresh air."

Grinning ear to ear, Schuyler walked away. Once he was safely beyond Choctaw Adams's reach, he danced a happy jig. Fists clenched, Adams watched him go with a growl rumbling deep in his throat.

Then he turned—and almost collided with Zach and Letcher.

"You Choctaw Adams?" asked Letcher.

"I am, and damned proud of it. Who wants to know?"

"I'm Doc Letcher. This is Zach Hannah."

"Hannah? Recollect hearing that name before." Adams rubbed his chin. "Mountain man, as I seem to recall. Got captured by the Blackfeet, hauled up into their country, and everybody wrote him off as dead. Only he managed to escape. That you?"

Zach nodded grimly. They were unpleasant memories, and he never liked them dredged up.

"All that true?" asked Choctaw.

"Pretty much."

Adams grunted. "Well, they say the Blackfeet are meaner than hell with the hide off. But I don't know about that. Never run across 'em. Still, I can't imagine they're any worse than the damned Comanches. Ever crossed paths with Comanch'?"

"No," said Letcher. "But I expect we will."

"How so?"

"We're going to Santa Fe."

"Are you now. What for?"

"Personal business. We're looking to join up with an outfit headed that way."

"Which explains why you're looking for me," said Choctaw. "You got any trade goods? A wagon? A team of mules?"

"No, none of that," said Letcher. "We don't have any money to speak of."

"Everybody who goes with me has to have a stake in the venture."

"We're going to Santa Fe," said Zach, "with a caravan or on our own."

"We just thought you might want two extra rifles along."

"Good rifles, too, I'll wager. But look here. It's eight hundred long, hard miles to Santa Fe. Fifty, sixty days. Every man must have some salt, about ten pounds of coffee, twenty pounds of sugar, fifty pounds of bacon, and fifty more of flour. That's the minimum per man on the trip. We hunt what meat we need along the way."

"We'll fend for ourselves," said Letcher. "Some meat and a little water is all I need."

"How about if we do the hunting for you?" asked Zach.

"The rules are the rules. Every man puts in an equal share of the goods and gets an equal share of the profit. That's the only way I've known it to work."

Zach looked at Letcher. "We're wasting our time. We'll go on our own." He started to turn away.

"Hold on a damned minute," growled Adams. "Would the two of you be willing to take an oath?"

"What kind of oath?" asked Letcher.

"That you'll see the trip through to the end, for one thing. I won't brook quitters."

"I've seen everything I've ever started through to the end," said Zach.

"There's more. You'll swear to submit to all the rules which the company as a whole sees fit to make. And that you'll obey my orders without question."

Zach and Letcher exchanged glances.

Adams grinned. "Makes you think twice, don't it?

You mountain men are an independent and on'ry bunch. Don't live by nobody else's rules."

"Where we come from, white man and Indian alike will follow a man if he gives orders that make sense," said Letcher. "If your orders are sensible, I'll abide by them."

"How about you, Hannah?"

"The last time I swore such an oath was ten years ago, when I signed on with Major Henry and the Rocky Mountain Fur Company. Because of that oath I had to take part in the Arikara Campaign, when all I wanted to do was stay home with my wife. But I went along because I felt obliged to do so. While I was gone my wife was kidnapped, and I didn't see her again for three years. I have answered to no man since, and have fared better for it."

Choctaw shook his head. "Just like I thought— on'ry. Fact is, as rawhide-tough and pure-dee mean as you two no doubt are, your chances of getting to Santa Fe on your own stick are mighty slim. Aside from the Comanch' you've got cutthroats lurking at every bend in the trail, on account of they know there is a lot of loot coming and going 'twixt here and Santa Fe. Strength in numbers is the answer. That's why we band together in caravans. Otherwise, precious few of us would make it there and back again."

"There is an old Chinese saying," remarked Letcher. "The grass must bend when the wind blows."

Zach knew that this homily was meant for him. It was Letcher's way of telling him to agree to the oath. This was their best chance of getting to Santa Fe alive. And they had to get there if they wanted to catch up with Sean Devlin.

"So if I take the oath, you'll take us on?" Zach asked Adams.

Choctaw nodded. "You'll do the hunting. You'll get no share of the profits once we get back here, though. That's when we divvy up."

"We won't be making the return trip," said Letcher.

"Fine." Adams shrugged. "I don't think I want to know anything about the business you have in Santa Fe. Once we're there, we part company. But I will say this. Call it friendly advice. The Mexicans want the goods we bring 'em, so they tolerate our presence. But if you step over the line down there they'll throw you in jail, and that's where you'll stay until you rot. And you'll get no helping hand, not from me or any other American trader. None of us want to jeopardize the trade. Too much money in it."

"Understood," said Letcher. "We wouldn't expect any help."

"No, not your kind," grinned Adams. "So what will it be? Do we have a deal? We're burning daylight, standing here jaw-flapping. And time is money."

"We have a deal," said Zach.

Chapter 16

Choctaw Adams told them to be at Council Grove in five days. There the caravan's individual elements would rendezvous. They would wait twenty-four hours if there were any stragglers, before heading down the trail for distant Santa Fe.

Council Grove was a hundred fifty miles west of Independence. The route took Zach and Letcher across the notorious "Narrows," a strip of bottomland between the Osage and Kansas rivers. As usual, spring rains had transformed this stretch into a morass of mud. The two mountain men spent half a day participating in the strenuous and messy task of extricating two wagons sunk to their wheel hubs in the quagmire.

On horseback, they arrived at Council Grove in three days, a trip that would take Adams and others who came by wagon at least two days longer.

Council Grove was a stand of timber a half mile wide, extending along the main branch of the Neosho River. The trees—stately oaks, towering elms, sturdy hickory, and magnificent walnut—were all the more remarkable for the fact that in every direction to the horizon stretched nothing but golden prairie.

Because the grove was such a landmark, Indians had used it for generations as a place where tribal envoys would meet to cut deals and iron out disagreements. For the same reason, the detachments of a caravan met here to select leaders and establish rules before embarking on the Santa Fe Trail.

Some of the men and wagons who would follow Choctaw Adams down the trail were already at Council Grove when Zach and Letcher arrived, as were elements of two other caravans. The mountain men agreed to camp apart from all the noise and clutter. Zach knew that Adams was two days behind, and he chafed at the wait. Every hour they squandered in lingering here meant Devlin was putting more miles between them. Letcher tried to rationalize.

"We stand a better chance of getting to Santa Fe with the caravan," he said. "Besides, we have an advantage. Devlin doesn't know we're after him. We may not even have to go all the way to Santa Fe. We might meet up with him on the trail, with him heading back to St. Louis. We're lucky Adams took us on."

"Adams knows what he's doing," said Zach. "He wasn't just being nice. He gets two hunters, and two scouts into the bargain—and he figures we're accomplished Indian fighters. He figures with us along those Comanches and the cutthroats he mentioned won't stand a chance of ambushing the caravan. Best of all, for him, is the fact that he gets all this for free."

They whiled away their time roaming through the grove. Many sought to engage them in conversation, but the mountain men kept their mouths shut and their eyes and ears open. Both had long ago discovered that a person learned precious little with his mouth open.

One of the first things Zach noticed were the inroads these Santa Fe traders, and all those who had come before in previous years, were making on the grove itself. Aside from the trees felled just for firewood, a supply of timber for axle-trees and other future wagon repairs was laid in. There was no good timber for the next six hundred miles. Zach wondered how long the grove would last. The ringing of axes, a sound that went on and on, from sunup to sundown, fell harshly on his ears. Again he felt keen apprehension for his distant high country. The axes and plows were inching inexorably closer to the mountains he loved. Nothing, it seemed, could stand in the way of progress. The beaver, the buffalo, the trees, the Indians, even the mountains themselves, could not resist this force—a force more powerful than nature.

On their second day at Council Grove, Zach and Letcher watched a caravan depart. Consisting of some sixty wagons, the company was over a hundred strong. In addition to the traders there were several genteel Easterners who called themselves "sportsmen." They carried fancy fowling pieces and dressed entirely too well for the trail that lay ahead. They looked forward to the trip as a lark, having contributed their fair share of trade goods just to purchase the opportunity to "shoot a buffalo and see a wild Indian," as one informed Zach. Zach was relieved to learn that Choctaw Adams did not permit such "loafers" to accompany his caravans.

The caravan also included three Spaniards traveling in a rockaway carriage—a young woman and an older couple. They were well dressed and well groomed, and the subject of much talk around the Council Grove campfires. From this talk Zach had concluded that the trio—husband, wife, and daughter—had fled Santa Fe during the 1821 revolution, by which the Mexicans had cast off the yoke of Spanish colonial rule. Now, it seemed, they were being permitted to return home. The man, it was said, had once been a wealthy grandee. There was nothing left of his fine Santa Fe estate. Yet he wished to go back. Zach wondered if they would make it. If the trail was as arduous as everyone said, he could not see the fragile rockaway coach reaching Santa Fee intact.

Choctaw Adams arrived the next day with his heavily laden wagon. That evening he called roll. Three men, with one wagon, had not yet arrived at the grove. Present and accounted for were forty-seven traders with eighteen wagons, not including Zach and Letcher.

Adams divided the caravan into divisions, one with ten wagons, the other with nine. Each division selected its own "lieutenant." This was a long, drawn-out process that took most of the next day, during which the last wagon arrived from Independence. The lieutenants were responsible for seeing to it that Choctaw's orders were transmitted, comprehended, and obeyed by the men in their respective divisions. Zach and Letcher found themselves under Choctaw's direct command. They would answer only to him.

On their fourth morning at Council Grove, Zach and Letcher, weary of inaction, were delighted to learn that the caravan would be setting out that day. Adams called out "Catch up!" and the lieutenants echoed the command. The wagoners caught up their mules and oxen and got them harnessed, in a race to see who would be the first to answer Choctaw's call with the reply of "All set!" When all the wagoners were ready, and all had made the reply, Adams yelled "Stretch out!" and got his wagon rolling. Whips cracked, men yelled, wagons rumbled, trace chains jingled. "Fall in!" yelled Choctaw, and the wagons began to roll out of the grove, one falling in behind the other, in an order already established by Adams and that would be adhered to throughout the journey.

Zach and Letcher rode on ahead. Near Diamond Spring they bagged two antelopes and pushed on twenty-five more miles to the Cottonwood fork of the Neosho. There, in accordance with Choctaw's instructions, they waited for the caravan to catch up. It was here that they would camp the first night out of Council Grove. The mountain men found abundant sign indicating that the previous caravan, two days ahead of them, had done so.

When the wagons arrived they were formed across the neck of a bend in the creek. Mules and oxen were let loose between the creek and the wagons. The five oxen teams were nervous and troublesome. Several days would pass before they were "trail-broken." Until then they would seize any opportunity to stampede for home.

Choctaw Adams was pleased to see that his two hunters had wasted no time earning their keep. Zach and Letcher had built fires and cleaned and spitted the game.

"Antelope are right hard to kill," commented Adams. "Leastways, that's been my experience. I seen one with a hind leg broke outrun a horse. How'd you manage it?"

Smiling, Letcher drew a strip of red cloth from his pack. "I tied this to the end of my rifle."

Perplexed, Choctaw rubbed his chin.

"We saw the herd, rode up to within a quarter mile or so, keeping our horses to a walk," explained Letcher. "Then we went on afoot."

"Antelope are curious creatures," said Zach. "They'll circle you until they figure out what you're up to. The red cloth really caught their eye, and brought a few of them within rifle range."

Adams grunted. "Well, just goes to show you aren't ever too old to learn."

"Antelope's not the best eating," admitted Letcher. "With any luck we'll come across some buffalo soon."

Zach and Letcher sat apart from the rest of the company while they ate their share of the meat. Someone broke out a violin and played a tune. The mountain men noticed that four of the wagoners were huddled together and talking in a conspiratorial way, throwing a few less-than-friendly looks their way.

"Wonder what they're up to?" mused Letcher.

"I don't know," said Zach. "But somehow I get the feeling they don't much like us."

"Know any of them?"

"That big one's named Hanrahan. One of Choctaw's lieutenants. I learned that much back at Council Grove. But I don't know him, or any of the others, and don't care to."

"Me, either. Which means it's our kind in general they don't care for."

Before long, Hanrahan and his three friends were up and crossing the camp to where Choctaw Adams sat on a wagon tongue smoking a pipe and gazing at the stars. An earnest conversation followed. Adams glanced across at Zach and Letcher a couple of times.

"I can't hear a word they're saying," said Letcher. "But I can tell they're talking about us."

Zach got up, wiped his hands on his buckskins, and picked up his Hawken rifle. "Let's go find out what they're saying."

They strolled over to Adams and the four grim wagoners.

"Is there a problem?" asked Letcher affably.

"These gentlemen don't think you two are necessary to the caravan," said Choctaw. Neither his expression nor his tone of voice betrayed his personal view on the issue at hand.

"Why not?" asked Zach, looking the surly Hanrahan straight in the eye.

"We can do our own huntin'," replied the hulking wagoner.

"In fact," said another, "we *want* to hunt."

"Yeah," said Hanrahan. "Me and the boys was lookin' forward to a buffalo hunt or two."

"For the hides," said Zach. It wasn't a question.

"Of course," replied Hanrahan. "Buffalo robes bring good money."

Zach turned to Choctaw. "As long as we're hunting for this outfit, only what's needed to keep the company fed will be hunted."

Choctaw glanced at Letcher. "Is that your position, too?"

Letcher looked at Zach, thinking it over. He didn't know why, but Hannah seemed dead-set on this. He was placing a condition on their further employment, and Letcher wasn't sure but that Choctaw Adams would send them packing as a result. After all, Choctaw's foremost priority had to be maintaining harmony among the caravaners. He didn't *need* a couple of mountain men to hunt and scout for him—especially if their very presence was going to cause friction in the company. Yet Letcher impulsively backed Zach Hannah.

"My stock floats with his," he told Choctaw.

"We'll have our fun," said the surly Hanrahan.

"You won't be killing buffalo just for their hides," said Zach. "Not while I'm around."

"Get in my way, buckskins, and I'll snap you in two like an autumn twig."

"That's enough," growled Adams. "Hanrahan, these two men will do the hunting. You'll stick to your wagon. Your job is to get those goods to Santa Fe. That's why we're on this trail. We're not doing this to shoot buffalo. We're not going to stop and gallivant all over this damned prairie for your sport. You savvy?"

Hanrahan glowered. But when Choctaw Adams came up off the wagon tongue, the wagoner nodded.

"You're the big augur, Choctaw," he muttered.

"You'd do well to keep that in mind."

Hanrahan and his cohorts returned to their campfire.

"Thanks," said Letcher.

Adams shook his head. "I didn't do it for you two. I'm the one who decides who goes along on this trip. Nobody else. So I won't have Hanrahan or anybody else question my authority. I brought you boys along, so he'll just have to live with that. But don't press your luck. Steer clear of Hanrahan and his cronies. I'll brook no feuding in this company."

The mountain men returned to their fire, apart from the others.

"What is it about a buffalo hunt that riles you?" Letcher asked Zach.

"Someday soon there'll be no more buffalo. No more beaver. No more wild country. Then what will people like you and me do, Letcher? Where will we go?"

Letcher looked up at the star-spangled sky. " 'There was a time when meadow, grove, and stream, to me did seem the glory and the freshness of a dream. It is not now as it hath been of yore. Wordsworth."

"That about says it," agreed Zach, impressed.

Letcher stretched out on his blanket. "Don't worry about it, Hannah. We'll be gone the way of the buffalo, too."

Chapter 17

The clouds rolled in overnight, obscuring the stars. Everyone was perfectly miserable. Zach and Letcher roamed well ahead of the caravan, looking for game, but saw not a single buffalo. The few antelope that they spotted took off running.

"I think word's gotten around about us among the 'plains goats,'" said Letcher wryly.

They managed to bag a mess of rabbits and a couple of sage hens. Slim pickings, indeed, and there was an undercurrent of displeasure, as well as a strong dose of Hanrahan stirring up some discontent among the rest of the traders. The big teamster had backed down from Choctaw Adams, but his obedience smacked of insincerity. He intended to make an issue out of the presence of the mountain men, and Zach had a hunch it had to do with more than a buffalo hunt. Hanrahan wanted to challenge Adams. He wanted to be in charge of the caravan. Zach could see it coming and he was already sorry he had taken the oath to stick with the caravan all the way to Santa Fe. It looked as though the liabilities involved in doing so would soon far outweigh the benefits. The last thing he needed was to get caught in the middle of a power struggle between Hanrahan and Choctaw Adams.

The afternoon of the third day out from Council Grove saw the rain stop and the sky clear. An hour later the mountain men spotted a small herd of buffalo off in the distance—perhaps a hundred head.

They dismounted and ground-hitched their horses—tying knots in the reins and burying the knots two hands deep into the ground. They then proceeded on foot, careful to move in downwind from the herd.

Bison have poor hindsight, and the half-dozen "pickets"—young bulls that positioned themselves at the rim of the herd—did not see them approach until they were about a hundred yards away. Then one of the bulls spotted them and sounded the alarm. Some of the other shaggies stopped in their tracks—they grazed on the move—and raised their massive heads to look. Zach and Letcher froze. The buffalo didn't run. They didn't know what to make of the two men just yet.

Both men realized that with the first shot the whole herd would stampede. They also knew that in all likelihood the shaggies would run in the same direction they were moving now. No words passed between Zach and Letcher. None were needed. They both knew what they had to do. Two kills were needed to feed fifty hungry men. Zach nodded at Letcher. The latter raised his rifle, aimed, and fired. One of the shaggies fell. The rest took off running as the rifle's report rolled across the prairie, shredded by the ever-present wind.

Zach had the Hawken to his shoulder and picked

a target. He led it a little, gauging wind, distance, and elevation. Then he fired. A cow somersaulted, shot through the brain. Turning away from the drift of eye-stinging white powder smoke, Zach reloaded and capped the Hawken. Done with that, he looked up to see the herd was already almost out of range, thundering across the prairie.

He and Letcher went back to fetch their horses. They rode closer to their kills before dismounting and ground-hitching the ponies a second time.

They proceeded to butcher the shaggies on the spot, working in tandem on one, and then the other. First they rolled the carcass over onto its belly. Then they made a cut from boss to tail. Pulling the hide back on both sides, they used their knives to chop the ribs apart.

The choicest cuts of the buffalo were the hams, tongue, liver, and hump meat. But with so many mouths to feed the mountain men stripped the carcass clean. Then they shoved the carcass over and pulled the hide completely off. Into this they piled the meat and used sinew to tie it up into a bundle.

Letcher stayed with the bundles while Zach headed back to the trail, turning east to meet up with the caravan. The meat was too much weight for them to haul, and it made life much simpler just to bring a wagon up. Letcher's task was to keep the scavengers away from the meat until Zach returned.

That night the wagoners were better pleased with their dinner than they had been the night before. Hanrahan lost some of his support. That did nothing to improve his disposition. He sulked for a while. Then he took a few slugs from the jug of ninety-proof bravemaker that he kept secreted away in his wagon, after first making sure Adams was nowhere around. Choctaw frowned on having hard liquor available on the trail. That was one of his rules. A man had to keep his wits about him at all times, according to Adams. But Hanrahan didn't care that he was breaking the rules. Fortified, he headed for the small fire, apart from the others, where he knew he would find the mountain men.

Letcher was the first to see him coming; Zach was busy sharpening his knife on a whetstone.

"We've got company," remarked Letcher.

Zach looked up. All he could see was a big, hulking shape in the darkness, silhouetted against the other campfires. But he knew who it was.

"I've been expecting it," he said, and went back to his knife sharpening.

"I doubt he's coming over to thank us for dinner."

A moment later Hanrahan was looming over them, hands on hips, his scowling features illumined by the light of the slow-burning buffalo-chip fire.

"I'll give you a dollar for both them hides," he said gruffly. "I hear you killed a cow and a young bull. They make the best buffalo robes, so I'm willing to pay a fair price for 'em."

"You call a dollar a fair price?" asked Letcher, incredulous.

"What're you going to do with those hides? Give 'em to your squaws?"

"I don't think I like the way you said that," said Zach.

"Like I give a damn," sneered Hanrahan.

"Look here," said Letcher, no longer amused. He

rose to stand toe-to-toe with Hanrahan. "Why don't you just walk away? All you really want is a fight. Or at least you *think* you do. But you really don't, my friend. You've been drinking, and it has clouded your judgment somewhat."

Hanrahan gave Letcher a hard shove. The mountain man almost tripped and fell, but caught himself. He started forward, fists clenched.

But Zach beat him to it.

Hanrahan was laughing at Letcher's stumbling attempt to keep his balance. The laugh was cut short as Zach sprang to his feet and charged, hitting Hanrahan low, in the breadbasket, driving him backward. Hanrahan tripped over his own feet and fell heavily. Zach came down on top of him, driving an elbow into the trader's chest. Hanrahan's sharp exhalation was so foul it made Zach wince. Zach put the blade of his knife to Hanrahan's throat, and the wagoner became very still.

"The hides," said Zach through clenched teeth, "are not for sale."

Hanrahan saw the anger blazing in Zach's eyes. He could almost feel the rage shooting down through the mountain man's arms and through the cold steel pressed against his throat. The razor-sharp blade bit into his flesh. He could feel a trickle of hot blood snaking down his neck.

Any sensible man would have been afraid. But finding himself so helpless, and so close to death, made Hanrahan angry. He lashed out with a lightning-quick left. A rock-hard fist slammed into Zach's stubborn jaw. The blow sent him sprawling. He almost blacked out, fought to stay conscious, rolling instinctively to put some distance between himself and Hanrahan.

With a roar like a wounded grizzly's, Hanrahan clambered to his feet and drew a knife from one of his mule-ear boots. Letcher recognized it as an Arkansas Toothpick, a wicked double-edge weapon. Figuring it was time to deal himself in, Letcher scooped up his rifle. Hanrahan was closing in on Zach. He didn't pay Letcher any attention. But Zach looked up and saw what Letcher was up to.

"It's my fight!" he said, and got unsteadily to his feet.

Hanrahan lunged. The blade of the Arkansas Toothpick caught the firelight as the trader tried to gut Zach. But Zach danced out of the way and parried the stroke with one of his own. Steel sparked against steel. Hanrahan was momentarily off-balance, and Zach started in, but the wagoner lashed out, keeping the mountain man at bay long enough to regain his balance.

The two men circled warily. Hanrahan was grinning, flipping the knife from one hand to the other. Zach knew what he was trying to do; he wanted Zach's attention drawn to the knife. But Zach knew that he had to watch the man's eyes. The eyes always gave a man away.

A crowd was gathering, men running over from the other campfires. Some of them shouted encouragement to Hanrahan. Others were laying bets. The rest stood silent and grim. Zach paid them no attention. He remained focused on Hanrahan.

The trader's eyes widened a split second before he made his move. That was what Zach was looking for.

He was ready when Hanrahan lunged. Again sparks flew as Zach parried Hanrahan's knife thrust. He swung a haymaker that connected solidly and sent Hanrahan reeling. Growling, Hanrahan shook his head to clear the cobwebs and charged wildly. Zach feinted to his left, dodged to his right, slashing with his knife. His blade cut deep into Hanrahan's arm. The trader let out a howl of pain. He dropped the Arkansas Toothpick, made a move to retrieve it. Zach kicked it into the darkness. Hanrahan, clutching his arm, pulled up short and stared at the knife in Zach's hand, the blade streaked with his own blood.

"You'd better kill me now," snarled Hanrahan. " 'Cause if you don't, I'll kill you later."

Zach smiled coldly.

He flipped the knife into the ground between them.

Hanrahan lunged for the knife. Zach hoped he would, and hit him with a left and then a right to the face. Hanrahan stumbled, but did not fall. He gave up on the knife and just bulled into Zach. He punched Zach in the stomach and drove a fist into Zach's face. Zach landed on his back, dazed, the copper taste of blood in his mouth. He kicked a leg out from under Hanrahan, and was back on his feet before the trader could get up. Zach put everything he had left behind a roundhouse right that snapped Hanrahan's head around and split his cheek open. The trader's eyes glazed over. On his knees, he pitched forward, out cold.

Breathing hard, Zach stood there a moment, rubbing his bleeding knuckles. The crowd was silent. The fight had obviously not gone the way most of them had wanted or expected. Shaking his head, Letcher walked up to Zach and looked down at the unconscious Hanrahan.

"You're crazy," decided Letcher. "You had him unarmed. He's twice your size, Hannah. And you toss your knife away?"

"What good's a fight if it isn't fair?"

"Fair is one thing. Dead's another."

Choctaw Adams pushed through the ring of onlookers, took one glance at Hanrahan and Zach, then turned on the wagoners.

"Fun's over, boys. Get back to your damned wagons. And those of you who lost a wager, pay up. One fight a night is enough."

The men drifted away. Choctaw walked up to Zach and Letcher.

"This is probably a stupid question, but who started it?"

"Hanrahan wanted to buy the buffalo hides," explained Letcher. "He wouldn't take no for an answer. He'd been drinking."

Adams nodded. "Not surprised. Probably got a jug or two stashed in his wagon."

"Then why don't you look and see?" asked Letcher. "Isn't that breaking the rules of this caravan?"

"I had no reason to look before tonight. I don't go looking for trouble. And you don't need to tell me my business."

Letcher was getting a little hot under the collar. "This man is dangerous. He's nothing but trouble. I thought you were a better judge of character. After all, you signed me and Hannah on."

Choctaw laughed. He turned to Zach. "You should've killed him while you had the chance."

"I reckon I'll get another," replied Zach.

Retrieving his knife, he went back to his campfire.

Chapter 18

During the next week there were no further disturbances, no more surprises. The caravan progressed twenty-five to thirty miles a day, on the average. The Little Arkansas slowed them down. So did Cow Creek. At both crossings the steep banks had to be excavated to provide "ramps" that wagons could negotiate. Muddy areas could be conquered by covering them with fresh-cut brush willow and cottonwood.

In the days following the fight, Hanrahan made no more trouble for Zach or Letcher. His fellow traders played some part in this, trying to restrain him from further rash action by means of reason and sound advice. Choctaw Adams let him know that further misbehavior would not be tolerated. "Hannah made you pay for it the first time," said Choctaw. "You'll pay me the next time."

Hanrahan bided his time. The general consensus was that he would seek revenge on Zach Hannah for humiliating him. Everybody who was acquainted with Hanrahan knew he was a poor loser. It wasn't a question of *whether* he would try to kill Hannah, but *when*.

Ten days out of Council Grove they arrived at the valley of the Arkansas. The mighty river, a quarter of a mile wide, was dotted with islands thick with cottonwood. The valley through which the river flowed, though, was virtually devoid of trees. This was due to frequent wildfires, caused primarily by lightning, which kept the growth down.

Zach had noticed that the farther west they traveled the more barren the prairie became. The soil went from fertile loam to sand and rock. The brush and trees were stunted and wind-scoured. The water became increasingly scarce.

The caravan followed the Arkansas River west for one day. They then crossed over and left the valley, to traverse a high plain. The sole landmark, visible from fifteen miles away, was Pawnee Rock. It was here, Choctaw Adams told the mountain men, that some time back an epic battle had been fought between the Pawnees and the Comanches. The Comanches had won, driving the Pawnees from their traditional hunting grounds. As a result of this victory, the Comanches reigned supreme on the southern plains.

These days Pawnee Rock was a place where travelers etched their names in the stone. It jutted skyward from the point of an arrowhead-shaped ridge. Choctaw urged his two hunters to make their marks on the rock.

"For posterity, as they say," remarked the trader. "Besides, many a man who put his name in the stone was never seen again. Might say he carved his own epitaph. Might say Pawnee Rock is the tombstone for quite a few good men whose bones are scattered somewhere out there on the prairie."

Zach declined to take Choctaw's advice. But Letcher inspected Pawnee Rock up close, accompanied by Choctaw. When he returned to Zach he was smiling like the cat that had eaten the canary.

"What's got you so pleased with yourself today?" asked Zach.

"Oh, I had a feeling I'd find something on that rock, and I did."

"Like what?"

"Sean Devlin's name."

Letcher was pleased by Zach's reaction to this news.

"And a date," he added. "June second. Choctaw says that was about a fortnight ago."

"A fortnight!"

Letcher nodded. "We're closing in on him, Hannah," he said with grim exultation.

Zach's excitement at the news of Letcher's discovery—concrete evidence that they were on the right trail—was tempered by a sobering realization: that once they found Coyote, Doc Letcher and he would become adversaries, for the simple reason that Letcher wanted to kill Devlin on sight, while Zach was resolved to deliver him alive to Redcoat McKenzie.

Fighting Letcher was not something Zach looked forward to. He could understand the man's obsession with vengeance. He could surely sympathize. And he figured Letcher was on the money in laying the blame for the death of his brother at Devlin's doorstep. Apart from that, Letcher was intelligent and capable. The kind of man you wanted on your side, not standing against you. Letcher had been canny enough to deduce that Sean Michael Devlin could not resist carving his name in Pawnee Rock. For posterity, as Choctaw said. Devlin had a problem with ego; he wouldn't travel down this trail, or any other, without leaving his mark.

The problem, thought Zach, *was that what Devlin usually left in his wake was heartbreak, destruction, and death.*

The next day, while out hunting, Zach and Letcher came across the sign of a half-dozen riders. The ponies were unshod. The trail was two days old. The riders were traveling from north to south. The mountain men followed it for an hour before finding what they were looking for. One of the riders had dismounted. The hunters closely examined the moccasin prints. The rawhide had been cut very close to the shape of the foot, tapering sharply at the front, with the upper's seam at the heel. There was fringe attached to the heel seam.

"Think it could be Comanche?" asked Letcher.

"Could be. I think we'd better find out exactly how much Choctaw knows about this bunch."

Letcher nodded. "Know thine enemy."

It turned out that Choctaw Adams knew quite a lot about Comanches.

There were several distinct tribal bands: the Penetekas, or Honey Eaters, the Quohadi or Antelope band, the Chaschotekas or Buffalo Eaters, and the Nocona. The Comanches had once inhabited the mountains near the headwaters of the Arkansas, along with the Northern Shoshone. The two tribes were related. A hundred years ago the Comanches had become acquainted with the horse, and the horse had changed their culture. The Comanches left their highland home, one band after another, scattering across the prairie and becoming the foe of everyone with whom they came into contact.

The Mexicans called them the *Komantcia*, which was the Ute word for "enemy." Indeed, the Comanches had become the enemy of the Mexicans, and the Utes, and the Pawnees. The only tribe to ally themselves with the powerful Comanches were the Kiowas. In fifty years time the Comanches were the undisputed rulers of the southern plains. Superb horsemen and fierce fighters, no one could stand against them, not even the fearsome Apaches. The Quohadi or Antelope band was, in Choctaw's opinion, the worst of the lot. He figured odds were good that the sign the mountain men had come across had been made by a Quohadi raiding party.

The Comanches were nomads. The buffalo was the keystone of their culture. In the summer, when the shaggies were fat from a springtime's grazing, the Comanches engaged in communal hunts. But fighting was their forte. The warrior enjoyed the highest status in the tribe. The chiefs of the different bands were invariably men who had won prestige as a result of battlefield exploits.

They were a proud and intractable people, who put much stock by individual freedom. As a result, it was difficult for the different bands, or even a single band, to act in unison on some matter. For that reason the war parties were usually small, and Choctaw assured Zach and Letcher that this was a good thing, because even a half-dozen Comanches were too much to handle.

They were, said Choctaw, a wild and reckless breed who made their own law. "Sort of like mountain men," remarked Adams wryly. In their society there were only two crimes: murder and sorcery. Thievery was unheard of. If a Comanche desired something owned by another of his kind he needed only to ask for it to possess it. Adultery was tolerated, as long as compensation was made. If a man slept with the wife of another and was caught red-handed in the deed, he was required to pay the husband, usually in horses. The wife might have her nose cut off, branding her an adulteress, but this extreme punishment was not often resorted to. "In a Comanche village," said Choctaw, "just about anything goes."

The way of the warrior was the ideal life of the Comanche male. Military prowess was the only road to success. As a result, Comanches were hard and reckless fighters, who never submitted to capture. They would always fight to the death.

The Comanche weapon of choice was a short bow, usually made from the wood of the Osage orange. Warriors were highly skilled in the use of bow and arrow. They could send an arrow completely through a full-grown buffalo, firing from astride a horse at full gallop. A few had rifles, thanks to the efforts of a group of Mexican traders called Comancheros.

Comancheros were unscrupulous villains, in Choctaw's book: Mexicans who profited from trading with Indians who in turn preyed on other Mexicans.

Worse still, the Comancheros exchanged weapons, whiskey, tobacco, and blankets for the bloodstained loot that their redskin clients had stolen from their victims: silverware, jewelry, dresses, coin, a family Bible or a pair of spectacles, a hand mirror or a man's watch and chain, lace curtains or a fiddle. All items that sold for top dollar in goods-starved markets like Santa Fe and Taos.

Sometimes the Comancheros acted as middlemen to secure the release of a person taken captive by the Comanches. But this service didn't come cheap. The Comancheros insisted on a high commission. It was rumored that they encouraged their Comanche friends to engage in widespread abduction. No question but that both they and the Comanches profited tremendously from this trade. Choctaw believed the Comancheros traded for Comanche captives, who were usually female, even when there was no ransom involved. Many young women taken alive by the Indians had seen their families slaughtered, and had no one left in the world who cared enough about them to put up a ransom. These women, if transferred in trade into the keeping of the Comancheros, were usually sold to brothel-keepers.

Armed with this wealth of information, Zach and Letcher rode out the next day and got firsthand evidence of the Comanche scourge.

The buzzards led them to the scene of the massacre.

The rockaway coach was tilted sharply to one side, an axle broken. The two bodies had been stripped. Dozens of turkey vultures were gorging themselves to

the point where some could not even fly when the
mountain men rode up. They darted into the scrub
brush with madly flapping wings.

Their horses shied away from the grisly sight.
Zach's stomach did a slow roll and he swallowed the
bile rising in his throat. He glanced at Letcher. It
was obvious Letcher was having a hard time keeping
his breakfast down, too.

They rode away from the carnage, dismounting a
safe distance away to secure their ponies in the
scrub, returning to the scene on foot. Both men
scanned the ground as they advanced. Zach wasn't
quite sure why he kept the Hawken in such a tight
grip, thumb on the hammer. Clearly the killing had
been done days ago. The killers were undoubtedly
long gone.

Nonetheless, his nerves were on edge. So were
Letcher's. When one of the bloated vultures broke
cover and tried to launch itself into the air, Letcher
whirled and raised his rifle. Zach reached out and
pulled the barrel of Letcher's rifle down before the
man could discharge the weapon, just in case
Letcher had a notion to shoot one of the buzzards
just for the hell of it.

"I hate those varmints," muttered Letcher.

"I'm thinking about Comanches."

Letcher nodded. Zach was right. A shot could
bring unwelcome company. Letcher resumed his
study of the ground. Zach did the same. They surveyed the scene thoroughly and met up to share
their observations.

"Comanches all right," said Letcher.

"Could be the same bunch whose tracks we saw yesterday. I count six."

"Me, too."

"They shot the man full of arrows," said Letcher. "Took his clothes and boots. Ransacked the coach. I don't think the woman died right away. I think they . . ." He glared bleakly past Zach at the sun-wracked, scrub-lined horizon. "The bastards."

"There were three people traveling in the coach. Remember the young woman?"

"Yes. I saw her back at Council Grove. A pretty girl." Letcher took a deep breath. "They took her, didn't they?"

"Yes."

"But what about the rest of the caravan they were with? Surely they didn't just leave these poor souls here."

"Looks that way," said Zach calmly. Behind his iron composure simmered a white-hot anger, but he tried to keep it corraled. "These traders care about only one thing: profit. I wouldn't be half-surprised if they didn't warn these people from the get-go that if that carriage broke down—which it was bound to do— they'd be on their own. I reckon these folks were desperate enough to accept that condition and take their chances. I was told they were going home to Santa Fe. Their only hope of getting there was to join up with a caravan."

"Agreement or not, to leave them out here, defenseless . . ." Letcher shook his head, speechless with rage.

"What's done is done."

"We can at least bury them."

"No."

Letcher stared at him. "Maybe I've misjudged you, Hannah. These people deserve a decent burial, at the very least."

"We waste time on the dead we'll lose the living."

"What does that mean?"

"The girl."

"You mean . . ."

"Yes. The Comanches killed these folks late yesterday. Probably on about sundown. They didn't go far, I wager, before camping for the night."

"God, that poor girl."

"Point is," rasped Zach. "They're only a few hours ahead of us, assuming they broke camp this morning at first light. We might be able to catch up to them."

"Just the two of us?"

"Who else? Do you think any of those traders will leave their wagons and take off in pursuit of Comanches just to save some woman they don't know?"

"Choctaw might."

"Choctaw is a decent man, I reckon. But I have a feeling he'll say she's as good as dead."

Letcher simply nodded. Everything Zach was saying made sense.

"If you don't want to go, I understand," said Zach, and started to turn away.

"Oh, I'll go," said Letcher. "What chance would you have against six Comanches, Hannah?" He glanced at the mutilated corpses. "I'm beginning to think maybe they *are* as bad as those Blackfoot devils we're accustomed to."

They headed back to their horses.

"You realize," said Letcher, "that if we get ourselves killed, Devlin will get clean away."

"I don't aim to get killed. I just want to get that girl away from those Comanches. If we don't try, who will?"

"Nobody *aims* to get killed."

"Look," said Zach. "I know that all you care about is catching Devlin. He as much as killed your brother with his own hands, the way you see it, and it'll eat away at your insides until he's gone under. An eye for an eye. But remember, he took my wife, just like those Comanches took that girl, and I know what Sky went through, all those years without hope. That girl is going to go through the same thing, and worse. I just can't walk away. We've got to try."

"All right," said Letcher, knowing what he had to do, but not liking it one bit. "If I get killed I'll just have to wait until Devlin gets to hell before I settle up with him."

Chapter 19

They caught up with the Comanches that night.

The sun was just setting, an orange-red ball of flame melting into the horizon, when they saw the campfire flickering in the purple shadows gathering beneath a line of cottonwoods and willows. The trees marked the passage of a creek, and it made sense that the Comanches had opted to camp there for the night. The day's journey had been a hot, dry one, without a spring or creek to be found.

Zach and Letcher checked their horses immediately upon seeing the pinprick of dancing flames. They were almost a quarter mile away, but dared not proceed closer on horseback. Their ponies hadn't smelled the water yet. The mountain men knew that when they did they would start acting up. So they dismounted and tied their reins to rocks heavy enough to keep the animals anchored in place. They then gave the last of their water to the horses. That done, they continued on foot.

It was full dark by the time they drew near the creek and the Comanche camp. They angled their approach to strike the creek two hundred yards downstream from the camp. After slaking their thirst, they moved on through the trees, making no sound.

All was going well until the woman screamed.

Both men dropped to the ground. Then Letcher looked across at Zach. His face was very pale in the darkness. His eyes were glittering with a strange and reckless light. Zach knew what he was going to do before he did it. So when Letcher started to rise, cursing under his breath, Zach lashed out and dragged him down.

"Don't do it," hissed Zach in a fierce whisper.

"We've got to . . ."

"Keep your voice down. We won't do her any good if we're shot full of Comanche arrows."

Letcher was silent a moment, his body rigid. Zach had a handful of his buckskin hunting shirt, and he didn't let go until Letcher nodded.

"You're right," he said.

"Come on."

Zach led the way. Single file they worked their way through the trees, pausing every few steps to crouch low and listen hard and search the dark shadows.

A few minutes later they could see the camp.

They could see all six warriors clearly in the firelight. Every one of them had painted his face red. Five of them wore headdresses adorned with the horns of buffalo. The one who didn't was younger than the rest. The latter was over by the horses, which had been tethered to a line strung between two trees. He sat on his haunches and watched his betters, who either stood or sat around the fire. Every warrior had his shield, lance, and bow and arrows near at hand. The shield was made of tanned buffalo hide, painted in bright colors and decorated with feathers. The lances were painted red. So were the horses; their heads and tails were carmine-red.

The warriors all had their hair parted in the center, and braided on either side, with a scalp lock on top. The side braids were adorned with strips of fur or bands of silver. They wore breechclouts and moccasins, and all but the young brave also wore fringed leggings. One of them wore a short green suede jacket. Zach had seen that garment before—back at Council Grove. It had been worn by the man whose remains they had discovered that morning.

The Comanches were going through the loot they had taken from the rockaway coach. A couple of valises were being rifled. They tossed articles of clothing to each other. One held a dress up to himself, and the others dissolved into laughter. Another was fascinated by a hand mirror and hairbrush. A scuffle broke out between two warriors over a pair of boots.

"Scavengers," muttered Letcher.

Zach didn't respond. He lay there in the night shadows, beyond the reach of the fire's light, watching every move the Comanches made.

"Do you see the girl?" whispered Letcher.

"On the other side of the camp," replied Zach. "See the blanket?"

Letcher shifted sideways a foot or two. Then he saw what Zach had already seen: the blanket-wrapped form, with only a bare leg visible. A horse-hair rope was tied at one end to the ankle, and at the other to a tree. Letcher's blood was boiling again at the sight.

"Let's do it, Hannah."

"Sit tight."

"No. Let's go in. We can kill two with our rifles, two more with our pistols, and then we'll do for the last pair with our knives. A couple minutes of good work and we'll have six dead Comanches to our credit."

"We might miss. We might not be fast enough. They might kill the woman. It's too risky."

"Look," rasped Letcher. "We came all this way to rescue her, didn't we? Then what are we waiting for?"

"A lucky break. And we just got one . . . *look.*"

Letcher looked.

The Comanches had discovered a scrolled-silver flask in one of the valises. A warrior uncorked it, sniffed at its contents, and yelped delight. He drank from the flask. In fact, he would have emptied it if the warrior beside him hadn't snatched it out of his grasp. Harsh words were exchanged. But the first warrior grudgingly agreed to share. The flask was passed around. Then it was passed around again. One of the warriors snatched up his lance and broke into an impromptu war dance. He stumbled, sat down hard. The others burst into raucous laughter.

"They sure can't hold their liquor," murmured Letcher.

The minutes crawled by. The liquor in the flask was polished off. The loot was divvied up. One of the warriors staggered over to the woman. Zach's grip tightened on the Hawken. If the Comanche had it in mind to molest her, he knew he would have to act.

But the warrior merely yelled at her and kicked her once. Letcher whispered a curse, but stayed put.

The woman made no sound that Zach could hear, nor any move that he could see. The Comanche returned to the campfire, obviously disgruntled.

An hour passed. It seemed like a lifetime to Zach. One by one the warriors rolled up in their blankets and went to sleep. Clearly they were off their guard, expecting no trouble, drunk with success. They left only the young brave on guard.

"I'm going to circle around," Zach told Letcher. "Cut the woman loose and get her out of here. You cover me."

"What about the guard?"

Zach realized it would be difficult to slip up on the young brave without disturbing the horses, which would in turn alarm the camp.

"I'll worry about him. You watch the others. If they wake up, start shooting."

"My pleasure."

Zach made his move.

He circled wide around the camp, coming in on the opposite side of Letcher, until he was a scant twenty feet from the tree to which the woman was tied. The move took another half hour. The guard was still awake. Zach resolved to wait at least another hour, in the hopes that the young brave might doze off. But he couldn't wait much longer than that. He wanted to put as many miles as possible between him and the Comanche camp before sunup—assuming he could get out of here with the girl and without any shooting.

His instincts paid off. It had been a long and arduous trail for this raiding party, and the young brave's stamina had been stretched to the limit. He yawned, something Zach was extremely happy to see. A little while later he rose and went down to the creek, out of Zach's sight. Zach considered moving in right then, but refrained. There was no way of telling how long the brave would be gone. No, he would just have to be patient. It was hard to do. There were no guarantees that he would have a better opportunity.

His gamble paid off. The brave returned and sat down near the horses, leaning against the trunk of a cottonwood tree. Eventually he began to doze off. Zach felt as though he had been waiting forever. In fact, less than an hour had transpired since his move around the camp. The brave struggled to stay awake. But he was fighting a losing battle. Finally his head drooped forward and stayed down.

Still Zach waited. He wondered about Letcher. The man was probably at the end of his rope. Well, he would just have to hold on a little while longer. Haste could be fatal.

Another half hour passed, with agonizing slowness. The guard did not stir. Neither did the other five Comanches. Finally satisfied, Zach crept forward, making no sound. Reaching the woman, he leaned his rifle against the tree and drew his knife. Then he stretched out on the ground next to her, and gently lifted the edge of the blanket that covered her face.

Her eyes popped open. Her lips parted, and Zach heard a sharp inhalation and knew she was about to scream. He clapped a hand over her mouth. She began to thrash around. The blanket fell away from her naked body. Her hands were bound behind her back.

"Quiet!" hissed Zach. "I'm here to help you. Don't you understand?"

But of course she did not understand. Panic had set in. All she could see was a man with a knife accosting her, and she continued to resist as best she could with her hands tied and one leg roped to the tree. Zach swore under his breath. This was something he hadn't calculated into his plan. He couldn't blame her for reacting so violently, after all she had been through.

The young brave awoke, jumped to his feet, and shouted an alarm.

A rifle spoke from the darkness. The brave crumpled, drilled through the heart.

The rest of the Comanches were up in an instant, grabbing their weapons, shouting at each other. Confusion reigned for one brief moment as they tried to figure out what was happening—a brief moment that was precious to Zach. He hated to do it, but he clipped the girl on the chin with a rock-hard fist, just enough to knock her cold. Then he slashed at the horsehair rope securing her to the tree. Sweeping her limp form up in his arms as he rose, he slung her over one shoulder.

Two of the Comanches were coming at him with their war lances. He dropped the knife, pulled his pistol, and fired point-blank at one of them. The bullet hit the warrior in the head and took the back of his skull off. A split second later Letcher's pistol spoke. The second warrior was struck squarely in the back. The impact sent him careening into Zach. Zach was braced for the collision, and the warrior fell backward, dying.

Zach turned, grabbed his Hawken, and ran for his life.

Despite the burden of the unconscious girl, Zach ran as fleet as an antelope through the woods. A hundred yards from the camp he stopped. Dropping to one knee, he deposited her as gently as possible onto the ground. Then he rose with the Hawken held at hip level, thumbing the hammer back.

Much to his surprise, there was no pursuit.

Three warriors left—but where were they? Zach listened hard for any telltale sound, scanning the darkness, hoping to see or hear something that would give him a clue to what had transpired. Everything had happened so quickly.

But the woods were silent once more. The creek murmured off to his left. It was time to get to the horses. Yet he was loath to leave the cover of the trees until he knew for certain where the Comanches were and what they were up to.

In time, though, he decided to chance it. Draping the girl back over his shoulder, he broke from the woods and headed across open, moonlit ground at a lope, his faultless sense of direction guiding him through the night to the place where he and Letcher had left their horses. He half expected to hear a Comanche war cry and the crack of a rifle. But he didn't. He reached the horses without mishap and found Letcher waiting there.

"Where are they?" gasped Zach as he bent to place the girl on the ground.

"They took off. Grabbed their horses and headed out."

"Are you sure?"

"Sure I'm sure. Probably figured there were a lot more than just two of us." Letcher was staring at the girl on the ground at their feet. Then he turned and pulled the rolled-up blanket from behind his saddle. This he shook out and threw over her. "Is she hurt bad?" he asked.

"Well, she's alive, at least. Let me have your knife."

Zach took the blanket and cut a slit a foot long in the very center of it. Kneeling beside her, he lifted her up into a sitting position, and managed to get the blanket over her. Her head fit through the slit and the blanket was transformed into a makeshift serape. As he worked he couldn't help but notice the ugly bruises and scratches on her alabaster-white skin. He shook his head grimly, remembering a time, not that long ago, when he had been the captive of the Blackfeet. Naked, bruised, and bleeding, just like the girl. A man named Bushrod Jones, an employee of the American Fur Company, had happened along and turned his blanket into a serape for Zach's benefit. Bushrod was dead—a victim of the plague that Devlin had carried into the Blackfoot country. Bad memories. It seemed to Zach that bad memories were the only kind he had.

"We'd better get moving," he said gruffly. "Those three might decide to come back and make a fight of it."

Letcher climbed aboard his horse. Zach lifted the girl and handed her up to Letcher. Letcher gave Zach his rifle, so that he could hold her securely with one big arm and take the reins in his other hand. Mounting up, Zach led the way across the darkened plain.

Chapter 20

"A woman's nothing but trouble in a company of men," grumbled Choctaw Adams. He noticed the smirk on Zach Hannah's sun-darkened features, and scowled. "Did I say something to amuse you, Hannah?"

"You sound a lot like a friend of mine," replied Zach, thinking about Shadmore.

The old leatherstocking who had been Zach's mentor had had his share of women—and of women trouble—in his day. Now, older and wiser, he seized every opportunity to wax eloquent about the trials and tribulations that females had a knack of visiting upon the male of the species.

"That's not very charitable of you," Letcher told Adams, sternly.

"Just telling it like it is," said Adams.

"She saw her folks murdered by those Comanches," snapped Letcher. "And then God knows what she suffered at their hands."

"I know what they did to her. We all do." Choctaw looked around at the circle of traders. He and the mountain men stood within the circle. Choctaw was holding a lantern. Its light fell on the woman who lay unconscious at their feet.

Zach and Letcher had ridden into camp after dark. The caravan had passed the scene of the Comanche ambush that day. The sight of the two mutilated corpses had put everybody's nerves on edge. The guards Adams had posted around the camp had come close to shooting the two mountain men in the darkness.

It had taken them a full day to get back to the caravan. The girl had lapsed in and out of consciousness. During her conscious moments she had been delirious.

"Fact is," continued Choctaw, "you would have done her a big favor by shooting her."

"Why you . . ." Letcher took a menacing step toward Adams, his fists clenched.

Zach stepped between them. "Back off, Doc," he said quietly.

"What's got into you, Letcher?" queried Choctaw. "You'd think this poor girl was kin to you, or something, the way you're acting."

"I thought you were a decent man," said Letcher bitterly. "I see now that I was wrong. You could at least show a little compassion."

Adams gnashed the tip of his pipe and fixed a flinty gaze on Letcher.

"Look, what happened is a damned shame, and I'm sorry as hell. But she'll just be a burden to us. And after what those savages did to her, she won't want to keep on living."

"You don't know that."

"I've seen it before."

"She'll be no burden. I'll take responsibility for her.

All I need is one of you to carry her in your wagon until she's fit enough to ride."

"She'll ride in my wagon if she rides in any," said Choctaw, and scanned the circle of traders again. "You men will keep clear of this woman, you hear?"

They made a place for her in Choctaw's wagon, shifting crates around and making a comfortable pallet for her using bolts of cheap cloth.

Late that night, after everyone but the guards had gone to sleep, a piercing scream woke the men. Letcher jumped up and bolted for Choctaw's wagon. Zach was right behind him. The entire camp was roused. Men grabbed their guns. Curses filled the night. A second scream brought them running to Choctaw's wagon. The girl was cowering beneath the wagon. Adams was holding the lantern aloft and knuckling sleep out of his eyes. When he saw Letcher he threw out an arm to stop the mountain man from getting any closer to the wagon.

"She's got a knife," he warned. "Stay back."

Zach saw it was so. The lantern's light glimmered off the blade. He figured she had to have gotten it from Choctaw's trade goods. Crouched beneath the wagon, she stared wildly at the congregation of men through a veil of disheveled black hair. Zach stepped forward.

"Watch yourself, Hannah," admonished Choctaw. "She's gone plumb loco. She'll gut you with that pigsticker, given half a chance."

Zach laid his rifle down and took another step closer to the wagon before hunkering down to extend a hand to the girl.

"Don't be afraid. You won't be . . ."

With a guttural scream she lunged, lashing out with the knife. Zach fell backward, barely escaping the blade. The girl had ventured out from under the wagon to make this attempt on his life, and now she backed up to press herself against the side of the wagon, looking frantically around for a place to run. But the traders completely circled the wagon. Most of them held their rifles in a way that made it clear to Letcher that if she made a move toward them with that knife they would defend themselves.

"Nobody shoot!" cried Letcher. He handed his rifle to Choctaw and stepped forward to stand beside Zach, who was picking himself up off the ground, shaken but unharmed.

"Everybody get back," growled Adams. "Give her room, damn it. If she wants to run off, then by God we'll let her."

"No," snapped Letcher.

He stepped forward, holding out a hand, palm turned up. The girl watched him with panic-stricken eyes.

"Careful, Doc," said Zach.

"Just back away. I'll handle this. She won't hurt me."

"He's as crazy as she is," declared Adams.

"Give me the knife," said Letcher, taking another step forward. His voice was calm. His hand was steady. He looked her straight in the eyes. "I'm your friend. We saved you from the Indians. You're safe now. I won't let anybody hurt you again. You have my word on that. Now, just give me the knife."

A single tear snaked down her cheek and broke Doc Letcher's heart.

He took another step. One more, and he would be within reach of her.

"I know they hurt you," he said. "But they won't anymore. It's all over. I . . . *no!*"

She slashed her wrist open.

"Christ!" breathed Adams.

The knife slipped from her grasp as she fainted. Letcher was there to catch her. He laid her gently down and closed one big hand around her delicate wrist. Bright red blood seeped through his fingers. As Zach rushed forward, Letcher looked up at him with a peculiar expression on his face.

"She'll live," he said hoarsely, as though by willing a thing he could make it happen. "Don't worry. She'll live."

The next day Zach rode out alone. Letcher had expressed his desire to stay with the girl, at least for the first day or two, and no one interested in his own health was going to object. Choctaw Adams certainly did not raise an argument, as Zach thought he might. After all, Letcher was along for the purposes of hunting and scouting. But Zach figured Choctaw's acquiescence was the result of the caravan leader's astute perception of Letcher's resolve. Doc Letcher was not going to be swayed, come hell or high water.

It turned out that the girl had failed to do serious damage to herself. The cut on her wrist was not deep. Zach felt sorry for her. But he had a hunch that Letcher's feelings ran much deeper than mere sympathy. Zach surmised that Doc Letcher was smitten. How had it happened? When had it happened? Probably during that long ride back to the caravan, thought Zach. After the rescue, when Letcher had held her tightly to him, her head against his chest. There was little point in trying to rationalize how these things came about, anyway. Zach could well remember how he had felt the very first time he had laid eyes on Morning Sky. One look, and his life had been changed forever. One look was all it took. He was living proof of that.

He returned to camp that evening to discover that Letcher had traded his flintlock pistol for a dress for the girl to wear. Zach knew then and there he was right about Letcher. Doc was in love, sure enough. Only a man in love would give up his pistol for a dress.

The girl was doing much better. Physically she was making a quick recovery. Emotionally it would take much longer. She seemed to realize, instinctively, that Letcher was her protector.

Within a few days time she was riding double with him as he returned to his hunting and scouting duties. Letcher knew he needed to find a horse for her. He wanted her with him, instead of back there with the caravan, and that was what she wanted, too. But horses were hard to come by.

In the evenings she shared the campfire of the two mountain men and slept on the ground, eschewing Choctaw's wagon, her blankets never far from Letcher's. She remained skittish in the presence of all the other men, although she tolerated Zach better than the others. Some of the traders offered her gifts—ribbons, a mirror, a hairbrush, a bracelet of copper and silver entwined together. The man with whom Letcher had traded for the dress returned Doc's pistol. Zach knew that they were giving these things out of the goodness of their hearts. They, too, felt sorry for her. They harbored no ulterior motives. But Letcher didn't seem to appreciate their generosity all that much. Zach figured jealousy lay behind his possessiveness.

Her name was Angelique Chagres. The only family she had left now was a brother, named Manuel, who was waiting in Santa Fe. It was Manuel who had persuaded Angelique's father to return home, after a long exile. For years after the revolution the Mexicans had persecuted full-blooded Spaniards. Such was no longer the case. Manuel had prospered because he had turned against his own kind to side with the peasants in their struggle for freedom from oppression. It had taken Angelique's father a long time to forgive his son for what he perceived to be a betrayal. Angelique had consistently defended Manuel. He was a young man sensitive to the tribulations of the downtrodden. The one thing Angelique had hoped for above all else in life was to see her father and brother reconciled face-to-face. Now she would never see that day.

In time they reached the Cimarron River. Much to their disappointment, they found the river at this point to be hardly more than a muddy trickle. The stretch from the Arkansas to the Cimarron had been a dry one. They were definitely in what the traders called a "water scrape." They pressed on, hoping for better luck with the Canadian. Their water kegs were almost empty. Men, mules, and oxen suffered in the desert heat on half rations.

But the day after putting the Cimarron behind them they had some luck. A summer storm rolled in. Zach, Letcher, and Angelique raced back to the caravan, not wanting to get caught out in the open. Angry black-bellied thunderclouds blotted out the sun. The wind whipped up something fierce. Zach noticed a green tint to the clouds, and figured on some hail. He was right.

The storm, when it struck, was a fury. Silver sheets of hard-driving rain coupled with hail the size of robin's eggs, and bolts of lightning that struck the prairie in conjunction with deafening blasts of thunder. Everyone took shelter beneath their wagons, after removing the lids from their water kegs. But the storm became so violent that the traders had to venture out to calm the mules and oxen left standing in their traces. A particularly large chunk of hail hit one man in the head and knocked him cold.

Gauged by the water accumulated in the kegs, four inches of rain fell in an hour's time. The storm passed quickly, as summer freshets do on the southern plains. The traders checked their cargoes for damage. Choctaw Adams decided they would stay where they were until the morning, and the men spread their goods out to dry in the stifling heat and blazing sun of the afternoon. It was discovered that a pair of mules had broken harness and escaped during the storm. Choctaw delegated to Zach the task of tracking them down.

Zach rode out on his errand—only to return in no time at all, empty-handed.

"I thought I sent you out after those damned errant mules, Hannah," groused Adams, who was not in the best of moods. Any delay rubbed him wrong. "What are you doing back here without them?"

"I wanted to warn you about the company we're about to have," replied Zach with unflappable poise.

"Company?"

Zach turned in his saddle and pointed.

At that moment a distant ridge suddenly bristled with a line of horsemen.

"Good God Almighty," breathed Choctaw Adams. "There must be a hundred of them."

"At least," agreed Zach, laconic.

"Comanches?"

"I didn't get close enough to get a good look."

Choctaw Adams stood up in the wagon box, turned to look back down the line of wagons, and raised a hand overhead to describe a large looping circle.

"Circle the wagons!" he yelled.

The call was carried down the line by the lieutenants. Men grabbed their rifles and shotguns. A scream drew Zach's attention away from the Indians. He saw Angelique running across the sagebrush flat. Letcher was in pursuit on horseback and quickly closed with her. He made a running dismount and grabbed her, wrapping his arms around her, holding her tightly to him. Forgetting about his horse, he led her back to the wagons on foot. Zach rode out to meet them. Angelique was sobbing softly against

Letcher's chest. Doc looked up at Zach, and his expression was bleak.

"Whatever happens," he said, "they won't take her alive. If anything happens to me, Zach, promise me that you won't let them take her alive."

Chapter 21

"Get back to the wagons," said Zach, and kicked his horse into motion, heading out across the flats to catch up Letcher's wayward horse.

"Promise me!" Letcher yelled after him.

But Zach pretended not to hear.

He caught up the horse without undue difficulty and turned back toward the wagons. He could see that Letcher and Angelique had reached the caravan. He could also see that a group of Indians—twenty, maybe twenty-five of them—had broken away from the rest, who remained on the distant ridge, and were coming straight at the wagons. Choctaw had belayed the order to circle up. There wasn't time. The traders took cover underneath and behind the wagons.

By the time Zach reached the caravan, the Indians were a couple hundred yards away. They had their ponies stretched out in a gallop. Thundering hooves kicked up a plume of dun-colored dust. Zach tethered both horses to a wheel of Choctaw's wagon and took the buckskin sheath off the Hawken to check cap and charge. Choctaw had dug a spyglass out of his possibles. He scanned the group of approaching

riders with the spyglass, and then the long line of Indians on the distant ridge. Finally he lowered the
spyglass and clambered back up into the wagon box
and yelled: "Hold your fire!"

As the lieutenants conveyed this order, Choctaw
jumped off the wagon and turned to Zach with vast
relief on his craggy features.

"I see women and children up on that ridge, Hannah, thank God."

Zach knew that was a good sign. Indians bent on
war did not bring their families along.

"What tribe?" he asked.

"Arapaho, I think. A whole band on the move. The
bunch coming up has our mules in tow."

The group of Indians checked their ponies fifty
yards from the wagons. One of them ventured closer,
raised his lance overhead, and uttered a piercing
yell.

"He's trying to tell us something," said Choctaw,
"but I'll be damned if I know what. I don't speak the
lingo and, frankly, don't know anybody who does.
The Arapaho language is entirely different from any
other Indian tongue."

The brave in advance of the rest hurled his lance
into the ground.

"Reckon that actions speaks louder than words,"
said Zach. "Is that a challenge? Or a way of telling us
he's come to talk and not fight."

"He wants to talk. Guess I'll mosey on out there
and see if I can figure out what the hell they want."

"I'll go with you," volunteered Zach. "I'm pretty
good with sign language."

Choctaw gave him a hard look. "We've got to go

out empty-handed, Hannah. You never can tell about Arapaho. They can be friendly as all get-out one minute and turn on you the next."

"I'll take my chances."

"Let's go." He glanced beyond Zach, as Hanrahan and the other lieutenant, a man named Gifford, came up to the head of the column for further orders. "You two make damned sure nobody shoots. If you do, those Dog Soldiers out yonder will make short work of us." He smiled coldly at Hanrahan. "And I know everybody would truly hate to see that happen."

"Don't worry, Choctaw," said Letcher, who had walked up behind the lieutenants.

Hanrahan turned and glowered at Letcher. Doc just stared back at him, impassive.

Choctaw and Zach divested themselves of all weapons and started out across the flats toward the bunch of Arapaho warriors, who awaited them on their prancing ponies.

Thirty minutes later they were back safe and sound with the wagons, the two errant mules in hand. It had been a long half hour for Letcher and the Santa Fe traders. Only when the Dog Soldiers turned their ponies and rode back toward the ridge did the caravaners ease off their triggers and breathe a collective sigh of relief.

"So what happened?" asked Hanrahan. "What did they want?"

"Just returning our livestock," said Choctaw.

"For nothing?" Hanrahan was skeptical.

"Well, they wanted guns, but we told them we had

none to spare. Offered them some blankets and knives and such, but they declined, and just gave over the mules. A show of good faith. Said they needed guns and nothing else, on account of they are at war with the Comanches."

"Good faith!" scoffed Hanrahan. "Injuns don't know what good faith is. They're up to something."

"Just because you can't be trusted," said Letcher, "doesn't mean the same is true of everybody else."

"You and I will settle," warned Hanrahan. He glanced at Choctaw Adams. "Once we get to Santa Fe."

"That suits me right down to the ground," said Letcher.

"When we get to Santa Fe you can do whatever the hell you want, Hanrahan," said Adams. "If you want to go and tangle with these two buckskin hellions you just go right ahead and get yourself killed. I won't stop you."

"Won't be me six feet under," growled Hanrahan, and stalked off.

Choctaw employed the spyglass to scan the ridge again.

"Looks like they're moving west. Reckon they'll hover around us for a while. I don't think they want a fight. But if we give them a shot at stealing these wagons they'll for sure do her. We'll just have to keep a close eye on them."

"There's one good thing to come of all this," said Zach.

"What might that be?"

"With all those Arapahos around, we won't be bothered by Comanches."

* * *

They moved on, and made five more miles before sundown. The Arapaho band, several hundred strong, traveled parallel to the caravan. That evening they came calling on the traders in small bunches. A group of young women circled the camp on the ponies, serenading the white men, while warriors brazenly strolled into camp, using sign language to profess their friendship, while their covetous eyes took inventory of the goods in the wagons.

Choctaw Adams saw through their ruse. Arapaho women, he told Zach, were on the whole quite fair of form and face, but notoriously free with their favors. These little jezebels, he said, were trying to distract the traders while their light-fingered counterparts made off with whatever they could pilfer. He roamed through the camp, admonishing the men to ignore the women and keep an eagle eye on the braves, who were trying their best to ingratiate themselves on the whites. At the same time Adams cautioned the company to refrain from violence. There were, he calculated, more than a hundred Dog Soldiers in the band, so the traders were grievously outnumbered.

The traders were understandably uneasy, and Zach was afraid that violence was inevitable. It was just a question of when. And after checking on Letcher and Angelique, he had a hunch it would be Doc who started the ruckus.

Angelique was the problem. The presence of the Indians upset her. It made no difference that they weren't Comanches. She was back to crouching under a wagon. It was all Letcher could do to keep her from panicking every time a fierce-looking Dog

Soldier appeared out of the darkness into the throw of the firelight. Needless to say, Doc Letcher was not in good humor.

Despite the tension, the night passed without mishap. Although most of the traders remained vigilant, some tobacco and a bolt of cheap calico were missing. Choctaw decided that the wise course was to ignore the theft. At least everyone was still wearing their hair.

That day Zach scouted alone, while Letcher stayed behind to watch over Angelique, who had suffered something of a relapse, thanks to the presence of the Arapahos. She did not want to leave the caravan, feeling that in numbers there was safety.

Zach came across a small herd of buffalo. He shot three. While he was butchering the first one out, a band of Arapahos appeared. He had been expecting them, and offered the other two kills to the Indians. The Arapahos were surprised and delighted.

Choctaw approved of Zach's generosity. "That was mighty diplomatic, Hannah," he said. "They must figure we're easy marks, now. They come in here last night and steal some of our goods, and the next day we make them a gift of two buffalo. I don't think they'll attack us. No, they'll just string along and try to steal us blind. Take advantage of us, for as long as they can."

A couple of days later the caravan reached the Canadian. The water kegs were filled, and they pushed on. Three days after that they reached Rabbit Ear Mound. Santa Fe was only a hundred miles away now.

The Arapaho stuck with them, visiting the camp

every night. By now each wagon had its own guard, the men taking turns watching over their merchandise in four-hour intervals. The tension eased, as the traders came to realize that the Indians were not likely to resort to violence. Some things turned up missing, but in such small quantities that the loss was inconsequential, and the traders were willing to let this petty thievery go unchallenged. They tolerated the Arapahos as they would pesky mosquitoes.

Zach continued sharing his kills with the Indians. The chief of the band came one evening to smoke the pipe of peace. Zach thought to ask for the gift of a horse. After all he had done with regard to feeding the Indians, the chief could scarcely refuse. The next morning Angelique had her own mount. From then on she and Letcher rode with Zach Hannah, well in advance of the caravan. A squad of Dog Soldiers usually shadowed Zach, but for their own amusement they tried to remain out of sight, and Zach was careful never to let on that he knew where they were virtually every minute of the day. This was better for Angelique than remaining with the caravan, with the main body of the Arapaho band constantly in sight to the north of the trail.

One day past Rabbit Ear Mound, Zach, Letcher, and the girl met up with a caravan embarked on the return trip to Independence. Zach got a good look at every man in the party. Sean Michael Devlin was not among them. Trading was brisk this season, they said. Better than ever. Their pockets were full of Santa Fe gold. There were three or four other caravans still in Santa Fe at that moment, and by all accounts everyone was making plenty of profit.

On they went, across desert plains studded with small mountain ranges, whose snow-clad peaks seemed to hover, disconnected, above the heat shimmer. The plain itself was cut by bluffs and deep barrancas. The whole was dotted with strips of scrub cedar. The air was so hot and dry that the wood in the wheels and axles shrank. At every stop the wagoners had to perform repair work, driving wedges between tire and felly, and bracing the spokes to the hubs.

Beyond the Point of Rocks they descended into the valley of the Canadian River. Here the river itself—eighty miles from its source in a range of mountains to the north—was scarcely thirty feet in width. The crossing was made without difficulty, as the river bottom was solid rock. The river was clear and cold, and Angelique found a private place to bathe. Zach had to admit she was right pretty with the dust washed off and her long raven hair brushed out. And he could see that Letcher shared that sentiment, in spades.

The next morning the traders awoke to find the Arapahos gone. The entire band had just vanished. Zach rode forth to examine their camp of the night before. He returned to inform Choctaw Adams that the Indians had apparently slipped away in quiet haste in the darkness of the early morning hours and headed north.

The sudden departure puzzled Zach, but Choctaw nodded as he listened to this report, as though he had been expecting such a development.

"Means we're going to have more visitors," he said.

"Either a large party of Comanches or Mexicans. Let's hope the latter."

He was right. Later that day they were visited by *ciboleros*—Mexican buffalo hunters.

Zach had never seen such a colorful bunch of characters. There were about forty in the group, including a dozen women. The men all rode on horseback. The women rode and drove two-wheeled *carretas* pulled by oxen.

The men wore flat-brimmed hats and leathern jackets and trousers decorated with quillwork or beadwork, fringe, and conchos. Their saddles were unusually high in the cantle and pommel, providing the rider with a most secure seat. They were dark, wiry plainsmen, and excellent fighters, for they often clashed with Comanches and Apaches, and in general were highly respected for their prowess by the Indians of the southern plains.

They hunted with lance and bow and arrow. The lance was carried in a case secured vertically to the saddle. The bright tassels decorating the tips of the lances fluttered high over the heads of the buffalo hunters.

Every year the *ciboleros* ventured out upon the plains to hunt the buffalo, providing their families, as well as the communities of Santa Fe and San Miguel and Taos with a supply of meat. The men performed the chase and the kill; the women followed to do the butchering. They cured the meat by cutting it into thick strips and spreading it out in the hot sun. The women kneaded the slices with their feet, a process they claimed preserved the meat. Salt was not needed for curing in this arid clime.

The *ciboleros* were delighted to meet up with the American traders. They confirmed that the prospects for trade in Santa Fe were excellent. Choctaw, who proved to have a firm grasp of the Spanish language, questioned them closely regarding the affairs of the custom houses and the identities of current revenue officers, and came away apparently satisfied with the state of things.

That night the buffalo hunters shared a camp with the traders. A few of them broke out their guitars, and the musically inclined among the Americans responded by brandishing fiddles and harmonicas. A couple of the Mexican women danced, and a few of the traders joined in. A good time was had by all.

Angelique was glad to have the chance to visit with people of her own race. The presence of the *ciboleros* animated her. She asked questions of them concerning her brother. Manuel Chagres was well known. He had prospered as a merchant and now ran a mining operation. He had many connections in Santa Fe. He was a hero of the revolution, so no one begrudged him his success, and chose to ignore his pedigree.

News of her brother and the realization that Santa Fe was so close energized Angelique. When Zach arrived at the campsite he shared with Letcher—as always apart from the rest of the caravan—he found the girl earnestly entreating Letcher to leave the slow-moving caravan behind and hasten to Santa Fe.

"If we leave at dawn," she said, "we can be there late tomorrow night. If we remain with the wagons it will take us two days."

"I'm inclined to do it," admitted Letcher. "I have my own reasons for wanting to get to Santa Fe as quickly as possible."

"Funny," said Zach, "but I was just talking to Choctaw Adams about that very same thing."

"What did he say?" asked Letcher.

"He suggested we go on ahead. He's willing to acknowledge that we've fulfilled our obligations, and release us from that oath."

"*He* suggested it? Why?"

"I think it has something to do with Hanrahan."

"Oh." Letcher nodded grimly. "We're not finished with that big son of a . . ." He caught himself, cast a sheepish glance at Angelique. Having spent the last ten years in the United States, she was fluent in the English language.

"Adams is hoping we can take care of our business and dust out of Santa Fe before Hanrahan gets there. He just wants to prevent bloodshed."

"Hanrahan's blood," muttered Letcher.

"Anybody's."

"You will not stay long in Santa Fe?" asked Angelique, searching Letcher's face.

Letcher didn't know what to say. The matter had never come up between them, and in truth, he had never thought past reaching Santa Fe and settling once and for all with Devlin.

So he stared at her, speechless, and she looked away, trying to mask her feelings.

"I am sorry," she said softly. "It is none of my concern what you do or where you go."

"So it's agreed?" asked Zach. "We leave in the morning?"

"The sooner the better," said Letcher.

Chapter 22

Entering Santa Fe separately from the caravan proved to be an advantage to the mountain men. The arrival of wagons filled with trade goods inevitably caused great excitement in the town, drawing the attention of many of its six thousand inhabitants as well as that of the local officials. Crowds would gather to see the *Americanos*. Customs inspectors would appear, courteous but firm and sharp-eyed.

The traders were required to present the officials with manifests listing every piece of merchandise in every wagon. This, for the purpose of calculating the *derechos de arancel*—the tariff imposts. These import duties were extremely high, as much as one hundred percent. But an experienced trader knew that a "bargain" could be successfully struck with the Mexican revenue officers, who were nearly always willing to consider arrangements by which they could provide for themselves a little "bonus."

Everything depends on the good sense of the trader. Many American caravaners had made the mistake of treating the Mexicans with poorly disguised contempt. Some unpleasant fate nearly always befell such unwise individuals, from paying the full tariff duties to ending up in some dank jail cell, shackled hand and foot. American contempt seemed to trigger Mexican resentment, which was ever-present but usually concealed in dealings with the gringos. Mexicans as a whole were envious of the prosperity of the Americans, and justifiably leery of Yankee greed. They desperately needed American goods, and for that reason alone tolerated the traders.

In spite of exceedingly high tariffs on their imported merchandise, the Americans still stood to realize a handsome profit. The goods were transferred to the customs house, where they were inspected by the customs officials. This process usually took a couple of days. The traders spent this time cutting deals with local merchants, so that by the time the goods were released, every piece was presold. The exchange was made, and the trader found himself with his pockets full of "hard chink."

Santa Fe spared no effort to get all of that money back. An American careless with his money could find himself broke before he knew it. Still, many of the traders flocked to the fandango, and spent wildly on women and whiskey. Some fell victim to thieves. A trader who awoke facedown in a dark alley with a knot on his head and his pockets picked clean would suddenly find Mexican sympathy in extremely short supply. In short, he would discover that a gringo with money would be greeted with a warm and concerned smile, while one without a peso to his name met only with cold stares. Rare indeed was the cutthroat guilty of preying on a Yankee trader brought to justice.

Zach and Letcher were hopeful of escaping most of this attention by entering Santa Fe separate from Choctaw's caravan.

Built at the western base of a mountain range, Santa Fe was a rambling collection of square adobe structures interspersed among fields of corn and wheat. The irregular streets were a maze, winding this way and that with no apparent design. The center of town was the public square. Here stood the *Palacio,* or Governor's House, the *Casa Consistorial* where the alcaldes of the city government conducted the business affairs of the municipality, the barracks with the adjacent *calabozo,* the much-feared local jail, the Customs House, and the Military Chapel. The major thoroughfares all radiated out from the public square, like the spokes of a wheel from its hub.

They reached the public square late at night, a circumstance that brought them to the attention of two soldiers who were on patrol in the vicinity of the *Palacio.* Neither Zach nor Letcher knew a lick of Spanish, so Angelique had to do all the talking. While she spoke, Zach noticed that the attitude of the soldiers gradually changed, from stern suspicious to open friendliness. They became very helpful and gave the mountain men a cheery salute when they moved on.

"What did you tell them?" Letcher asked her.

"I told them who I was. The sister of Manuel Chagres. I also told them that the two of you had rescued me from the Comanches. They were very impressed."

"Looks like your brother is a big augur around here," remarked Zach.

Just beyond the ring of buildings around the public square they found a street where, according to the soldiers, Manuel Chagres had a house.

The Chagres home was quite a bit larger than most of the other dwellings they had seen in Santa Fe. Surrounded by a high adobe wall, it was a rambling one-story affair with galleries all around. The heavy timbered carriage doors of the main gate were shut. A storm lantern on the wall beside the gate was lighted. The pull of a rope jangled a bell hanging in an iron frame atop the wall.

Across the street a stream tumbled down over a rocky bed. Born in the snow-topped mountains looming above the town, the creek joined the Rio del Norte twenty miles to the southwest. Zach listened to the rush of the icy waters—and wondered if Devlin could hear that same sound at this very moment. Was Coyote here in Santa Fe tonight? Was the manhunt almost concluded? Zach thought about Morning Sky and little Jacob. For weeks now he had tried very hard *not* to think of his family, because such thoughts hurt his heart. He longed to see them both again. He had lost track of the days that had passed since he had taken his leave of them. He did not worry about their well-being, though. Shadmore had promised to look out for them, and the old leatherstocking was the only man Zach Hannah fully trusted.

There was a small door cut into the gate. This swung open, and an old man appeared to squint at them and ask them what they wanted.

"You do not recognize me, Felix?" asked Angelique. "But no, you would not. I was but a little girl when I went away."

"*Madre de Dios!*" The old man's eyes widened. "Angelique!"

She leapt off her Indian pony and into Felix's embrace. They held each other a long time before he broke away, trembling with high emotion and wiping a tear of joy from his cheek.

"Come, come, my child," he said. "Your brother is inside." He looked at the two rough-hewn mountain men. "But who is this? Where are . . . ?"

"They are dead," said Angelique flatly. "The Indians killed them, Felix. These men saved my life."

"*Muerte!*" The old man's expression had changed from joyous to grief-stricken. He crossed himself.

Angelique put a hand on his shoulder.

"I know, Felix. I know. I can still hardly believe it is true. I wake in the mornings and look around to see them. And then I remember and I feel as though I could die." Seeing the old man's pain almost broke the control she sought to exert over her own emotions. Yet she managed somehow to force back the tears and smile. "Come, open the gate and let me see my brother."

Felix did as she bade him do. Angelique led her horse into the courtyard. Zach and Letcher rode in behind her. As they dismounted and tethered their ponies to a heavy iron ring in a cedar post buried in the ground, a man emerged from the house.

"Who is it, Felix?"

"Your sister, *patron*."

The man came closer, a slender young man, well

groomed, wearing doeskin trousers and a short jacket handsomely embroidered. He stared hard at Angelique, as though he didn't believe Felix, or thought it was some kind of trick. But then he recognized her, in spite of all the years that had passed since last they had seen each other, and he rushed forward, and Angelique cried out in joy as he threw his arms around her.

Zach looked away, feeling like an intruder at this very private moment of happy reunion. He glanced at Letcher. Doc was watching Angelique and her brother, and he didn't look very happy. Zach had a hunch as to why. Angelique was home, and that meant she was no longer in Letcher's keeping. He had delivered her safely to Manuel, and soon he would have to leave. But she would stay, of course.

Angelique told her brother the bad news of their parents' deaths. He took it bravely. And when she introduced the mountain men to him, explaining that they had rescued her from the Comanches, Manuel shook their hands and warmly expressed his heartfelt gratitude.

"My house is your house," he said in passably good English. "If there is anything I can do, I will do it. I owe you both a debt I could never fully repay."

"Well, there *is* something we'd like to know," said Zach. "We're looking for someone. We think he's here in Santa Fe."

"Then you will find him. I will see to it. Come, you can tell me all about it inside. Felix will see to your horses."

* * *

The Chagres house was furnished with heavy, age-blackened pieces of furniture, fine rugs on the polished oak floors, gilt-framed paintings adorning the walls. Chagres offered the mountain men brandy and cigars in a big room dominated by a fireplace large enough, thought Zach, to burn a full-sized tree in. He realized he could have stood almost upright inside the hearth. It was surely a true wonder.

While Zach declined both brandy and cigar, Doc Letcher accepted. "Mr. Chagres, you have done well for yourself," said Doc.

Manuel's shrug was humble. "I began as a merchant. But not until I became involved in mining did I prosper. The mine is called El Real de Dolores. It is a half day's ride south of Santa Fe. It is not the quantity, but the quality of the ore which is taken from the mine which makes of the venture a success. The gold is uncommonly pure. It brings about twenty dollars American a troy ounce."

"Is yours the only gold mine in these parts?"

"The only one of any consequence, yes. Traces of gold can be found almost anywhere in this country, but the major veins are difficult to find. I am lucky to have found one. I do not seek to monopolize the business. Many *gambucinos* work their own little *labors,* and they find enough placers of gold to survive. But another vein has not yet been found.

"I do what I can for the *gambucinos*. When the Dolores was discovered there was what you would call a gold rush into the mountains. Men killed each other over a piece of land. I persuaded the alcaldes to institute some provisions, enforced by soldiers. Now a *gambucino* cannot stake a claim nearer than ten paces from another. His claim is registered for a small fee to the alcaldes. Unless he abandons his *labor*, no one may interfere with him.

"I also offer to pay twenty dollars an ounce for any gold they bring to me. I make no profit from these transactions, you understand, but the *gambucino* is happy with one or two reals in his pocket, enough to buy food for his family, and he knows he is better off bringing his gold to me rather than the merchants in town, who will try to cheat him."

Listening to Chagres, Zach got the feeling he was a little defensive about his success. Perhaps it was due to his high-born background—perhaps Manuel deemed it necessary to go to great pains to demonstrate that he was not just another Spanish aristocrat who did not care one whit for the common man.

Manuel deftly changed the subject. "But that is enough about me. Tell me what has brought you to Santa Fe. You say you are looking for someone. What is his name?"

Letcher was careful not to look at Angelique. They had never discussed the purpose of his journey to Santa Fe. He had been reluctant to do so, afraid she would think less of him if she knew his mission was vengeance.

But what did it matter now? Soon they would go their separate ways.

Feeling oddly empty, Letcher said, "His name is Sean Michael Devlin. He is a trader, who should have arrived in Santa Fe more than a fortnight ago. Have you heard of him?"

Manuel was frowning. "Yes, I have heard of this man."

Letcher's pulse quickened. "Is he still here?"

"Oh, definitely. He is still in Santa Fe. Tell me, what business do you have with this Devlin?"

"I aim to kill him," replied Letcher.

Chapter 23

"I will see what I can find out," said Manuel. "You will know by morning where to find this man."

"You're not going to ask me why I want to take his life?"

Manuel shrugged. "I am sure you have your reasons. Whether they are right or wrong reasons does not matter. It is not my concern. I only know that you saved my sister's life, and for that I am in your debt. I must pay my debt. I will locate Devlin for you."

"I have a question," said Zach. "How is it you've come to hear about Devlin, anyway?"

"There was some trouble."

"With Coyote there usually is."

"Coyote?"

"That's how he's known up in the high country, Mr. Chagres."

"There was trouble at a cantina. An argument over a woman, between Senor Devlin and one of the soldiers from the garrison here."

"What happened?"

"Nothing. Calmer heads prevailed. No blood was shed. But that won't be the end of it, I think. One thing an American should not do in Santa Fe is make a nuisance of himself."

"So we've heard."

"Devlin has made enemies."

Zach smiled, but there was no humor in it.

"He has a knack for doing that."

"You speak as though you know of him."

"Reckon you could say we used to be friends. But no more."

"Now you want to kill him, too?"

"That's what Doc here wants. I want to take him back to the high country alive. He'll face his judgment day there."

Letcher gave Zach a long, indecipherable look. "Reminds me that our partnership is close to being dissolved."

Manuel showed them to their rooms.

Zach took one look at the four-poster bed with its canopy and plump goosedown mattress and knew he couldn't sleep in the contraption. Many years had passed since he had slept in an honest-to-God bed, and he had gotten completely out of the habit. The room itself was claustrophobic. Tall, narrow French doors opened onto the gallery that ran the length of the rear of the Chagres house. Zach opened them and stepped out into the night. From somewhere up on the lonesome, cedar-cloaked slopes of the foothills, a coyote wailed a mournful lament. Doc Letcher had already stepped out of his room, which was adjacent to Zach's.

"I haven't changed my mind about Devlin," said Letcher.

"Neither have I."

An uncomfortable silence fell between them. Zach had grown to like Doc Letcher, and he wasn't looking forward to having him for an enemy. He didn't know it, but Doc Letcher was thinking similar thoughts.

"Do you want to settle it now?" asked Letcher.

"I never cross a bridge before I come to it," said Zach. "I'll see you in the morning."

As he turned to go inside, Letcher said, "Good night, Hannah."

Zach pulled the coverlet off the bed, stretched out on the floor, threw the coverlet over his legs, and went to sleep, the Hawken beside him.

Later that night stealthy footsteps woke him. Reaching for the Hawken was pure reflex. He had left the French doors open, and somehow he knew that it was from the gallery that the sound had come. Yet he saw nothing out of the ordinary. He waited, motionless, listening hard, but heard nothing else. Had he been dreaming? Zach considered that possibility, then discarded it. Someone had slipped past those doors. He was sure of it.

He rose and, silent as a ghost, moved toward the doors, rifle ready. Stepping out onto the gallery, he scanned the night shadows. Nothing. The doors to Letcher's room were still open. Zach moved to them, walking on the balls of his feet, and peered inside.

Letcher was asleep in the bed.

Angelique, clad in a long white cotton nightdress, was curled up on the floor beside the bed.

Zach couldn't tell if she was aware of his presence on the gallery—if she was, she pretended to be asleep.

Shaking his head, Zach went back to his room. He wondered what Manuel's reaction would be if and when he discovered that his sister had spent the night in Letcher's room.

But he didn't worry about it, or about Devlin, or about the prospects of conflict with Doc Letcher. Tomorrow would take care of itself. It always did, and worrying about it never changed that. He rolled up in the coverlet again and went promptly back to sleep.

He was awake at first light, to the sound of angry voices, and he sighed, not surprised. Rising, he stepped out onto the gallery to see Manuel and Angelique squared off in front of Letcher's room. They were speaking in Spanish, but Zach didn't need to comprehend the language to know that they were having a disagreement.

"It is not . . . not *proper,* what you have done!" sputtered Manuel, red-faced.

"I could not sleep unless I was close to him, Manuel."

"Sister!"

Angelique stomped a bare foot. "You just do not understand!"

"I understand what I see. And I do not like it, I can tell you."

"I do not feel safe without him."

"But you *are* safe. You are at home. I will protect you."

Some of Angelique's anger subsided. "I know what you say is true. But I cannot help the way I feel."

"But people will talk."

"No one will know."

"You do not understand my position," said Manuel, exasperated. "You have your reputation . . ."

Angelique's laugh was bitter. "It is not my reputation you are concerned about. Don't you remember? The Comanches took me, Manuel. They—"

"Enough! I do not want to hear it."

"What about my feelings?"

"Look," said Manuel, engaging in an epic endeavor to calm himself, hoping he could explain the situation to his headstrong sister. "The word *will* get around. People work for me in this house, Angelique. They pretend to see and hear nothing, but they know everything. It is not proper for you to sleep in the American's room. You could not help what the Comanches did to you. But you can help this. It is bad enough, what you have done. But with an American?"

"What is wrong with Americans?" exclaimed Angelique, outraged. "You want their goods, you try to take all their money, and then you spit on them. I thought you were better than that, brother. But you have changed. You are just like the rest."

Manuel's attempt to control his temper had by now failed abysmally. He wagged a finger under Angelique's defiantly raised chin.

"You will not do this again! I will not permit it!"

"You cannot tell me what to do."

Letcher stepped out of his room, scowling at Manuel. His expression alarmed Zach, who rushed forward. Brother and sister had conducted their quarrel in Spanish, so he didn't know what had been said, but Manuel's tone of voice had grown ever more strident and ugly as the argument progressed. That alone was enough to set Letcher off, reckoned Zach. The fact that Doc didn't know what Manuel was threatening made it even worse.

"You'd better start talking in English," Letcher warned Manuel.

"Stay out of this, senor."

"Don't reckon I will."

Zach was thinking: *We need Manuel Chagres to find Devlin, and Doc is a tick's hair from ruining everything.*

Another consideration that prompted Zach to intervene was the probability that Letcher—and maybe his gringo partner—would end up in the *calabozo,* sentenced indefinitely, if any harm came to Manuel.

"If there's a problem," said Zach, "I'm sure we can work it out between us."

"*Sí,*" replied Manuel, in a cold fury. "There is a problem, senor. My sister is in love with this man."

"Oh!" cried Angelique, hands flying to cover her crimson cheeks. With a glance at a dumbfounded Doc Letcher, she took off running.

Letcher took two steps, a hand outstretched, as though to go after her. "Angelique!" But he stopped and turned on Manuel.

"You should know one thing," he rasped. "Your sister and I never . . ."

Manuel held up a hand to stop Letcher.

"Do not bother professing your innocence to me, senor."

"Why you little stuffed shirt . . ."

Zach stepped between the two.

"Back off, Doc," he said sternly. "Try to remember where you are and why."

Zach's caveat gave Manuel Chagres an idea.

"I will make you a deal," said the Spaniard.

"What kind of deal?" asked Zach.

"I sent some people out to find this man Devlin. They have found him. In the jail. Apparently, the charge is very serious. It concerns a woman from one of the fandangos. They say he beat her badly. The soldiers arrested him."

"Sounds like this could have something to do with that quarrel he got into the other day, with a soldier. Wasn't that over a woman?"

"Yes, I am sure it is connected in some way."

"So what will happen to him?"

Manuel shrugged, as though Devlin's fate were of absolutely no consequence to him.

"They will let him spend some time in chains. Then they will fine him. The amount of the fine will depend entirely on how much *dinero* he has in his possession. After that, he will be tried, found guilty, and sentenced."

"You sound pretty sure he'll be found guilty."

Manuel raised an eyebrow. "But of course. He is a gringo."

Zach thought, *I'm beginning not to like it here in Santa Fe.*

He said, "How long of a sentence?"

"I do not know. But a long one, I think. Five years, maybe ten."

Zach glanced bleakly at Letcher.

"But then," said Manuel, "if I were to say the right word to the right person, and give a little charity"—he rubbed thumb and forefinger together—"then Devlin could be released."

"I think I see what you're getting at," said Zach.

"Me, too," said Letcher. "What's the price for your help?"

"I will arrange it so that Devlin is handed over to you. Once you leave Santa Fe you can do with him what you will. The condition is this." He looked sternly at Letcher. "You will leave this city and never return. You will not see my sister again."

Zach said nothing. He would leave it up to Letcher, and abide what the decision Doc made. It was clearly a difficult choice for Letcher, and Zach wondered what he himself would do, faced with such a dilemma.

Manuel could tell by Letcher's expression of agony that he now had the upper hand. He smiled coldly.

"Think about it, both of you. I will wait to hear your decision."

With that, he walked away.

"Do you love her?" asked Zach.

Letcher looked like he wanted to hit somebody. Anybody.

"If I don't accept his condition we'll never get Devlin, will we?"

"Well, we could always try to break him out of jail."

"This is no time to be funny, Hannah."

"No, it isn't. I'm sorry. I guess we wouldn't get Coyote if you don't accept the condition. But I'll tell you, Doc. If you choose Angelique I'll go along with it, and Devlin can just rot in this jail for the next ten years."

"What about McKenzie? What about all the trappers, and trying to buy some time for them by handing Devlin over to the Blackfeet?"

"I haven't forgotten. But there was never any guarantee McKenzie's scheme would work, anyway. The fight is going to happen, sooner or later."

"What about you? Everything Devlin's done to you?"

"I figure I'll never have any peace of mind as long as he's alive. I know my wife won't. Makes no difference if he's in jail, for five years or ten or twenty. If he survives, I've got a problem as soon as he's cut loose. But you're not listening, Doc. What I want doesn't matter. I'll live with it. Thing is, what about avenging your brother?"

"Yes." Letcher's voice was hollow. "I made a solemn vow on my brother's grave."

"Can you give it up?"

"I don't know."

"Want some advice? Forget vengeance."

"You're one to talk."

"I want Devlin dead because he's a threat to my family now. Not because of what he did to me in the past. Don't you see that? When I escaped the Blackfeet, all I could think about was killing Devlin. I did my damnedest, too. But he got away. That's when I decided to let it go. I couldn't spend my whole life trying to take *his* life. I tried to go forward, and not look back. But not long ago I realized Devlin was there in front of me, too."

"I swore . . ."

"Let it go. Choose Angelique. Don't worry about

her brother. I reckon she'd go anywhere with you. Go get her, and let's ride out of here."

Letcher stopped agonizing over his decision. That much, at least, Zach could see. Doc turned abruptly and entered his room, to emerge a moment later with rifle and pack, a determined look on his face. Zach was waiting for him, with his own gear, on the gallery.

"What are we going to do?" asked Zach.

"We're going to get Devlin," was Letcher's bleak reply.

"Doc . . ."

"We're going to get him. And I hope I don't have to, Zach, but I'll go through you, when the time comes, if you get in my way."

Chapter 24

For a long time they waited in a barren room, its dirt floor hard-packed, its peeling adobe walls fly-specked. Along one wall was a narrow wooden pew. Zach sat there, on and off, but he could never will himself to remain seated for any long period of time. Letcher never once sat down. He spent his time standing in the doorway, staring out at the sun-hammered inner courtyard of the notorious *calabozo*.

Two men were being punished in the courtyard. Their heads and hands were enclosed in heavy timbered yokes, which were secured to sturdy posts buried deeply in the ground, at such a height that the prisoners could not kneel down without choking to death. As a result they had to stand bent over in an extremely uncomfortable position. On the occasion that one of them fainted from the heat and lack of water, one of the guards would saunter lazily out from a strip of shade and hurl the brackish contents of a water bucket on the unconscious man, reviving the latter in time to prevent him from strangling.

As the day wore on, one of the prisoners began to babble incoherently. Zach wondered if his mind was gone. He wondered, too, what kind of crime these men had committed that would earn them such torture.

Letcher did not seem to notice the suffering prisoners. He was lost in his thoughts. Zach figured those thoughts had a lot to do with Angelique—and the life Letcher had turned his back on the moment he had accepted Manuel's condition.

Zach had a bad feeling about the whole business. The cruelty being visited on the two prisoners in the courtyard, and Letcher's stony silence, made him uneasy. This place, as well, contributed to his discomfort. These walls fairly reeked with the smell of fear and hopelessness and death.

One other thing bothered Zach: the knowledge that Sean Michael Devlin was under this very roof, and that, presumably, they would soon stand face-to-face. The prospect of this confrontation was a keenly unpleasant one. Apart from the fact that most, if not all, of the misery that Zach had suffered in the past ten years was the result of actions taken by Devlin, there was as well a sense of betrayal. Devlin had been a friend once. More than a friend. They had become blood brothers ten years ago, that day in St. Louis when Devlin had befriended a friendless youth from the backwoods of Tennessee. Yes, in a way, Devlin was like a brother to Zach—a brother who had gone bad. And that made all of his treachery that much worse.

They waited for hours, and not a word passed between them. There did not seem to be anything left to say. As soon as they got Devlin out of here, mused Zach, Letcher was going to try to kill him. Which left Zach with a tough decision. Letcher had chosen vengeance. His mind was made up. For that Zach envied him. Now Zach had to choose. He, in turn, would have to kill Letcher to stop him, in order to take Devlin back to the high country and deliver him to Kenneth McKenzie, as he said he would.

Was Devlin alive worth Letcher dead?

Miserable, Zach sat for a while, then paced for a while, then sat back down again. He was restless. This interminable wait was wearing on his already frayed nerves. He wanted it to end, but then in another way was in no hurry for it to be finished. Because when the waiting was over he and Doc Letcher would have to settle their differences once and for all.

The hours dragged by. Occasionally, a stern guard with suspicious eyes would swing by to look in on them. He would say nothing, just stare coldly and then move on.

It was well past noon before Manuel Chagres appeared with an officer. The captain was a paunchy man with thinning hair, a pockmarked face, and furtive eyes. His uniform was in a perpetual state of dishevelment. His breath reeked of *aguardiente*.

"The arrangements have been made," said Manuel, addressing Zach. He studiously ignored Doc Letcher. "I have even made a horse available for Senor Devlin. All that remains is that you positively identify the prisoner. Once that is done he will be released into your keeping."

Zach nodded. "What about our rifles?" Their weapons had been confiscated at the gate of the *calabozo*.

"They will be returned to you when you leave. But

remember. There will be no killing while you remain in Santa Fe. Wait until you are out of the city. If you fail in this all of you will end up in here. Quite possibly for the rest of your lives."

Zach glanced at Letcher. He knew then that he had to stop Letcher, somehow, from fulfilling the vow he had made over his brother's grave. The last thing Zach wanted was to rot in this hellhole.

The rattle of chains reached Zach's ears. He turned to face the door, his heart pounding. A soldier entered first, followed by a bearded apparition in tattered clothes. A second guard brought up the rear. The prisoner's head was bowed. Heavy iron shackles decorated his wrists and ankles. He shuffled along, barefooted. For one horrifying moment Zach thought, *This isn't Devlin! We're on the wrong trail. Always have been. All these weeks away from Sky—for nothing!*

Then the prisoner raised his head, as though it took tremendous effort just to do that much, and shamrock-green eyes locked on to Zach and flashed with recognition.

"Hello, Zach. Fancy meeting you here."

The shock of seeing Sean Michael Devlin in the flesh rattled Zach. For a moment he was speechless. That terrifying nightmare—Devlin grinning at him as he held Morning Sky's scalp aloft—shook him to the core as he stood there and stared at Coyote.

"You look like you've seen a ghost," said Devlin, pleased by Zach's reaction. "But I'm not dead yet. Oh, no. These damned bean-eaters can't kill me, though I can't argue that they haven't tried."

The captain barked a sharp command to the soldier behind Devlin. The latter promptly drove the stock of his rifle into the small of Devlin's back. Devlin fell, his face twisted with agony, his mouth gaping—but no cry of pain emerged. He bent over, then straightened up. The soldier shouted at him to get to his feet. Devlin managed to do so. And then he flashed a taut, pain-wracked smile at Zach.

"Now are you gonna let them pick on a fellow American like that, Zach?"

Zach said nothing. This was a much tougher Devlin than he remembered.

"You would do well to keep silent," Manuel warned Devlin, with poorly disguised contempt. "The captain has told you that prisoners are not permitted to speak unless spoken to."

"I don't savvy the lingo," sneered Devlin.

The soldier raised his rifle as though to strike again. Manuel snapped at him, and the soldier refrained. Zach noted that the captain did not seem to care that Manuel Chagres was ordering his men around, and figured this studied indifference meant the commandant had already received his "charity."

Manuel turned to Zach.

"Is this Devlin?"

Zach nodded.

"Your horses are outside," said Manuel curtly. He turned to Letcher. "I have done my part. Now you will carry out your end of the bargain. Adios."

He nodded at the captain, turned on his heels, and marched out of the room. The captain ordered his soldiers to depart, and was the last to exit, leav-

ing the three mountain men—Devlin still shackled—
alone.

Devlin extended his arms.

"Wouldn't happen to have a key to fit these, would
you, Zach?"

"I'm taking you back to the high country, Sean."

"Are you? That suits me. I was getting plenty tired
of that dirty black hole they call a jail cell. I'd like to
see the mountains again. This desert isn't for me.
How's Morning Sky? And my son?"

Zach grimaced. "Jacob isn't yours."

"He's my flesh and blood, and nothing can change
that."

"It doesn't make him your son. I was there when
he came into this world. Sky and I have raised him.
He's not your son. And you'll never see him again."

"I think I will. I do believe I've got the luck of the
Irish, Zach. I mean, here you are in Santa Fe getting
me out of a jail I figured I'd spend the rest of my
days in. What else would you call it, besides luck?"

Zach shook his head. "If so, your luck's run out.
You're going to be turned over to the Blackfeet."

"What?" Devlin was incredulous.

"I'm going to give you to McKenzie, and he's giving
you up to the Blackfeet. Just like you gave me up to
them winter before last."

He saw a glimmer of fear in Devlin's eyes. Devlin
tried to cover it with indignation.

"You think you're a long sight better than me, don't
you, Zach Hannah? But you're not. You're no different than I am." He looked at Letcher. "Who are
you?"

"Me?" rasped Doc, who had been staring at Devlin

all this time. "Why, I'm the man who's going to save you from those Blackfeet."

Devlin's eyes narrowed suspiciously. "Huh? I don't know you. What are you saying?"

"I know you." Letcher took a menacing step closer. Devlin backed up, sensing danger. Then he braced himself, always self-conscious of any display of the cowardice that ran deep in his soul.

"You're the man who killed my brother. Hampton Letcher."

Devlin paled. "I never knew any Hampton Letcher. I don't know what—"

Letcher lashed out and grabbed a handful of Devlin's tattered, grime-blackened buckskin tunic.

"The Blackfeet murdered him. They're on the war-path, on account of what happened at Whirlwind's village."

"I didn't—"

"Yes you did!" roared Letcher. He slammed Devlin against the wall, and his hand closed around Devlin's throat. Zach rushed forward and pried Letcher's hand loose.

"You want to spend the rest of your life in this place, Doc?" asked Zach. "They'll lock us up and throw away the key if you kill him here and now."

Letcher hurled Devlin to the ground and stepped away, disdainful. He went to the door, paused to look back.

"Let's go," he said. "Let's get it over with."

And he walked out into the hot white afternoon.

"Are you going to let him kill me, Zach?" asked Devlin, trying to sound calm and almost succeeding. " 'Cause that's what he aims to do, isn't it?"

"I reckon."

"I'm sorry about his brother. But, Christ! How was I to know those blankets I gave to Whirlwind's people had the plague in them? You can't hold me responsible for that! It's not my fault."

"I'm not blaming you. Letcher is."

"But . . . but that isn't fair."

"Life isn't fair. Get up."

"I'd just as soon stay here."

Zach lost his temper. He dragged Devlin to his feet and slammed him into the same wall to which Letcher had pinned him a moment before.

"Look," said Zach. "I'm taking you back alive, and what Doc Letcher wants doesn't matter. But I'll tell you this. Give me any excuse, and I'll hand you over to him and just walk away. Just remember: I'm the only thing that stands between you and the hereafter."

Devlin nodded.

Zach gave him a hard shove, propelling him toward the door. With his feet shackled, Devlin nearly fell. He caught himself against the frame of the door and smiled at Zach. There was no bravado in that smile. It was not meant to aggravate. Rather, it was tinged with what seemed to be genuine regret.

"Won't be the first time, Zach."

"For what?"

"You saving my life. I remember when those Absaroka Crows had me. They were going to lift my hair and cut my throat for sure. But you showed up, and here I am, still breathing."

"Believe me, many's the time I rued that day."

"Well, I admit, I've done wrong by you. I guess I deserve everything that's coming to me."

"You never spoke truer words, Sean. Now get moving."

Chapter 25

True to his word, Manuel Chagres had arranged to have a horse available for Devlin. Letcher was already mounted. He watched with a marked lack of sympathy as Devlin tried to get mounted in his shackles. Devlin grabbed hold of the saddle pommel and pulled himself up until he could slide one shackled foot into the stirrup.

Zach had a hunch that Letcher expected Devlin to make a break for it once he was mounted. The iron gate across the courtyard was open. All Devlin would have to worry about were the two armed sentries posted there. But Devlin made no desperate, foolish moves. He was relying on Zach Hannah.

They rode across the dusty, sun-hammered courtyard, with Devlin in the middle. At the gate, Letcher and Zach were reinvested with their weapons.

"What about my gear?" asked Devlin. "I had a rifle, too, when they hauled me in here. Not to mention over two thousand dollars in gold."

"Shut up," said Zach.

"You won't need gold where you're going," added Letcher.

Emerging from the Calabozo, the three riders

found themselves in a narrow street not far from the
public square of Santa Fe. They turned away from
the center of town, heading for the outskirts. Letcher
took the lead and Zach brought up the rear, with
Devlin between them. Devlin turned his face skyward and grinned at the sun's warmth on his face.

"God bless you, Zach Hannah," he said. "If I have
to die, at least it won't be in that filthy hole where
I've been the past week."

Zach did not reply.

Up front, Letcher checked his horse sharply. A
lane every bit as narrow as the one they traveled
branched off here, and Doc used this space to turn
his horse around and draw up alongside Zach.

"This is where we part company," said Letcher.

"What?"

"You're on your own."

"I don't follow."

"It was Virgil who said that love conquers all
things. I reckon he was right on the mark."

Then it dawned on Zach what Letcher was doing.
Zach grinned. A great weight was lifted from his
heart. He stuck out his hand. Letcher took it.

"It's been an honor to ride with you, Zach. Especially with you being a legend and all."

Zach laughed, vastly relieved. "Wish I could stick
around for the wedding."

Letcher's expression was rueful. "So do I, in a way.
I have a hunch Manuel Chagres is going to kick up
some dust about this. I mean, I'm not keeping my
end of the bargain. So I'll give you a little time to get
clear of Santa Fe before I show up on his doorstep.

Then all hell will break loose. But I don't care. Nothing he can do will keep me and Angelique apart."

"I'm proud to hear you say that, Doc."

"I'm right proud to say it."

"Where will the two of you go?"

Letcher shook his head. "I know we can't very well stay here. I know that, just like I know now that I can't leave without her."

"You're making the right choice."

"Yeah." Letcher glanced at Devlin. "The end of the road is just up ahead for you, Coyote. Sorry I can't be there to witness it. But I've got better things to do with my life."

"Best wishes to you and the lady," replied Devlin. "Don't worry about me. As long as I'm alive there's a chance. Zach here's living proof of that."

"Don't let him get away from you this time," Letcher told Zach.

"Not this time."

Letcher was turning his horse when the shot rang out.

The pony let out a shrill whinny and fell. Zach's horse, unnerved, jumped sideways, crow-hopping. For a moment it was all Zach could do to keep in the saddle. Even as he tried to bring the animal under control, Zach was aware of everything happening all at once around him. Devlin was kicking his horse into a gallop, hoping to make his escape. Letcher had tried to jump clear of his dying horse—and failed, to have his leg pinned beneath the animal's carcass. And coming up the street was the hulking Hanrahan, powder smoke still trickling from breech and barrel of his percussion rifle.

"Get Devlin!" roared Letcher, his voice taut with pain. "Don't let that bastard get away!"

As he spoke, Doc dragged the pistol from his belt, aimed at Hanrahan, and fired.

The bullet struck Hanrahan in the thigh. It staggered but did not stop him.

"I told you we'd settle!" growled Hanrahan. He kept coming on, limping now, the slick stain of blood spreading on his stroud trousers. "I told you . . ."

He gave up trying to reload his rifle, tossed it away, and brandished his own pistol.

Zach jumped to the ground and let his horse go. The pony galloped down the side street.

"What the hell are you doing?" exclaimed Letcher. "Devlin . . . for God's sake . . . !"

Zach tossed him his own pistol.

Letcher and Hanrahan fired simultaneously. Zach couldn't be sure if the trader was firing at him or Doc, but either way, Hanrahan missed his shot. Letcher didn't. This time he caught Hanrahan square in the chest. Hanrahan took one more step forward, then two back. He stood there a moment, swaying precariously. Then the pistol slipped from his grasp, and he pitched forward to lay dead in the dusty street.

Zach did not see any of this. He was relying on Letcher to deal with Hanrahan. Turning his back on Doc and the trader, he brought the Hawken's stock to shoulder and drew a bead on the fleeing Devlin.

Coyote was fifty yards away and moving fast. He was bent low over the neck of his stretched-out pony to make of himself a smaller target. Zach fleetingly considered shooting the horse out from under him.

But the angle was wrong for a clear killing shot, and Zach realized that there was nothing to be gained by killing an animal just to spare Devlin's life.

"Hell," muttered Zach, and squeezed the Hawken's trigger.

Stepping out of the powder smoke, automatically reaching for his cartridge pouch to begin the process of reloading, Zach watched Devlin slide sideways off the galloping pony and sprawl limp in the street.

Remembering to breathe, Zach exhaled sharply and shook his head.

So much for Redcoat McKenzie's plan, he thought, feeling oddly empty.

Zach finished loading and capping the Hawken and then turned to see how Letcher was doing.

"Anything broken?"

Letcher was flat on his back, one leg pinned beneath a half ton of dead horse, the other draped on top of the carcass.

"I don't think so," said Letcher. He twisted his upper body, trying to get a look up the street at Devlin. "Is he dead?"

"I'll go make certain."

Letcher nodded. "Take your time," he said wryly. "I'm not going anywhere."

Zach started up the street. He figured Devlin was done for. Sky and Jacob were finally free. And he would finally get some peace of mind, no longer wondering what tomorrow would bring. It seemed to him that he ought to feel immense relief, if not downright elation. Instead, all he felt was numb.

Until he reached Devlin and saw him move.

Startled, Zach sat on his heels beside Devlin and

gaped at the bloodstain on Coyote's shirt. The bullet had caught Devlin high in the shoulder and passed clean through below the clavicle. It was the fall, deduced Zach, that had knocked Devlin out cold, and he was just now coming to.

"Maybe you do have the luck of the Irish," muttered Zach.

But he wondered about his own luck, and how far it would stretch, as he looked up to see a squad of soldiers running down the street toward him.

They reached Letcher first. All but one, a sergeant, carried muskets with bayonets attached. At the sergeant's order, two of the soldiers menaced Letcher with their bayonets. Doc threw the empty flintlock pistol away and lay very still. Saber flashing in the hot sun, the sergeant led his three remaining soldiers toward Zach.

Uncertain of what he should do, Zach stood up. All he could think about at first was being locked up in some dark cell for the rest of his life. That made him give consideration to running for it. But he couldn't abandon Doc Letcher, and he damn sure couldn't leave Santa Fe without Devlin. Now that he had Coyote he didn't hanker letting him slip out of his grasp. And making a fight out of it didn't strike him as a very smart idea, either. Chances of coming out of a scrape alive, under these circumstances, were slim and none.

In the end, he did nothing, and the soldiers surrounded him, putting their bayonets to his chest, and the sergeant barked something at him that didn't sound too polite. Zach didn't know the lingo, but he fully comprehended the meaning of the words, and moving very slowly, not wanting to give the soldiers any excuse to turn him into a pincushion, he surrendered the Hawken.

He spent but an hour in a cell, yet that was quite enough time for him. A heavy chain connected the shackle secured to his left ankle to an iron ring set into the wall. He could lie down on the floor, or sit with his back to the wall, or get up and stretch, but he couldn't walk around. The chain was only three feet long. Not that there was much room for walking around anyway. The cell was scarcely six by eight feet. There was no window, and no light, except what little leaked through the barred, foot-square window in the heavy door made of timbers braced with strap iron. The floor was strewn with rank-smelling straw. Something rustled around in the straw over in a far corner of the cell. Zach couldn't see what it was. A mouse, maybe.

Zach tried not to think about what the future held. He couldn't imagine anything worse than being chained in this stinking claustrophobic cell for any length of time. Even death would be preferable. This was too much like being buried alive. It didn't suit him at all. He figured he would go stark raving mad in here.

When the cell door opened the last person he expected to see was Doc Letcher. The latter limped slightly as he entered the cell. He stepped to one side to allow a soldier to enter. The Mexican set to work opening the stubborn padlock that secured the shackle on Zach's ankle to the heavy chain.

"What's going on?" Zach asked Letcher.

"They're letting us go."

"They are?" Zach was stunned. "Why?"

Doc smiled. "Angelique had something to do with it."

"How?"

"Seems as though she talked her brother into getting us out."

The soldier had triumphed over the recalcitrant lock. The shackle fell off Zach's ankle. He sat there, rubbing the circulation back into his foot. The soldier left the cell without looking at either one of the mountain men. He left the door open.

"How did she do it?" asked Zach.

"You remember how worried Manuel was about word getting out that Angelique had spent the night in my room?"

Zach nodded.

"She made it plain she'd tell everybody herself, unless Manuel fixed it so we could walk out of here."

"What about Devlin?"

"Him, too. They've called in a doctor and patched him up. He's not in too bad of a shape. I reckon he can ride. If the wound opens up and he bleeds to death I won't shed many tears."

"I'm glad Manuel Chagres is so concerned with his reputation." Zach stood, testing his foot. "I've been meaning to ask you something, Doc."

"Go ahead."

"About last night. You didn't know Angelique was in your room?"

Letcher threw back his head and laughed. Zach was relieved, not knowing how Doc would react to such a question.

"Sure I knew. I heard her cat-footing into the room. But I pretended I was dead asleep. I was scared to death she'd climb into the bed with me."

Zach smiled.

"You'd better get over that fear, Doc."

"You're getting a little personal, aren't you?"

"Where do you reckon you and she will go?"

"I've been giving some thought to California. Never been there. And at least she knows the lingo."

"What about the high country?"

Letcher shook his head.

"There's going to be a lot of killing in the mountains before the year is out, Zach," he predicted. "I'm not inclined to take her there. You get back there in a hurry, my friend. Hand Devlin over to McKenzie if that's what you're set on doing, and then get home to your family and look out for them, because all hell is going to break loose."

"I will." Zach stuck out his hand. "Guess I'll say so long a second time."

Letcher took the proffered hand and shook it. "It's as a nail from the flesh."

"What?"

"When friends part. I don't recall who said that."

"Whoever he was," said Zach, "he was right."

Chapter 26

Zach rode due north out of Santa Fe. The search was over. He had found Devlin. Now he could head for home. He wanted to see Sky again so bad it hurt. Two months had passed since he had taken his leave of her. It seemed like two years. All he had to do now was deliver Coyote to Redcoat McKenzie. Then he would waste no time leaving Fort Union and heading back to that little cabin high on a lonesome mountainside where Sky and little Jacob were waiting. He would not even stick around to make sure Devlin was handed over to the Blackfeet. Maybe that was a mistake, but he couldn't help it. He told himself that if the Indians didn't take care of Devlin once and for all, the American Fur Company surely would. After all, Coyote had stolen plews and left his own brigade to meet its fate. Like Letcher, Zach believed that war would come very soon. When it did, his place was with his family.

He took no chances with Devlin. Before leaving the Santa Fe jail he had asked that Devlin's shackles be removed. Then he had used rawhide to bind Coyote's hands behind his back. Devlin's feet were tied

to the stirrups. Zach used a long lead rope to tug
Devlin's horse along behind.

That first day out Devlin did not say a word to
him. It was all Coyote could do to stay conscious in
the saddle. He was in severe pain from the gunshot
wound, but to his credit he did not complain. Zach
was dutifully impressed. Sean Michael Devlin had
grown some hard bark somewhere along the line.
The Devlin he remembered had never been one for
hardship. His own personal ease and comfort had always been foremost in his mind. Even wading waist-
deep in some ice-cold creek to set or recover a
beaver trap had been something Devlin had consistently sought to avoid by any means possible. He had
changed quite a lot since then, Zach observed—an
observation that made Zach that much more watchful. Devlin had always been dangerous. With this
added toughness, he was doubly so.

The day was old before they put the outskirts of
Santa Fe behind them, so they did not travel far prior
to nightfall. Zach chose to camp in some rocks above
a spring-fed pool. He did not build a fire, though desert nights, even in summer, were cool. They ate jerky
and slaked their thirst in the pool, which looked like
blood in the crimson light of the dying day. Before the
last thread of daylight was gone, Zach checked Devlin's gunshot wound. The Santa Fe doctor had done a
workmanlike job of dressing it. After hours on horseback over rough terrain Devlin had started bleeding
again, but not severely.

"I thought you were a better shot," remarked Devlin.

"So did I."

"You were really trying to kill me, weren't you?"

"You sound surprised."

"We're still blood brothers, no matter what."

"Counts for nothing in my book," replied Zach, irritated. "For a long time I felt like I owed you for sticking with me that winter, when Major Henry sent us out after that French Canadian, Chavanac, and I broke my leg, and the blizzard came."

Devlin smiled faintly. "Those were high times, weren't they, Zach?"

"But I stopped feeling beholden when you stole Morning Sky."

Devlin was silent for a while. Full night had descended, with the suddenness that always accompanied nightfall in the desert, and Zach could no longer see Coyote's face.

"How is the boy?" asked Devlin finally, soft-spoken.

"Well."

"I'd like to see him once. Before I die. Reckon he's gotten pretty big."

"He has that."

"I've made some mistakes in my life, true enough. But I count that to be the biggest."

"You mean having a son?"

"I mean letting him go like I did. Him and Morning Sky."

"You never loved her."

"You can't say . . ."

"You took her because she was my wife."

"The boy's my son."

"Not anymore."

A curtain of silence fell between them again, and

again it was Devlin who spoke first, a few minutes later.

"How did you find me, Zach?"

"It made sense that you'd take those stolen plews back to the Mississippi River, where you could get top dollar for them."

"You tracked me all the way back to St. Louis?"

"All the way to Oak Alley."

Another moment of silence as Devlin recovered from his surprise—and then he chuckled.

"Susannah," he said fondly. "How does she fare these days?"

"She thinks you're really coming back. That you'll marry her, and live happily ever after."

"What? And get poisoned for my trouble? It was pleasant while it lasted, old friend, but I know when to fold a busted hand. Susannah, you might say, floats on an uneven keel. Women are wonderful creatures, Zach, but also very dangerous."

"You should know. A woman got you thrown into that jail back in Santa Fe."

"Treachery. I was framed."

"That dog won't hunt."

"Honestly. I never laid a hand on her. I suspect that soldier—the one with whom I had the altercation—struck a deal with her. I believe he's the one who put those bruises on her face, and then he persuaded her to accuse me of the deed. Perhaps he threatened her with worse than beating if she did not. Or maybe she got a handsome share of the two thousand dollars in gold which used to belong to me."

"It doesn't matter now."

"No, I guess not."

"What happened to Montez?"

"Who?"

"When you stole those plews, Shadmore sent a man after you."

"Never saw him."

For some reason, Zach was inclined to believe this. Devlin would profit little by lying. If anything, consistent with past history, he would have bragged about taking Montez on and prevailing in the fight. So what had befallen the Spaniard? Zach figured his fate would remain a mystery. Montez had spoken little about himself, and as a result Zach had known almost nothing about his life. Now it seemed he would know nothing of the Spaniard's death. And Zach was fairly certain he was dead. He would have returned had he been able. There were many ways a man could lose his life in the high country.

Northward they traveled, without incident of note, for several days, up the desert valley of the Rio Grande, where the river ran its serpentine course at the bottom of windy gorges, while snow-peaked mountain ranges, cobalt-blue in the heat-hammered distance, rose on either side, the San Juan Mountains to the west, the Sangre de Cristo to the east.

In time they parted company with the Rio Grande, which curled off to the west. The next few days were pure hell, as they pushed on across waterless alkali flats where it seemed only sagebrush could survive, and sometimes not even that, and the only life to be seen was the rattlesnake, the scorpion, and the buzzard. They ran perilously low on water. Zach had no idea where the waterholes were in this country—if indeed any existed. He had never ventured this far south of the high country. But he kept the Sangre de Cristo range off his right shoulder, and marveled at the sand dunes that had accumulated at the foot of the mountains. Instinct told him that these peaks were the tail end of the Rockies.

And when, finally, they reached the high country proper, Zach Hannah's heart sang with joy. Through a high pass they rode, and then down into the valley of the Arkansas. This river they followed to its source, only to negotiate yet another high pass. Beyond this lay another river, this time the mighty Colorado, and on they pressed, past the Medicine Bow Mountains, and thence down into the Great Divide Basin, a high sagebrush plain.

It was then that Zach felt like he was home. To the northwest was the Wind River Range. Beyond it, the Absaroka Mountains. Due north lay the Bighorns. Zach knew every peak, was familiar with every valley. From here on he could find his way blindfolded.

Shortly after crossing the Sweetwater they came upon a brigade of trappers. Seven men in all, with two Indian women, one a Shoshone, the other a Flathead. Their pack animals were laden with furs. The booshway's name was Briggs. They were employed by the American Fur Company.

Learning of this, Zach grew leery. He still could not forgive or forget the alliance between the American Fur Company and the Blackfeet. His reluctance to let bygones be bygones had little to do with his ordeal as a Blackfoot captive—a direct result of that unholy alliance. Rather, it was the ghosts of the dozens of trappers who had lost their lives beneath the Blackfoot knife because American Fur Company scouts had led Blackfoot war parties to the trapping grounds of the Rocky Mountain Fur Company brigades.

Zach did not object to alliances with Indians on the whole. In fact, he had long hoped that white man and red could live together in peace—a hope that reality made appear rather forlorn at times. But it had always been his view that the Blackfeet could not be trusted, that they hated all foreigners, red and white alike, with a passion, and that they waged war for war's sake. Long before the first white trapper had ventured west the Blackfeet had been engaged in prolonged and brutal conflict with almost every Indian tribe with which it had come into contact, from the Nez Percés to the Absaroka Crows. Zach had believed that all-out war with the Blackfeet was inevitable, and that the defeat of that tribe was a prerequisite to peace in the region. And so he had scorned the American Fur Company for striking a deal with the Blackfeet solely for the purpose of crushing its competition in the fur trade: the Rocky Mountain Fur Company.

Yet these men were friendly—especially so when they learned the identities of the two men who rode into their camp as the purple twilight of day's end blanketed the land.

"Mr. McKenzie has told us to keep an eye peeled for you, Hannah," said Briggs, a gruff and rawboned character with a patch over one eye. "He said to give you any assistance you needed."

"I'm not used to getting help from the American Fur Company," confessed Zach. "Truth is, I've usually gotten just the reverse."

"Times change. You're welcome to share our camp and our grub."

Zach set aside his prejudices and accepted the booshway's offer.

They sat around the fire and shared the prairie goat that Briggs himself had bagged that day. Zach untied Devlin's hands so that he could eat, too.

"Don't fret none about him trying to make a run for the tall timber," Briggs told Zach. "If he tries, we'll all shoot him."

"I'd like to take him back alive."

"I know. Hannah, we're in the same stew together, now. Once it was us and the Blackfeet and you Rocky Mountain boys and them Absaroka Crows. Now I reckon it's every last one of us against the Blackfeet. I reckon that after what happened to you, you're not too inclined to trust us, and I can't fault you for that. I'd feel the same was I in yer moccasins. I never much cared for that bloody business Major Vanderburg dreamt up, but I went along with it, on account of I hankered after that brown gold, and it sounded like an easy way to get rich quick. So I ain't exactly as pure as the driven snow, I admit, but I'm sorry for it, all the same."

"It caused some bad blood, sure enough," said Zach, noncommittal.

"Well, I like McKenzie's idea better." Briggs looked

at Devlin. "Especially the part about turning this two-legged snake over to the Blackfeet."

"As you can see, Zach," said Devlin, "you just can't trust the American Fur Company. After all that I did for them, they turn on me like this."

"Has nothing to do with this company or that," snapped Briggs. "Has to do with you runnin' out on yer brigade like you did. Yore a poor excuse for a booshway, Sean Devlin, and not much of a man, in my book."

Devlin shrugged, as though he could care less what Briggs thought of him, and made no rejoinder.

"What's happened out here the past couple of months?" queried Zach.

"Been mighty peaceful. *Too* quiet, if you want my opinion. Word is them Blackfeet are planning a big raid. Hundreds of warriors, maybe more than a thousand. Piegans and Bloods, too. If true, it'll be the first time all the villages could get together for a fight. Lord knows, a little raiding party is bad enough. I don't even want to think about the whole damned Blackfoot nation on our backs."

"Your back is all the Blackfeet will see," remarked Devlin.

Briggs shot to his feet, fists clenched. The other trappers froze, watching their booshway with eagle eyes, their bearded faces grim and gaunt in the flickering firelight.

"By God, Coyote, if McKenzie didn't want you alive, I'd snuff yer candle right here and now."

"He's just trying to rile you," said Zach wearily, well acquainted with Devlin's tactics.

"He's doing a bang-up job of it, then."

"If he can stir things up, he might get the chance he needs to escape. Just ignore him."

"Well, he's one to talk about running," sneered Briggs as he sat back down.

"Are you heading for Fort Union?"

"Naw. There's a rendezvous coming up, hoss, a fortnight from now, up in the Teton Basin. That's where we're going. But McKenzie's still at the fort, last I heard. Seems he's convinced the headmen of the Blackfeet to come in for a palaver. Whether they smoke the peace pipe, now that's something else again. I hear tell Red Claw might even show up."

"Red Claw?"

"Yeah. Young hothead war chief. He's the one more and more of the warriors are listening to. He says the whole Blackfoot Nation can rise up and drive the white man out of the high country forever. They like that kind of talk, especially since Whirlwind's village got wiped out by the plague." Briggs paused to give Devlin another ugly look. "Some of the older chiefs aren't so sure about a big war. But every day, Red Claw becomes more and more powerful."

"If this Red Claw is so dead-set on war, why is he going to Fort Union to talk peace?"

"He ain't interested in peace."

"But you said . . ."

"He's going to stir up trouble, and to make sure the old chiefs *don't* smoke that peace pipe. McKenzie's lookin' for you to bring Devlin pronto. Devlin's his ace in the hole. If he can give up Devlin to them, that might make all the other chiefs think twice about all-out war, at least for a while. Otherwise, I think the Blackfeet will listen to Red Claw."

Zach nodded. "When is this palaver suppose to take place?"

"Ten days before rendezvous."

"But Fort Union is at least a week away. I won't make it in time."

"Well," drawled Briggs, like all mountain men a fatalist at heart, "like a dog, you can try. Iffen you don't, I guess the killin' starts."

Chapter 27

Jim Bridger was sound asleep when Kenneth "Red-coat" McKenzie came busting through the door of the small room at one end of a barracks buildings. Old Gabe came out of his rope-slat bed with a pistol in one hand and a knife in the other, with such sudden ferocity that McKenzie took a hasty step backward and threw up his hands.

"Whoa, Bridger! It's considered bad form to shoot the host."

Bridger blinked, belatedly recognized McKenzie, and lowered his weapons. There was a sheen of cold sweat on his forehead. He glanced beyond the Scotsman, through the door at the pearl-gray light of dawn.

"Looks like I overslept," said Bridger. "I was dreaming about Blackfeet."

"Your dream has come true," said McKenzie wryly. "The red devils are here."

His expression grim, Old Gabe belted knife and pistol, turned back to the narrow bed to retrieve his percussion rifle. For years now he had been sleeping with it.

"I'm ready," he said.

McKenzie preceded him out of the room.

Fort Union was bustling with activity. The gates were closed. Men were running hither and yon to take up their posts. Bridger admired the way McKenzie ran things at the post; the Scotsman imposed military-style discipline. Every trapper knew his place on the ramparts.

Old Gabe followed McKenzie up a ladder to the roof of the barracks building, which backed up to the northern palisade. They traversed this, climbed another ladder, and gained the western rampart, above the main gate.

"Looks more like a war party than a peace delegation," remarked McKenzie.

Bridger had to agree.

There were about sixty Blackfoot, Blood, and Piegan warriors in the bunch. The ponies were painted. The braves were in full regalia: painted faces, shields, bone breastplates. It was a parade of savage splendor. Not a single woman or child among them. But there was one white man. A grizzled, wiry character kicked his horse forward and neared the gate, to peer up at McKenzie.

"Mornin' to ye, Berger," said the Scotsman.

"Mornin', McKenzie."

"Have they come to fight or talk?"

Berger glanced over his shoulder at the warriors arrayed a hundred feet behind him. They sat their ponies, silent and watchful. Berger shrugged and flashed a wolfish smile up at McKenzie.

"You can never be sartin with these fellers, can you?"

"True words, old friend."

"I reckon they'll talk. But that ain't to say they wouldn't try to take the fort, and every scalp within its walls, if they saw a chance to do it."

"One thing must be made clear," replied McKenzie sternly. "I'll permit nary a one of them inside the stockade, for any reason. We'll do all our talking out there."

Berger nodded, whipped his horse around, and rode back to the Blackfeet. The men in the fort looked on as the old mountain man discussed matters with the chiefs.

"That one there," McKenzie said to Bridger, pointing. "That's Red Claw."

Bridger nodded. He knew which one McKenzie meant.

The warrior had three eagle feathers dangling from his topknot. That told Old Gabe that Red Claw was one tough customer in a fight. To wear one eagle feather a Blackfoot warrior had to distinguish himself in battle. To wear two meant he was quite accomplished indeed. Three feathers was a signal honor exceedingly few warriors attained. Red Claw had evidently performed with conspicuous bravery in many a scrape. He had slain many foes.

While Berger jawed with the three older chiefs, the young Red Claw sat tall and disdainfully on his pony, which was painted with three parallel crimson lines on withers and haunch. They resembled the marks a bear or mountain lion might have made. Which Bridger supposed was the intent. Red Claw acted as though the discussion between Berger and the chiefs was of no consequence to him; that what was being decided would not bind him if he did not approve of the decisions. His superior attitude seemed to say: *Talk all you want, and make all the empty words you wish to—none of it will matter—I will do what I want to do, and all the braves will follow me—I answer to no one.*

While the words flowed, Red Claw studied the fort, paying particular attention to the men who lined the ramparts. Bridger had a hunch he was counting rifles and planning some future assault on the stronghold.

"That one's a heap of trouble," he muttered.

"Aye," agreed McKenzie. "No doubt about it. I'm of half a mind to shoot him dead right here and now. If any one man can bring about this war, it's him."

"You shoot him, and the war is on."

"Perhaps. But what do you do when you come upon a rattler, Mr. Bridger? You cut off its head. He'll whip around for a spell, but he's no real danger to you anymore. Those other warriors believe Red Claw has powerful magic. Seeing him dead on the ground would take some wind out of their sails."

"I wouldn't take the chance," said Bridger. "The idea is to buy some time—at least until all the brigades are gathered for the rendezvous, and the messengers you sent out alert every trapper of the danger. You've postponed bloodshed by negotiating with them, McKenzie. You got them to come here, instead of going on the warpath. It would help if the fight is put off until next year. If that isn't possible, at least a few more days would be nice."

"But I have nothing to offer them except words— and words wilna be enough to hold their attention for long. I was hoping against hope your friend Hannah would've returned by now—with Devlin."

Bridger took a deep breath. The idea of turning a white man—even Devlin—over to the Blackfeet made him uneasy. "If anyone can do it, Zach can. Until he shows up, you've got to play for time."

"Aye, that I do. But Red Claw there doesna strike me as a very patient fellow. I've got only one card to play. And it's not without risk."

"What's that?"

McKenzie's smile was taut. "Firewater. I've got my still, you know."

"Give 'em likker?" Bridger was incredulous.

"As a last resort."

"You never can tell what an Injun will do when he's got a bellyful of likker."

"Well, we'll start with blankets and tobacco. But I don't know how long that will keep them here. Wish me luck, Bridger, and keep me covered. And then, if you think of it, say a little prayer."

McKenzie left him then, to walk a moment later through the gate, alone and unarmed, with the carefree stride of a man out for his morning constitutional. A red three-cornered Nor'west blanket was slung over his shoulder. This he spread out on the ground in front of the still-mounted Blackfeet. Then he sat cross-legged and with a grand gesture invited the chiefs to join him.

Three chiefs, along with Berger, dismounted and sat around the blanket. Red Claw dismounted, too, but he did not sit in. Instead, he chose to stand at the head of his pony and listen. His standoffish attitude signified disapproval of the goings-on.

Bridger couldn't hear what McKenzie and the chiefs were saying. He figured a little praying wouldn't hurt, after all.

God, I dunno if you're in the habit of listenin' to sinners of my caliber, but iffen you are, and you hear me now, I'd be beholden for one small favor. I sure would like to see Zach Hannah's ugly face—before it's entirely too late.

The chief's name was Two Snakes. He had survived more than eighty winters. Exactly how many he wasn't sure. His memory of days long past was dimming, but he could recall vividly a particular event that had occurred a little more than a year ago. The blanket had triggered the memory. He fingered the Nor'west blanket, rubbing the red wool between gnarled thumb and forefinger. Sadness deepened his walnut-brown skin, and his dark, deep-set eyes glistened as he looked up and across at the hairface he knew as Redcoat.

"Whirlwind's village—all gone. The people get sick and die. From blankets like this one. Blankets given to us by you, Redcoat."

McKenzie was conversant in the Blackfoot dialect, and his response was quick and fluent.

"I did not send those blankets to Whirlwind."

"One of your buckskins did."

"But I did not sanction it. Even so. You are a wise man, Two Snakes. You must realize it was not intentional. No one could have known those blankets were infected with the plague."

"Some believe that," replied the old chief gravely. "But then some say it was meant to happen. They say the hairfaces try to kill us with bullets first, and then they try to kill us with a great sickness."

"That just isn't true. No one is sorrier than I about what happened to Whirlwind and his people, Two Snakes."

Two Snakes shrugged. One of the other chiefs, Crooked Knife, spoke up.

"Redcoat, I have heard it said that the plague fell upon Whirlwind's people because they had done wrong in taking the white man called Longshot, whose magic was greater even than the shaman Blue Elk's, and so they were punished . . ."

A shadow fell between McKenzie and the three chiefs. The Scotsman squinted up at the scowling visage of Red Claw. The morning sun seemed to sit on the warrior's shoulder. Red Claw's cheeks were badly scarred. McKenzie had been told that Red Claw had disfigured himself with the talon of a hawk.

"Those who say such things are nothing but scared old women," snapped Red Claw. His words dripped with scathing contempt. "It is never wrong to take a white man and kill him."

"They did not kill him," said Crooked Knife.

"Then I say that is why they were punished."

Crooked Knife shook his head. McKenzie sensed the old chief was angered by Red Claw's interference, but the Indian's face was a stony mask of impassivity. The Scotsman had a feeling the old chief was aching to put the upstart Red Claw in his place, but was afraid to. And that worried McKenzie.

"There was no honor in the way they treated

Longshot," said Crooked Knife. "He is a great warrior. He deserved to die like one."

"All the hairfaces who invade our land deserve to die like dogs," said Red Claw. "And they will."

"We don't want war," said McKenzie, relying on reason and compromise. "Not that we don't think we could win—because we would. But we prefer peace. We do not want your land. We only . . ."

"You want only to kill the beaver and the buffalo," said Red Claw. "When they are all gone, the Blackfeet will die. I say it is better to die in battle than to starve to death, or waste away with a sickness brought by the white man."

"There are many coming behind you, Redcoat," said Two Snakes. "This we know from the Arikaras and the Sioux. Is it not so?"

"Look," said McKenzie, choosing to ignore Red Claw and direct his plea to the older chiefs. "I will give you Coyote, to show you that we do not want war. Berger gave you my offer. You came here, and now you hear it from my own lips. You know I have never lied to you."

"That is so," said Two Snakes, nodding. "Coyote was once friend to the Blackfeet. But no more. He brought death to Whirlwind's village. The ghosts of those who died because of that cry out for vengeance. Their souls are lost until Coyote pays with his own blood."

"Show us that you are sincere, Redcoat," said Crooked Knife. "Bring Coyote before us."

McKenzie grimaced. "Longshot himself is bringing Coyote here to give to you. I ask only that you be patient."

"How long do we wait?" cried Red Claw, incensed. "Until the snows come? Then it will be too late to wage war. Are you too old and blind to see what he is doing, Crooked Knife? He lies. The hairface never gives up his own kind. He wants to avoid war now, because when another winter has passed there will be many more white men here to fight us."

"Crooked Knife, you know me," said McKenzie. "I do not lie to the Blackfeet. All I am asking for is a little more time. Coyote is fast and clever. He ran far away. Longshot has traveled many suns to find him. But he will bring Coyote here. He has promised to do so. And Longshot is a man who keeps his promises."

"Only fools would hear these words," sneered Red Claw.

"I have tobacco," said McKenzie. "And whiskey. If you will wait, these things I will make gifts to you."

Red Claw barked a laugh. "He thinks he can make us drunk with his firewater, and then his men will fall on us with their knives."

"Redcoat is a man of honor," said Crooked Knife, his tone sharp.

"How long would you have us wait, Redcoat?" asked Two Snakes.

"Ten suns," said McKenzie, knowing that to ask for more would be futile.

"We will wait three suns," said Two Snakes.

The other two chiefs nodded agreement. McKenzie knew it would be pointless to ask for more time. They had made up their minds. It was three days or nothing at all.

Chapter 28

On the morning of the third day, Zach Hannah arrived at Fort Union, Devlin in tow.

For two nerve-wracking days McKenzie had played host to the Blackfeet. He plied them with gifts. They would not accept blankets, and considering what had occurred in Whirlwind's village, that came as no surprise. They persistently asked for guns and powder, but of course McKenzie was not going to fall for that. Instead, he gave them tobacco and doled out some whiskey. Most of the garrison thought that to be a rather poor idea, but no one challenged Redcoat.

Instead, they manned the barricades and kept an eagle eye on their Blackfoot guests. It seemed like the only Indian who didn't drink was Red Claw. Aloof and sternly disapproving, he watched his brethren become ever more inebriated as the days went by. McKenzie tried to ration the liquor carefully, seeking to give them just enough to dull their senses and make them foolish, and not so much that they became belligerent.

In most cases he succeeded. Some scuffles broke out between the warriors over a jug, and a few even rode up to the very walls of the fort and screamed drunken epithets and taunts at the men on the ramparts above them. McKenzie repeatedly admonished his men to exercise restraint. He knew he was asking a lot of them. Their nerves were stretched to the snapping point. Their fingers were tight on the triggers of their rifles. The drunken braves often fired their rifles into the air, which didn't make anyone feel more relaxed about the situation. But McKenzie's orders were strict: no one was to shoot unless the Blackfeet actually attacked the fort. Every trapper knew that if he failed to abide by those orders he would suffer greatly.

In the end, the trappers came through for McKenzie, though they were severely tested time and again. Meanwhile McKenzie himself took great personal risks. Only he and Berger ever ventured from the protection of the fort. They conferred daily with the principal chiefs. The Scotsman was perfectly aware that if the Blackfeet decided to fall upon him his chances of survival were nil. The men in the fort would not be able to save him. On several occasions, a warrior made threatening gestures; in each instance it was in response to Redcoat's smiling refusal to supply more firewater. He lied straight-faced, apologetically explaining that his still simply could not produce enough liquor to meet the demand.

All in all, thought McKenzie, *his gamble paid off.* As long as the Blackfeet could anticipate more whiskey on the morrow, they were inclined to go along with Two Snakes and Crooked Knife and wait. As a result, they shut their ears to Red Claw, who moved tirelessly among them exhorting them to forsake the old chiefs and follow him to bloodstained glory on the warpath. Red Claw tried cajolery, reason, threats, ridicule. McKenzie was convinced the liquor turned the tide. A warrior would not follow a chief unless he believed it was in his best interests to do so. Blind loyalty was not an Indian trait. But by agreeing to be patient and stick with Two Snakes and Crooked Knife, the braves could expect more whiskey—so they stuck.

McKenzie owned a brass-mounted spyglass. Men took turns, in one-hour stints, roaming the ramparts and scanning the horizon with the instrument. On the morning of the third day, as Redcoat was preparing to venture out once more into the midst of the Blackfeet, the lookout yelled out that two riders were coming. McKenzie bolted up the ladders, his heart in his throat. He dared not even hope. He bulled through the crowd of eager trappers who had gathered round the lookout. He snatched the spyglass away. He cursed softly when he realized that even with the spyglass he could not identify the riders— they were too far away. Minutes crawled by. The wait was every bit as harrowing for McKenzie as the past two days had been. He tried to prepare himself for disappointment. Tried to convince himself that if this wasn't Hannah and Devlin all was still not lost. But it didn't work. He knew better.

So when the riders were finally close enough, and he saw that it *was* Zach Hannah and Sean Michael Devlin, McKenzie let out an earsplitting whoop of joy and danced a little jig.

A minute later the whole fort was celebrating.

* * *

When he saw the Blackfeet, Zach Hannah's gut instinct was to turn right around and head for the tall timber.

Memories came flooding back—memories of the terrible ordeal he had survived, barely, as a captive of the Blackfoot Nation. Those memories had not dimmed with time. It was just that most days he could push them to the back of his mind. One thing that *had* faded from his memory was the depth of his hatred for this tribe. Yes, and fear.

It was all he could do to keep going. Briggs had warned him that the Blackfeet were probably at Fort Union, and the booshway had told him they were here to talk, not fight. So Zach steeled himself and steered his horse for the gate.

As a captive he had run a gauntlet. The entire population of Whirlwind's ill-fated village had turned out to greet Scar's war party—and the notorious Longshot. Hundreds of men, women, and children, with clubs, stones, and switches.

Now here was another Blackfoot gauntlet he would have to run, and Zach broke into a cold sweat as he drew closer. He was half expecting Devlin to make some snide comment about how nervous he looked. But a glance over his shoulder revealed that Devlin was too anxiety-ridden himself to pay any attention to him.

Some of the warriors jumped on their ponies and galloped out to meet them. The Blackfeet rode circles around the two white men, brandishing their weapons and yelling shrill taunts. Zach tried to ignore them. He also tried to appear as though their truculent antics weren't bothering him in the least.

He reached the main body of the Blackfeet. A young warrior with three eagle feathers in his top-knot and scars on his cheek vaulted aboard his painted pony and kicked the animal into motion, rushing forward to block Zach's path.

Zach reined up.

Red Claw pointed with his rifle at Devlin. "Is this Coyote?"

Morning Sky had taught Zach the Blackfoot dialect. He responded with "Who asks?"

"Red Claw." He said it as though the name alone ought to be sufficient to make Zach jump to do his bidding.

"This is Coyote."

"Give him to me."

"No."

Red Claw fumed. "You will do as I say."

"I have brought Coyote to Redcoat. If you want him, you will have to ask Redcoat for him."

Red Claw glowered. Zach stared right back, cold-eyed. While they were staring each other down, Kenneth McKenzie was running toward them. The gates of Fort Union remained open behind him. Some of the Blackfoot braves took note of this. But none chose to act on it. Heavily armed mountain men boiled out of the gate in McKenzie's wake. They did not venture far afield, but rather spread out, so that every man could have a clear shot.

When McKenzie reached Zach and Red Claw he was only a few steps ahead of Two Snakes and Crooked Knife.

"By God, Hannah!" he exclaimed. "You're a sight for sore eyes."

"Nice of you to come out and meet me. I'd have gotten to the fort, except this feller got in my way. I'm trying to decide if I should go around him or through him."

"It's killing we're hoping to postpone here."

"It's just that I don't have much nice to say about Blackfeet."

"I can understand that. Truly, I can. But just bear in mind what we're trying to accomplish."

"He wants me to hand Coyote over to him."

McKenzie glanced at the scowling Red Claw, and smiled coldly.

"Well now, I'm sure he would, come to think on it. I expect if you had done so, Hannah, Devlin would be dead at this very moment."

"How do you figure?"

"Because in a manner of speaking, Devlin stands between Red Claw and the war he wants." McKenzie turned his attention on Zach's prisoner. "I didna think I'd ever see your smiling face again, Coyote. And I wouldna care to, if the truth be known, except that I need you to die so that others can live."

"Well," said Devlin, trying hard to keep a brave face. "I'm glad, at least, that I'm not a good-for-nothing."

McKenzie turned to the old chiefs.

"Two Snakes, Crooked Knife, as you now see, I have kept my word. Here is Coyote, as promised. I give him to you. Let all the Blackfeet—the Bloods and Piegans, too—see that it is to the two of you, and not Red Claw, to whom I give Coyote."

The significance of what McKenzie was doing did not escape the old chiefs. The Scotsman was making a statement that all the Blackfeet present would comprehend—that the chiefs, not Red Claw, were the legitimate leaders of the tribe.

"We see that Redcoat has a true heart," said Crooked Knife. "It is good. The white man and the Blackfoot do not agree on many things. But as long as you are chief of the hairfaces, we have hope that someday our people *will* agree."

"I say kill Redcoat!" cried Red Claw. "Kill Longshot and Coyote. See—the gates are open. I say we fight now. The Blackfeet have always made war on our enemies. Anyone who invades our land is our enemy. We do not hope to agree with them. We do not want to live in peace with them. We kill our enemies. It has always been so. I say . . ."

"When you are a chief among the Blackfeet we will listen to what you have to say, Red Claw," snapped Two Snakes. "You are permitted to speak to our councils because you are a great warrior. But that is a privilege we can take away."

Red Claw was stunned. It was as though Two Snakes had slapped him across the face. Rage twisted his scarred features. He violently whipped his pony around and rode away at the gallop, scattering other Blackfeet, shaking his rifle at the sky and shrieking insults at everything and everyone.

Two Snakes snapped an order at one of his warriors. This brave guided his pony alongside Zach's. He held out his hand. Zach realized he wanted the lead rope.

Zach hesitated.

He glanced back at Devlin. Second thoughts assailed him. If he surrendered the lead rope to the Blackfoot warrior he was sentencing Devlin to a horrible death.

It wasn't that this was the first time he had considered the consequences of what he was doing. But always before he had pushed those second thoughts away, and steeled himself with recollections of all the pain, physical and emotional, which by his actions Devlin had visited upon him.

For some reason, though, at this the moment of truth, that technique failed him. This was wrong. No matter what Devlin had done. No matter how much Devlin might deserve it. Maybe the pilot, Jenks, had been right in saying that it was downright uncivilized to give Devlin to the Blackfeet.

"Hannah?"

It was McKenzie. The Scotsman was worried.

Zach drew a deep breath. Wrong or not, it was too late to back out now. He had come too far. There was no way out.

"Sorry," he said, forcing himself to look Devlin square in the eyes.

Devlin smiled. "Don't worry about it, Zach. I did the same thing to you. Fair is fair."

Zach gave the lead rope to the Blackfoot warrior. Then he kicked his horse into a gallop and headed for the gate of Fort Union.

He looked back only once, as the Blackfeet raised a great hue and cry. Crooked Knife and Two Snakes were walking through the Indian camp, the brave in charge of Devlin behind them. Coyote sat tall on his pony as the warriors swarmed around him with insults and threats.

Feeling sick to his stomach, Zach Hannah turned his back on the scene and rode into the stockade.

Chapter 29

When the Blackfeet rode away, the celebration at Fort Union began in earnest.

Kenneth McKenzie preached caution. One could never tell about the Blackfoot Indians. They were very changeable sorts. They could get a few miles away, have a sudden change of heart, and come storming back to attack the fort. The Scotsman deemed it unwise to let down his guard. But the trappers were too relieved to listen to his admonitions. They broke out the fiddles and the harmonicas—and the whiskey—and before long there was a full-fledged shindig being conducted. Everybody wanted to join the party, so it was all McKenzie could do to keep a half-dozen men on the parapets to serve as lookouts in the event of Blackfoot deceit.

McKenzie looked for Zach in the crowd. Failing to find him there, he searched the buildings, and finally found Hannah, along with Bridger, in the latter's quarters. Old Gabe was sharing his powder and shot with Zach.

"You came through for us, Hannah," said the Scotsman, elated. "Every trapper in the high country owes you a debt of gratitude."

Zach gave him a hostile look.

Perplexed, McKenzie glanced at Bridger, eyebrows raised in silent query. Old Gabe just shook his head.

"It was the only thing you could do, Zach," said Bridger.

"No it isn't. I could have stayed up on my mountain to begin with and not taken part in this. It leaves a bad taste, Jim."

"I know. I had my doubts about it, too. Not just whether it would work or not, but whether it was the right thing to do."

"If you're speaking about handing Devlin over to the Blackfeet," said McKenzie, "the proof, seems to me, is in the pudding. I'd say it worked out very well. We've at least postponed the outbreak of the war we all know is coming. In this case, I would have to argue that the ends justify the means."

"Do they?" asked Zach. "That doesn't make me feel any better about what I've done."

"You knew how it would end when you agreed to go after Coyote."

Zach nodded bleakly. "I can't deny that. But I tried not to think about it. I kept reminding myself of all the misery Devlin had caused me. That kept me going. I'm not laying any blame on your doorstep, Mr. McKenzie. Or on anyone else."

"You're blaming yourself," surmised Bridger.

"I'm the one who brought him back."

"Where did you find him?" asked McKenzie.

"Santa Fe."

"Santa Fe! Indeed, you've had a long trail. I was confident you would find him on the Mississippi."

"He had been. But when I got to St. Louis I was

a couple of weeks too late. Devlin had signed on with a caravan headed down the Santa Fe Trail."

"And Doc Letcher?"

"Met up with him near St. Louis."

"What happened to him?"

"He's on his way to California, I think."

"California? Why California?"

"He met a girl named Angelique. Decided he had better things to do with his life than waste it all on revenge."

McKenzie rubbed his chin, bewildered.

"That's bloody amazing. I figured Letcher would track Devlin to the ends of the earth, if need be. I was afraid you might have to tangle with him somewhere along the line, as dead-set as he seemed to be to kill Coyote."

"I thought so, too, for a spell. But it didn't work out that way."

"Where are you headed now?" asked Bridger.

"Home."

"Sky and the boy aren't there, Zach."

"Where are they?" asked Zach, alarmed.

"At rendezvous by now, I reckon. Before you start getting riled, let me tell you that it was Sky's idea in the first place."

"How do you know?"

"I passed that way a while back. Just dropped in to see how everybody was doing. Shadmore wasn't too happy. Seems Sky had her mind set on getting down off that mountain and going to the Teton Basin."

"Why?"

"Part of it was for Jacob's sake. She said he needed to meet other children. She figured there'd be more

than a few at rendezvous. Always are. And she was
hoping some of her people, the Absaroka Crows,
would be there."

Zach's expression was downright somber. "I reckon
it has been hard on her, stuck up there on that
mountain with just me to talk to."

"And not even that for the last two months."

Zach nodded.

"You're not mad?" asked Bridger.

"Got no call to be."

"Shad will be awful relieved to hear that. He kept
telling her you'd have his scalp if he took her to the
Teton Basin."

"Well, I'd best get started."

"I'd like to ride along, if that's all right with you."

"I'd be obliged for the company, Jim."

"The both of you can ride with me," said
McKenzie. "In a few days I'll be going that way myself. Got to get the wagons loaded. And make sure
those Blackfeet are long gone. I think I'll send out
some scouts to track them for a day or so. Once I'm
convinced they don't plan to double back I'll feel better about leaving a skeleton crew here at the fort."

"I don't care to wait," said Zach. "I've been away
from my family too long as it is."

McKenzie stepped forward, a troubled frown on
his ruddy face.

"You harbor no hard feelings toward me, I hope,
Zach."

Zach shook his head. "You did what you thought
was best for all concerned."

"I know it may have struck you as cold-blooded,
but . . ."

"It was that. But I guess it worked out."

McKenzie extended a hand, and Zach shook it.

Devlin wondered if he would make it to the Blackfoot country north of the Missouri River.

The first day away from Fort Union they let him keep his pony. At least twenty warriors galloped up and struck him with their fists or slammed the flat of their tomahawks against his back and shoulder or lashed out with their quirts of braided rawhide. They had been prohibited from taking his life by the edict of Two Snakes and Crooked Knife. But they meant to inflict as much pain as they could.

Devlin was quick to comprehend that the game was to knock him off his horse. His hands were tied behind his back, yet his feet were no longer lashed to the saddle stirrups. Thus it was difficult for him to stay aboard. When he did fall, several more warriors would descend upon him, brandishing tomahawks and quirts or prodding him with the barrels of their rifles. It didn't take Devlin long to realize that he cut the pain inflicted upon him by at least half if he stayed in the saddle.

All day long the Blackfeet counted coup on him, so that at day's end he was one solid bruised and bleeding ache.

That night they took his clothes and tied him, standing, to one of the willows that lined the creek by which the camp had been made. They took turns seeing how close they could come to shooting him. Devlin figured that at least half the bunch used him for target practice that night, by the light of a big fire.

It was, to say the least, a nerve-wracking experience for him. Rare indeed was the Indian who could legitimately claim to be a crack rifle shot. A chronic shortage of powder and ball prevented the majority from indulging in sufficient practice to acquire expertise.

Another factor that bode ill for Devlin was the fact that most of the Indians were armed with old flintlock rifles or muskets. Very few carried the newer percussion rifles. Devlin was of the opinion—shared by most—that the old rifles were not nearly as accurate as the new models.

All these factors combined led him to conclude when the shooting match began that he was gone beaver for sure. But then he didn't see that it made much difference, getting accidentally killed here or intentionally tortured to death at some future date.

He had never possessed the patience to master any Indian dialect, but having spent several years in the employ of the Hudson Bay Company trading with the Blackfeet, he had absorbed some of their language in spite of himself.

So now he was able to discern that the old chiefs had decided to make a spectacle of their celebrated captive. Each chief insisted upon the privilege of parading Coyote through his own village. When all that was done with, they would decide by council the time and place of his spectacular demise. The entire Blackfoot Nation would participate in the ritual murder of Coyote. Whirlwind's village would be avenged. At the same time, Coyote's death would serve as a symbol of the ultimate Blackfoot triumph over the white interlopers. It would bring all the villages together in common cause. Internecine squabbles would be laid aside for the greater good. There, over Coyote's mutilated corpse, they would seek the guidance and blessing of the Great Spirit in whatever scheme they then devised to rid the land of the white man forever.

Knowing that the fate they planned for him was very much the same as the one they had intended for Zach Hannah last year was cold comfort to Devlin.

He considered it nothing short of miraculous that the Blackfoot marksmen failed to hit him, though they did shoot the willow tree all to hell. The warrior who won the contest hands down was the last to shoot—Red Claw. Devlin said his good-byes to the world when he saw this particular Blackfoot toe the mark and raise his rifle. He had overheard Kenneth McKenzie voice his opinion that Red Claw's purpose was best served with Coyote dead. But Red Claw didn't drill him through the heart, as Devlin expected. Instead, he shot a piece of Devlin's left ear off. He was the only brave who managed to draw blood. The other warriors were visibly impressed by this marksmanship. None of them had dared sling their lead so close to the prisoner, for fear of drawing the wrath of the old chiefs down upon themselves.

They left him there, tied to the tree, all night, and did not bother to offer him food or water. To hear the nearby creek purling was sheer torture for Devlin. He was truly parched. But he did not beg. He had not done so all day, and he didn't intend to start now. He was cut, bruised and bleeding, dying of thirst, but he wasn't going to utter a sound.

This was because he knew he was going to die. Since that was the case, this would be his last chance to show a little backbone. Always before, when in peril, he had seen a way out through chicanery or rank cowardice. But there was no way out of this.

He tried not to think about all the bad deeds he had performed. For sure he was going to hell. That realization in itself was possessed of a certain inescapable irony. Before, he had denied that heaven or hell even existed. He had refused to believe that man had to pay for his sins. It was convenient, in his case, to stick to this refusal. Now, suddenly, faced with certain death, he knew he had been fooling himself all along. There *was* a God. There *was* a heaven and a hell. And, furthermore, he was destined for the latter place.

So he was sorry for all his misdeeds. Not because he thought being sorry now would earn him a divine reprieve, but genuinely sorry for a misspent life. Had he known life was so fleeting he would have made better use of his own.

Had he been a better man he might have won Morning Sky's love legitimately. Instead, he had been forced to steal it. Had he been a better man he would have been able to raise his son. Instead, Zach Hannah would have that pleasure. Not raising Jacob—and he knew he alone was to blame for it—was what he regretted most of all in life.

The next morning they put a rope around his neck and made him walk. A warrior had won his horse in a wager. By noon his feet were a bleeding mess. By midafternoon he was falling down with disturbing regularity, dizzy from the heat and lack of water. When he fell, the warrior in possession of the rope tied around his neck kept dragging him until he got up. After the tenth or eleventh fall—he wasn't counting—he didn't bother trying to get back on his feet and let the rope slowly choke him into unconsciousness.

When he awoke it was night again.

He was surprised to be above snakes. Then he saw Red Claw bending over him, a knife raised, and he knew he wasn't going to be that way much longer.

Red Claw clapped a hand over his mouth.

Devlin closed his eyes.

He snapped them open as he felt Red Claw roll him over on his side and slice the rawhide binding his swollen, bleeding wrists together.

"You speak with Blackfoot tongue," said Red Claw.

Devlin nodded.

"Take this knife and go. There is your pony."

Devlin looked around, suspicious. The Blackfoot camp was sleeping. The buffalo-chip fires had burned down. Each warrior slept with his horse nearby, the horsehair reins tied around a wrist. Close at hand stood the pony he had ridden all the way up from Santa Fe. And over there lay a Blackfoot brave, sprawled facedown on the ground. Devlin took a closer look at the knife that Red Claw was offering him. There was blood on the blade. And it wasn't *his* blood.

"You killed the guard?"

Red Claw's smile made chills run up and down Devlin's spine.

"You killed him, Coyote, when you escaped."

"You must want war pretty bad to kill your own kind," said Devlin.

"Run, Coyote."

Devlin took the knife and got to his feet.

"I guess you and the rest of your brothers will be after me in the morning."

"Ride fast."

Devlin led the horse an arrow's flight away from the camp before mounting up and riding off into the night.

"You were fools to trust the white men!" cried Red Claw, getting in the face of the stoic Crooked Knife. "Their hearts are black with treachery."

At their feet lay the body of the slain warrior.

The rest of the braves formed a circle around them, some on foot, holding their ponies, others mounted. All were grim and silent and warily attentive, for they knew that this was the moment of truth, when Red Claw challenged the authority of the principal chiefs.

"I think it is your heart which is the blackest of all," replied Crooked Knife.

Red Claw searched for the hidden meaning behind the old chief's words. He had a feeling Crooked Knife suspected the truth of what had transpired last night. But he had no proof. Red Claw smiled coldly. He stepped back and, lifting his head defiantly, addressed the assembled warriors.

"You see what happens when you do not listen to me? Redcoat makes fools of all of you. The white men are laughing at us now. I say we listen no longer to the white man's lies. I say we do now what the Blackfeet—and their Blood and Piegan brothers—

have always done to their enemies. *I say we kill the white men!*"

The warriors brandished their weapons over their heads and yelled approval.

Gloating, Red Claw turned back to Crooked Knife.

"Go back to your lodge, and I, Red Claw, will bring you the scalps of the white men."

He called out the names of three warriors and dispatched them to their respective villages, with orders to round up all of the braves and bring them, with all haste, to the falls of the Wind River.

From there they would strike due west, through the high pass, and descend upon the trappers gathered in the Teton Basin.

Chapter 30

Zach and Bridger reached the site of the annual rendezvous on the evening of the seventh day out of Fort Union.

From a distance it was quite a sight.

The sun had long since dropped behind the magnificent snow-clad peaks of the mighty Teton Range. The first stars were glimmering in the purple sky. The indigo shadows of night were gathering in the verdant valley. Dozens of campfires, tiny flickering pinpricks of light, delineated the sprawling encampment. Beyond the camp, the lake was a vast expanse of inky black, rimmed by a towering forest.

They approached the camp with caution, concerned about the sentries that they suspected had been posted. By now, word of the Blackfoot threat had surely reached the trappers congregated here.

"Don't sound like they're too much worried about Injuns," remarked Bridger.

Zach had to agree. Raucous sounds drifted across the valley to their ears, distorted by distance, but still identifiable as lusty male voices raised in anger or song or laughter, the wail of the fiddles, an occasional gunshot bouncing off the stony flanks of the mountains encompassing the picturesque basin.

A black shape rose suddenly out of the waist-high grass a stone's throw in front of them. Their horses snorted and shied.

"Don't shoot!" bellowed Bridger. "We're trappers."

"Who goes there?" came the nervous query.

"Jim Bridger and Zach Hannah. Ease off that trigger, hoss."

"Gawd A'mighty, I done come close to pluggin' you boys."

"Is that you, Joe Meek?"

"It's me, Old Gabe, sure 'nuff."

The frontiersman shoulder-racked his rifle and waded through the grass toward them.

Joe Meek was a big, bearded, grinning character, tall and broad-shouldered, full of pluck, and the most consistently good-natured man Zach had ever met. It was hard not to like Joe Meek, he was so full of the joy of life. He was rough-hewn but courteous. A natural-born fighter who could be as gentle as a lamb. He had few enemies, and he had proven himself to be the kind of man you would want siding with you in a scrape.

Born in Virginia, he was only twenty-two years of age, and yet he was as experienced a mountain man as any currently on hand in the Teton Basin. At eighteen he had run away from home, being less than fond of his stepmother. The autumn of '28 had found him wandering around in St. Louis, penniless and ragtag yet undaunted in his determination to seek fame and fortune on the frontier.

It had been his great good fortune to run into William Sublette. At that time Sublette had been one of the new owners of the Rocky Mountain Fur Company, as that concern's original founders, Major Henry and William Ashley, had cashed in their chips after seeing the company through its rough beginnings and making a handsome profit in spite of numerous setbacks.

Sublette had just returned from the summer rendezvous. He had sold the furs gathered from the Rocky Mountain brigades and was in the process of selling them and buying up trade goods to haul back out west for next year's rendezvous.

"So you want to see the Shining Mountains, do you?" Sublette asked the runaway Virginian.

"Yessir."

"You got a rifle?"

"Nossir."

"A hoss?"

"Nossir."

"Where you from?"

"Virginny."

"You walked all the way from Virginny?"

"Not all the way. I hitched me a ride in a wagon every now and again."

"Know anything about Injuns?"

"Nossir. Only seen a couple."

Sublette shook his head. "Boy, you will get yourself kilt before you even get halfway to the high country."

"Then I reckon I'll be dead. But that won't stop me from trying."

Sublette laughed at that. He couldn't help but admire Joe Meek's spirit, and in the end he signed the

lad on. The following spring, Joe headed west with
Sublette and his merchandise-laden wagons.

He joined up with the brigade of Milton Sublette,
William's younger brother. He and Milt became fast
friends and shared numerous hair-raising adventures
together.

"Joe, you look better dressed and better fed than I
remember," said Zach. "Where did you come by all
that fancy beadwork on your huntin' shirt?"

Joe looked positively sheepish. He mumbled
something in reply.

"What? Speak up, Joe?"

"I done got squawed up."

"Say it isn't so!"

"Shoot, Zach, I figured if it was good enough for
you and Milt, I might as well give it a go."

"Wonders never cease," laughed Bridger. "What
tribe does she hail from, Joe?"

"Nez Percé."

"Looks like married life suits you."

"I can't complain."

"Yeah," said Bridger. "I guess it's one of those
things every man ought to try at least once."

"When you gonna get hitched, Old Gabe?"

Bridger chuckled. "When I'm tired of livin'."

Zach leaned forward in his saddle. "Morning Sky.
Is she here, Joe?"

"Sure. Look, fellers . . . I've been hearing talk
about the Blackfeet . . ."

Bridger shook his head. "Smooth down your hack-
les. Last bunch we saw was headed north, back to
their villages."

They rode on into camp.

Nightfall had not curtailed the festivities. There was still a good bit of gambling and wrestling and tall-tale swapping going on. But most of all there was a great deal of "passin' round" jugs of liquor. At every campfire sat or stood a group of trappers. The Indians roamed freely among the white men. There were Shoshones, Flatheads, Nez Percés, and of course a sizable contingent of Zach's friends, the Absaroka Crows.

Many were the men who left their fires to step out and greet the two mountain men as they rode by. Not one failed to ask about the Blackfeet. Everybody wanted to know what those devils were up to. And Zach seldom missed a chance to ask after Morning Sky's whereabouts. Most of the men didn't know. Some admitted they knew she was present, but they weren't sure where she could be found.

The camp itself covered a vast amount of ground. There were hundreds of trappers and Indians present, with more coming in every day, and no rhyme or reason to the way things were laid out. Some of the trappers had fashioned lean-tos for shelters. But many of them slept on the ground, beneath the stars. Quite often it was a case of their lying where they fell, stone-cold drunk.

One who intercepted them was Thomas Fitzpatrick—the legendary mountain man the Indians knew as Broken Hand. Along with Bridger, Milton Sublette, Henry Fraeb, and Baptiste Gervais he was one of the third generation of part owners of the Rocky Mountain Fur Company.

Fitz was aware that Bridger had of late been at Fort Union to witness the meeting that Redcoat

McKenzie had arranged with the Blackfeet. He wanted to know what had happened. Though Zach was impatient to continue his search for Morning Sky, he lingered to exchange greetings with Broken Hand.

"Hear tell you went out to find Coyote," said Fitzpatrick. "A feller named Briggs, a booshway with the American Fur Company, came in a few days back and said you had done so."

"Yes, I found him." Zach was not at all eager to discuss the matter.

"Did them pesky Blackfoot devils show up at McKenzie's post?"

"They showed," replied Bridger. "And when they left they were riding north for the Missouri."

Fitzpatrick's rugged countenance lit up. "You don't say! Well, that's damned good news indeed. I figured for sure we had a full-fledged war on our hands. Didn't give McKenzie much of a chance with them redskins. But I guess he came through for us all. Is he coming to rendezvous, Jim?"

"He'll be along."

"Good. Quite a few of his boys are already here. We all seem to get along a lot better than we did a year ago. I reckon I'll have to shake Mr. McKenzie's hand."

"Fitz, have you seen my wife?" asked Zach.

"Shore did. Went by to pay my respects just this mornin'. She's stayin' with the Sparrowhawk people." He pointed to the west.

"And Shadmore?"

"He's stickin' to her like fleas to a redbone hound."

Zach thanked him and rode in the direction he had indicated. Bridger rode along with him.

The Indians who attended the annual rendezvous traditionally raised their lodges on the outskirts of the encampment. They mingled with the mountain men, but did not live among them. This year the Nez Percés and Flatheads were camped to the east, while the Absaroka Crows were camped to the west, nearer the lake.

Most of the trappers preferred the company of the Nez Percés to other Indians. This proud and friendly tribe had proven themselves to be trustworthy allies. The Crows, on the other hand, had a reputation as conniving, light-fingered sorts. The reputation was well deserved. The Absarokas were inveterate thieves. They thought it great sport to steal. They particularly enjoyed giving gifts and then stealing them back again. As far as they were concerned, a man who did not think enough of the gift he received from them to guard it from thieves did not deserve Crow largesse in the first place.

Zach Hannah would have been the first to admit that the Absaroka Crows had their faults. Yet, while he had never officially gone through the ritual of becoming a blood brother to the Crows, Zach was, among all the mountain men, the one most admired by the tribe. Iron Bull, the principal chief of the Sparrowhawk people, regarded him as a father would an adopted son. His role as the inveterate enemy of the Blackfeet, who were the arch-foes of the Crows, was also a factor in the closeness of the relationship between Zach and the Sparrowhawk people. That he had escaped certain death at the hands of the Blackfeet, and killed the notorious Blackfoot warrior named Scar in the process, only served to enhance his stature among these people. The Crows were convinced he had great magic.

So it was that Zach Hannah's arrival in the Crow camp resulted in a joyous hue and cry, as the Absarokas poured from their lodges and left their evening fires to congregate around him. Zach recognized several faces in the crowd and spoke his greetings. One was a brave named Deer Stalker.

Deer Stalker had been one of a small band of Crow warriors who, while out on a horse-stealing excursion last year, had captured Sean Michael Devlin. Zach had interceded on Devlin's behalf, and persuaded Deer Stalker and his brothers not to take Coyote's life—an intercession Zach had lived to regret, as not long after that incident Devlin's treachery had led to Zach's capture by the Blackfeet.

Seeing Deer Stalker again reminded Zach that one of the warrior's friends had gone by the name of Red Claw.

"You must tell your brother Red Claw that I have met his Blackfoot namesake," said Zach cheerfully in the Sparrowhawk tongue. "I prefer the Crow version."

Deer Stalker's expression, bright with pleasure at seeing Zach, changed suddenly to one etched deep with grief.

"I wish I could tell him," said Deer Stalker glumly. "But several moons ago my friend left our village and never returned. I found his body—and Blackfoot sign."

"I am truly sorry, Deer Stalker."

"But as for the Blackfoot they call Red Claw," said the warrior, and his voice grew harsh, "I will kill him when I am given the chance. His existence blackens the name of my good friend."

"How is Iron Bull?"

"He lives."

"And Sky? Where is Sky?"

"We raised a lodge for the woman of our white brother, Zach Hannah. It stands near the lodge of Iron Bull in the center of the camp."

Zach and Bridger moved on. The crowd stayed with the two mountain men. As some of the Crows called their greetings and dropped out of the mob, others rushed up to take their places.

As they approached the center of the camp a familiar voice reached Zach's ears above the din made by the Indians.

"Zach! Zach Hannah!"

Shadmore bulled his way through the press.

Zach jumped off his pony and threw his arms around the old, gray-bearded leatherstocking. They pounded each other on the back, then held each other at arm's length. Both men were grinning from ear to ear.

"Yore a sight for sore eyes, scout!" exclaimed Shadmore.

"So are you, old coot."

"Sky and the boy are fine, Zach. I . . ."

"I knew they would be, with you to look out for them."

"I tried to talk her out of coming here, you know, but . . ."

"Don't concern yourself about that. Once Sky's

made up her mind about something, a team of wild horses couldn't drag her off course."

Shadmore nodded, grateful. "Did you find what you were lookin' fur?"

"I did."

"Wahl, you kin tell me all about it later. I reckon you'd like to see yer woman and younker."

"Very much, yes."

"Gangway, you heathens!" bellowed Shadmore. He began to carve a path for Zach, shoving and elbowing his way through the Indians. They laughed good-naturedly at him. The louder he cursed, the more they laughed.

"The Lord had an easier time partin' the Red Sea!" lamented Shad at the top of his lungs.

But then they were through the crowd, and as Zach took a step toward the lodge directly in front of him, the deerskin flap of the tepee's entrance moved—and Morning Sky emerged.

The sight of her stopped Zach Hannah dead in his tracks.

"My God," he breathed. "You get prettier every time I see you, Sky."

"Father!"

Little Jacob burst from the lodge and charged straight at Zach, who tossed his rifle to Shadmore and scooped the boy up in his strong arms before walking closer to Sky. He reached out to touch the raven-black hair that draped her shoulders and framed her lovely face. He noticed that her violet-blue eyes were wet with unfallen tears.

"It's done," he said, his voice thick with emotion. "I will never . . ."

She put a finger to his lips.

"Do not say it, Zach," she whispered. "You are home. That is all that matters."

She put her arms around him, then, and as they embraced, a laughing Jacob squeezed between them, the Absaroka Crows raised a squall of rejoicing loud enough to reach the snowy windswept heights of the looming peaks.

Chapter 31

When the Absaroka Crows erected the lodge for the use of Morning Sky, Shadmore had slept that first night on the ground in front of the tepee entrance, rolled up in his blankets. That morning, emerging from the lodge, Sky had tripped and fallen over his prostrate form.

"Why do you sleep here on the ground?" she asked the old leatherstocking, after she picked herself up and stopped laughing at the stricken expression on Shad's grizzled features.

"Where else would I sleep?"

"In the tepee, of course."

"No, ma'am. That thar wouden be proper."

She laughed again, remembering how Shadmore had started out sleeping on the porch of the cabin after Zach's departure on the hunt for Devlin. It had taken her a few days of persistent nagging to persuade him that he could unroll his blankets on the floor of the cabin. The bed she shared with her husband was screened from the rest of the one-room abode by blankets depending from a rope strung between two big iron hooks hammered into rafters.

"But we slept under the same roof on the mountain, Shadmore."

"True 'nuff. But this here situation is some different. For one thing, thar's lots of folks around, and you gotta be keerful about the notions they might get."

"Nonsense."

"No it ain't."

"No Absaroka Crow would insult me."

"It ain't Crows I'm worried about. It's them other trappers. You know how loose their tongues can get when they're likkered up. Way it'd end up, I'd have to kill one or two of 'em for talkin' bad about you. No, I'd just as soon step around the water as fall right into it and muddy it up."

And so it had stood, with Shadmore sleeping at the entrance to her lodge, like a watchdog at its master's door.

But on the night of Zach Hannah's return, Shadmore scooped up little Jacob and gathered his possibles, giving every indication that he was leaving the premises permanently.

"Where are you going?" asked Zach.

"Well, scout, yore back, so I'm no longer needed here."

"You're taking our son?" asked Sky, smiling.

"What? Oh, I thought little Jacob here would like to go camp down by the lake tonight. Then mebbe we'd git our lazy bones up jist 'fore daybreak and do us a little fishin'. What d'ya say, lad?"

Jacob was keenly interested, and Zach gave his approval. When Shad and the boy had gone, he turned to Sky, suddenly nervous.

"It's just you and me now," he said lamely.

"I think that was Shad's idea."

Zach looked around the lodge. The fire in the center, ringed with stones, was burning down to ashes and embers.

"Reckon I'd better go fetch some more firewood," he said. "It'll be right cold tonight."

"I don't need a fire to keep me warm tonight," she said.

She took his hand and led him to the buffalo robes where she slept, and when she looked at him there was smoldering desire in her eyes.

"I have you, my husband," she added.

A minute later Zach had forgotten all about firewood.

Late the next morning Shadmore and Jacob returned from the lake with a mess of perch. Zach was just emerging, shirtless, from the lodge as they walked up.

"You look like a feller's just been on his honeymoon," remarked a grinning Shadmore.

Zach felt his cheeks burn.

"Look what we caught!" exclaimed Jacob.

"Looks like breakfast."

Morning Sky came out of the lodge behind Zach. "Jacob, come and help me gather some wood."

"I'll do that," said Zach.

"No, you and Shad have a talk."

She and Jacob headed back toward the woods.

Zach and Shadmore cleaned the fish. Then the old leatherstocking settled back and broke out his clay-bowl pipe. He packed it with tobacco mixed with willow bark.

"I want to thank you for looking out for my family, Shad."

"Warn't nothing'."

"It was to me. You missed out on trapping this season. You had no plews to trade."

"Oh, I did me a little trappin' thar in yer valley, Zach. 'Course, I allus took Sky and the younker along with me. You know I wouden leave them alone for a minute."

"Find any brown gold?"

"Some. That valley ain't completely trapped out."

"Then how come you're still cutting your tobacco with willow bark? If you had plews to trade with?"

"I traded 'em. Got me some Dupont powder and Galena lead, and I got Jacob a book from a feller named Nathaniel Wyeth."

"Wyeth? Who's he?"

"Feller come west from New England, with a few other Yankees. Says he's bound for the Oregon country. He fell in with Sublette a few days out of Independence." Shadmore was smirking. "Seems Mr. Wyeth and company got themselves lost right off. He don't know the first thing about the frontier, but he's an educated cuss. Talks fancy. Nice enough, I reckon. He sold me a book to give to Jacob. That younker, I swear, he's shore got a strong hankerin' to learn. Allus askin' questions. Pestered the dickens out of me sometimes with his askin' about this and that. Finally I told him I'd buy him a book with all the answers in it. He's a lot smarter than you'd figure a boy who's only seen—what?—five winters should be."

"You're a true friend, Shad," said Zach, realizing that Shadmore had been forced to choose between tobacco for his pipe and the book for Jacob. He remembered, in the old days when Shad had been a member of his brigade, the old leatherstocking's first purchase with the credit he received for his share of the brigade's plews was tobacco. Other men spent their hard-earned money on whiskey or women, but Shadmore's greatest pleasure in the autumn of his life was a good smoke.

"I hear tell you found Coyote," said Shad. He could sense that Zach wanted to talk about Devlin, but for some reason couldn't bring himself to broach the subject.

Zach nodded, and looked morosely at his hands. "I found him."

"Whereabouts?"

"Santa Fe."

Shadmore grunted. "The feller shore got around. Did he give you much trouble?"

"No. He was in jail."

"Who'd he shoot in the back?"

"Nobody. It concerned a woman."

"Figures. What about Montez?"

"He never caught up with Devlin."

"And never come back to us. Reckon he's crossed the river."

"Reckon so."

"You turned Coyote over to McKenzie?"

"I did."

"And McKenzie gave him to the Blackfeet?"

"Yes."

"That seems to bother you some."

"Can't deny that it does. There at the last minute I almost backed out of the deal. Probably would have, except that it was too late."

"Too late? How come?"

"There were about fifty Blackfeet there who wouldn't have gone for it."

Shadmore was staring at him, incredulous.

"I dunno 'bout you sometimes, scout. Have you forgotten what-all Coyote's done to you?"

"No. I could never forget."

"What you should've done was put a bullet in his brainpan right then and there when you met up with him thar in Santa Fe."

"I couldn't do that."

"You mean you wouldn't. I know that. You're too decent-minded. Now, I don't mean that in a bad way. Yore just a better man than me. I would've kilt him dead on the spot. That way I'd never have to fret about what style of mischief he was plannin' to throw at me."

"Well, we don't have to worry about that now. If he isn't gone under, he soon will be."

Shadmore snorted. "You reckon it's that easy? The rascal's got the devil's own luck."

"You think he could get away from the Blackfeet? They wanted him something fierce, on account of what happened to Whirlwind's village."

"Yeah, and they wanted yer scalp so bad they could taste it, too. And what happened? You got clean away with a whole skin, didn't you? Coyote's the slipperiest scoundrel I ever had the misfortune to meet. That's why I say you'd've done better killin' him yerself."

Zach shook his head. "I don't reckon we'll see him again."

"I hope yore right, but I got my doubts. Iffen you *are* right, I say good riddance. Zach, you done the right thing. For some reason that I ain't got all the way figured out yet, you've been walkin' all around gettin' rid of that two-legged snake. Had more'n one chance these past years. Mebbe it's 'cause he stuck with you that winter ten year back, when you busted yer leg a thousand miles from nowhere."

"No. He didn't do that for me. I know as much. But I think it's because I always had this feeling he could've made something of himself. That it wasn't altogether his fault, the way he was."

Shadmore nodded. "I know that sometimes the world will roll right over a person. But the man who says he's gone wrong on account of life not givin' him a fair shake is blamin' the fiddle for the music instead of the fiddler. I ain't never met a man who's had more hard knocks than you have had these past ten years or so, Zach, and I don't see you off makin' life miserable for all creation."

Zach shook his head. He had hoped that Shadmore would convince him that he had done the right thing, and the old leatherstocking had given it a game try. But Zach found, much to his dismay, that he still wasn't convinced.

"So what do you aim to do after rendezvous?" asked Shadmore. "With Montez gone there's not much left of the old brigade. Jubal Wilkes and MacGregor and me. That's it."

Zach shook his head again. "I'm done with trapping, Shad."

"Then what will you do? What else *is* there to do?"

"If McKenzie's scheme works, we might not have a war this summer. But that just puts it off till next green-up. I think I'm going to take my family out of harm's way."

"You could live with these Crows. I know Iron Bull's been after you to do as much."

"The Crows will be right in the thick of this fight. They see it as their big chance to destroy the Blackfoot Nation once and for all. For years they've been fighting the Blackfeet on their own. Now they've got help."

"True enough. What, then, for you?"

"I recall Jedediah Smith tellin' about the Oregon country. You say this feller Wyeth is headed that way?"

"That's what he says."

"No Blackfeet in Oregon."

"No, they'd have to go through the Nez Percés to get there, and such ain't likely. But then you got the British to worry about. I hear tell there's trouble brewin' up there in that Oregon territory over what country holds title to it."

Zach smiled wryly. "Seems like folks are always quarreling over who owns the land."

"And so it will be till Judgment Day."

Zach was silent for a spell. Shadmore waited, moodily puffing on his pipe.

"I think I'll talk to this Wyeth feller," said Zach, at length. "Maybe go take a gander at Oregon."

"Hmm" was the full extent of Shadmore's noncommittal reply.

Zach stood up. "Old coot," he said, "wouldn't you like to see Oregon before you go under?"

Shadmore bounced to his feet, quite spry for a man of his advanced years.

"Scout, I thought you'd never ask."

Chapter 32

Nathaniel Wyeth was a tall, spare man. His long, lantern-jawed face and somber expression attested to his Puritan bloodline. He wore a black frock coat, trousers, and flat-brimmed hat, and this somber garb contributed to his aura of austerity. The first thing Zach wondered was if the man knew how to smile. He didn't look like the sort who practiced smiling much.

When Shadmore brought Zach to Wyeth's tent to introduce the two men, Wyeth was sitting in a folding canvas camp chair, impervious to the hot sun, perusing a book. When he shut the book, his place marked with a red ribbon, Zach saw the title on the spine: Plato's *Republic*.

"Mr. Wyeth," said Shadmore. "This hyar's Zach Hannah."

Wyeth nodded gravely. "I believe I have heard the name mentioned."

"That book I bought from you was fur his boy."

"Ah, yes. Parson Weem's life of Washington." Wyeth fastened coal-black eyes on Zach. "Are you interested in books, Mr. Hannah? I brought a great many along with me. More, it seems now, than I should have. They are a burden to me, as well as to the mules which pull my wagon."

"Don't know much about books, Mr. Wyeth. I haven't been around too many of them."

"Your grammar is fair. You have had some schooling?"

"Not much. They had a hard time keeping me in school."

"I see." Wyeth raised the heavy tome he had been reading. "This is a splendid work. You should read some of Plato."

"What's he write about?"

"The rational relationship between the soul and the state and the universe at large. You see, Plato believed that the human soul was both rational and immortal. He also believed in what you might call a world soul. It is his premise that virtue exists in the harmony of the human soul and the world soul. This insures order in an ever-changing world. Only a man in tune with this harmony can understand the universe in which he lives. Do you think that premise is sensible, Mr. Hannah?"

"Might be. I've had the feeling, at times, when I'm one with this country, and all its creatures, that I can almost hear the mountains and the streams talk, and I'm at peace. But when I turn my back on that— when I let myself get drawn into the affairs of others—that's when I start losing my way."

"Fascinating." Wyeth seemed suddenly and keenly interested in the tall, buckskin-clad frontiersman. He appeared pleasantly surprised that such a sentiment could come from a man as rough-hewn as Zach.

"Ask me," said Shadmore, only half joking, "yore

soundin' like an Injun, scout. Been hangin' around them Absaroka Crows a damn sight too long."

"What about the wolves?" asked Zach.

"Wolves?" queried Wyeth. "What wolves?"

"Seems like every time I'm up to my eyebrows in trouble, a pack of wolves, led by a big silver-back male, shows up."

"And what happens?"

"Well, one time, two of us were caught in a blizzard. I had broken my leg, and it was beginning to look like we were going to starve to death. Then the wolves came along. We shot one, ate it, and had the strength to go the rest of the way."

"What else?"

"When I escaped from the Blackfeet, and in need of food and clothing, the wolves showed up and killed a young shaggy. I got my dinner and a buffalo robe to wear."

"Don't forget that spirit-wolf Sky insists came callin' on her one day," said Shadmore, shaking his head.

The ghost of a smile touched the corners of Wyeth's stern mouth. "I do believe you are a skeptic, Mr. Shadmore."

"I believe what I kin see with my own two eyes, and not much more."

"A shame. But you, Mr. Hannah, believe in things you cannot always see, don't you?"

"I reckon there's a lot we don't see. That doesn't mean it isn't there."

"Very true. So it is books, ideas, that you are interested in?"

"I'm interested in the idea of the Oregon territory, Mr. Wyeth."

"Have you been there?" asked Wyeth, leaning forward eagerly.

"No. I've only gone as far as the Nez Percé country."

"Ah. So you know the mountains between here and there fairly well."

"Fairly well?" echoed Shadmore. "Wagh! Zach here spent years alone wanderin' the high country, back when most of these hyar valleys had never felt the tread of a white man's foot, and the mountains had seldom heard the sound of a white man's voice. I dare you to come up with anybody who knows these mountains better than Zach Hannah."

"Is that true, Mr. Hannah?"

"I know my way around."

"Alas, I do not. Neither do my companions. We are all rank greenhorns. We were fortunate that Mr. Sublette came along when he did. I had a compass, but lost it in a river crossing."

"You still had the stars to guide you."

"Yes, and some acquaintance with steering by them. But we had almost a week of overcast, and by the time the skies had cleared, I knew we were well off our course. That is about all I knew for a certainty."

"Sounds like you could use a guide."

"Indeed. Mr. Sublette brought me this far, and with great patience and courtesy, I might add. But he did not volunteer his services to see me through these mighty mountains to my destination, nor did I deem it proper to prevail upon his good nature to do so. So it is an example of the rational order of the universe, of which Plato writes, that brings the two of you here today to volunteer your services to my endeavor. You are volunteering, too, aren't you, Mr. Shadmore?"

"Yore a right smart man, Mr. Wyeth."

"In some things. Human nature, for instance. You and Mr. Hannah have forged a very strong bond of friendship. Where he goes, thither will you go, too. Is that not the case?"

"I reckon I'd follow him to hell."

"Fortunately, it is Oregon, not hell, for which we are bound. And Oregon, my friends, is about as far from hell as you can get without being in God's glorious heaven. Yes, I am smart in some ways, but woefully ignorant in others. Woodlore, for example. We all have our gifts. I hail from the Commonwealth of Massachusetts, and city-born. I suppose the Almighty did not think it necessary to bestow upon me the gifts which both of you no doubt possess in that regard."

"Why do you want to go to Oregon?" asked Zach.

"I am an entrepreneur."

"A what?" puzzled Shadmore. "I thought you was an American?"

Wyeth smiled tolerantly. "I seek to establish a trade on the Columbia River."

"Trade with whom?" asked Zach.

"I will trade with the natives first. But my intent is to establish a fort near the mouth of the Columbia and engage in the China trade."

"China?"

"A nation of tremendous untapped wealth across

the Pacific Ocean. Centuries ago, Marco Polo was the first to establish a trade route to China overland from Europe. There was an immediate, virtually insatiable demand for the silk and spices and jewels with which China is abundantly endowed. So much so, in fact, that it was the desire to find a sea route to the Orient which led to the discovery of this great nation of ours."

"How you figure?" asked Shadmore.

"The Europeans were tired of paying tribute to Muslim overlords in return for safe passage of the overland caravans. So Spain and Portugal, once free of the Moors, dispatched seagoing explorers to find a sea route to the Orient. Da Gama, Magellan, and the like. The Dark Continent, Africa, was discovered as a result. As was the Americas, by a fellow named Columbus. Columbus thought he had found the Orient. He had no idea that this vast continent stood between him and his goal.

"It has taken us three hundred years since the time of Columbus to traverse this land. You fellows have played an integral role in conquering America. Now nothing but an ocean stands between us and the fabled Orient. Not too many years ago, John Jacob Astor sent a merchant ship around the Cape Horn and across the Pacific. The vessel reached China and returned laden with a fortune in exotic goods. Upon that single cargo Mr. Astor built a fabulous fortune."

"Why don't you just send a ship on the same route?" asked Zach.

"The Cape Horn is the southernmost tip of South America. It is an extremely long and perilous journey.

By establishing a post at the mouth of the Columbia River, I will cut that distance by far more than half. I will have a great advantage over those back east who dream the same dreams that I do."

"You have a ship?"

"Indeed I do. It is bound for the Horn as we speak. In a month's time it should arrive at the Columbia, where I am to rendezvous with it."

"What about the British?"

"Yes, indeed," said Wyeth. "What about them? The very same John Jacob Astor built a fort on the Columbia twenty years ago. It was the only instance in which his luck failed him. For war soon broke out between the United States and Great Britain, and he could not hold the fort against a superior British force."

"From what I've heard," said Zach, "we might have to fight the British again over Oregon."

"There is that possibility. Would that there was not. But every venture carries its own risks. I will face that challenge when and if it arises."

"Yeah," said Shadmore. "Like Zach here says, you can't cross a bridge until you come to it."

"So what do you say, my friends?"

"I'd like to talk it over with Zach for a minute," said Shadmore.

"Please do."

The frontiersmen walked off, far enough to be out of earshot.

"What do you think?" asked the old leatherstocking.

"I think I'm bound for Oregon, Shad."

"You like Wyeth?"

"He talks straight."

"Fancy, too. What's grammar?"

Zach laughed. "You'll find out."

They returned to Wyeth.

"Reckon we'll be going along," said Zach. "But I've got to talk it over with my wife first."

"Of course."

"And there's one condition."

"Name it."

"I won't sign a contract, or give my word to stick with you, except for getting you through the mountains to Oregon. Beyond that, no promises. I might take one look at the country and turn around."

"I doubt that. But I readily accept your condition, Mr. Hannah."

"Goes for me, too," said Shadmore.

"Naturally."

"It's just that every time I make a promise like that I'm soon wishing I hadn't," explained Zach.

"Agreed."

"When do you want to set out?"

"The sooner the better."

Zach nodded. "I'll be back before sundown with the word. If Sky's willin', we can leave tomorrow."

"Excellent."

"I'll want to check out your horses and your gear. It's a rough trail."

"We have two wagons."

Zach shook his head. "Wagons won't make it from here on out, Mr. Wyeth. We'll have to pack your gear over the high passes on the backs of horses or mules."

"I defer to your expertise."

As the two frontiersmen walked away, Shadmore said, "What was that he said thar at the end."

"Whatever we say goes."

"Like I said, Mr. Wyeth is a smart man."

Chapter 33

Zach Hannah didn't have a clue as to how Morning Sky would react to his suggestion about going to Oregon with Nathaniel Wyeth and company. Her reaction turned out to be unreserved enthusiasm—so much so, in fact, that Zach was surprised by it. He told Shadmore, who nodded sagely, as though he had known all along that Sky would be for the move.

"What's she got to hold her here?" he asked Zach. "No family, exceptin' you and the boy. Oh, she's got a Blackfoot brother, but from what she's told me, he'd just as soon see her dead."

"Ten Bows. Since she's been with the Crows, she's an embarrassment to him."

"So she's got a choice between that cabin up in the high lonesome or a new life in Oregon. Natcherly she'll choose Oregon."

"Then I'll go tell Wyeth."

At that moment Jim Bridger came running through the Crow camp. Zach could tell by the expression on Old Gabe's face that something was plenty wrong.

"You won't believe who just rode into camp," said Bridger.

Somehow Zach knew the answer. Only one man had such bad timing. Here he was, with his heart set on putting the past behind him and getting a fresh start in a new country called Oregon, and then . . .

"Devlin," he said, his voice hollow.

Bridger gaped. "How'd you know?"

"Had to be," replied Zach bitterly.

Bridger looked beyond Zach, at the lodge, and Zach turned to see Morning Sky standing there, her body rigid, her features taut with fear and dismay, and he knew she had heard everything that had been said.

"You'd better stay here, Sky."

She said nothing, turning to duck back into the te-pee.

With a fatalistic sigh, Zach grabbed his Hawken rifle. He and Shadmore followed Bridger out of the Absaroka camp.

At least fifty frontiersmen, and a few Indians, had gathered around Sean Michael Devlin. Through this strangely silent crowd pushed Zach, Shadmore, and Old Gabe. When they saw Hannah, some of the trappers began to make wagers among themselves.

They knew the story of Zach Hannah and Sean Devlin—how the two had once been friends, until their falling out over Morning Sky, and Devlin had abducted her. A disillusioned Hannah had disappeared into the mountains for years. He had finally gotten her back. And then there was the question about little Jacob's parentage, though no one dared address that subject in Zach's presence. They knew, too, about how Devlin's treachery had led to Hannah's capture by the Blackfeet. Again Zach Hannah had been written off by everyone, only to reappear after engineering an epic escape from those red rascals. And finally they knew how Hannah had turned the tables on Devlin, tracking Coyote down and turning him over to the Blackfeet, who wanted Devlin's hide as bad as they had ever wanted Hannah's.

It was a tale of vengeance and betrayal that was already a legend among the mountain men. The odds were ten to one that Zach Hannah would write the final chapter of that saga right here and now by killing Devlin. The look on his face as he pushed through the crowd indicated that such was going to be the case.

When he reached the center of the ring of frontiersmen, Zach stopped dead in his tracks.

Devlin sat on a log, dirty and haggard and naked, his skin burned by exposure to the sun. The man standing over him, rifle pointed with calculated carelessness at Devlin's head, was Briggs, the American Fur Company booshway Zach had met on his way north to Fort Union.

"I was on guard duty," Briggs explained to Zach, "when this rode in, bold as brass. All he had on him was this knife." Briggs indicated the weapon now stuck in his belt.

Devlin nodded at Zach, smiling faintly. "I am sorry to be so unpresentable, but the Blackfeet took my clothes. If someone could spare me a blanket . . . ?"

Bridger turned to the crowd. "One of you men fetch a blanket."

"How did you get away?" Zach asked Devlin.

"Red Claw."

"What do you mean?"

"Red Claw helped me escape."

"That makes no sense," said Briggs.

"He killed the brave who was guarding me and cut me loose. Even provided me with a horse. The rest of the bunch were sleeping. I just rode away."

"And they didn't go after you?"

"I've stayed one jump ahead of them. But then it's not me they're really after."

"You mean the Blackfeet are right behind you?"

"You led them savages right to us," growled Briggs.

"You don't understand . . ."

"We'll just give you right back to 'em," said Briggs.

"Listen to me—"

"Hold on a minute," said Zach.

"Why would Red Claw help him escape?" came a skeptical query from the crowd.

"It *does* make sense," insisted Zach. "Red Claw wants war. He didn't like it one bit when the old chiefs fell for McKenzie's scheme and headed home with Coyote as their prisoner. McKenzie told me himself that Red Claw preferred Devlin dead."

"Then why didn't he kill him?" asked Briggs. "We'd all be better off."

"Because the old chiefs wanted him alive for the time being."

"Red Claw's clever," said Devlin. "This way he can say it was all a trick by the white men from the very beginning."

Fitzpatrick came through the crowd, gave Devlin a frosty look, and turned to Bridger.

"What's happened here, Old Gabe?"

"Devlin got away from the Blackfeet."

"And they're on their way here," added Briggs.

"But they're not coming after me," said Devlin, exasperated. "Don't you understand? I could have headed south instead of coming here, and Red Claw and his bunch wouldn't have wasted their time tracking me. They're headed straight here. I managed to stay ahead of them. Came to warn you."

The man who had gone to fetch a blanket returned. Zach took the blanket from him and gave it to Devlin.

"Thanks," said Coyote. He draped the blanket over his shoulders and held it closed in front.

"How many Blackfeet?" asked Broken Hand.

"About fifty with Red Claw. But they held up at the falls of the Wind River."

"When was that?" asked Bridger.

"Yesterday, about noon."

"They're waiting for more warriors," guessed Zach. "I reckon Red Claw sent riders to some or all of the villages to gather up those who wanted to fight, and picked the Wind River falls as the rendezvous."

"Sky," breathed Devlin.

Zach looked at him sharply, then followed his gaze to Morning Sky, who had slipped through the press of mountain men.

She stepped forward, raised the flintlock pistol Zach had given her a long time ago. He had worked patiently with her to make sure she was proficient in its use. But at this range she did not need to be proficient. She pointed the pistol at Devlin's head, at point-blank range. All she needed was the nerve to pull the trigger.

"Sky, no!" yelled Zach, jumping forward.

Devlin sat stone still, unflinching. He looked her right in the eye. He could have tried to knock the pistol aside, but he didn't. Before Zach could reach her she had a split second to do the deed. She couldn't bring herself to do it. And Zach pulled her arm down, then wrested the pistol from her limp grasp. With a stunned expression she turned slowly away from Devlin, a single tear snaking down her dusky cheek—and into Zach's comforting embrace.

"I know I've done wrong by both of you," said Devlin. "I'm not asking for forgiveness. What I've done, no one could forgive."

"This man needs some food and clothing," said Fitzpatrick.

He said this to all those assembled. Being one of the big augurs in the Rocky Mountain Fur Company, he had a right to make his desires known and, having done so, to expect the others to work it out among themselves how to get it accomplished. One man would donate an extra hunting shirt, another a pair of moccasins, another some leggins, while someone else would volunteer to fetch some vittles.

"I'd be obliged for a rifle and some powder and shot," said Devlin.

"Perhaps in time," said Fitzpatrick. "You have wronged many people, Devlin. But I take into account the fact that you have come to warn us."

"You believe this lyin' bastard?" asked Briggs, incredulous.

"I'm inclined to, yes. Why would he come here among us, knowing that there are several here present who would like nothing better than a shot at him. You, for one, Briggs." Fitzpatrick paused and glanced at Sky before continuing. "Yes, I believe he is telling the truth."

"Just give me a rifle and I'll go," said Devlin.

"No chance," snapped Briggs. "I'll hold him until McKenzie gets here. This man abandoned his whole brigade and stole plews belonging to the American Fur Company."

"The rightful ownership of those plews," said Zach with a cold smile, "is open to debate."

"Look," said Devlin, "I'm not running away. Give me a rifle so I can head back to the Wind River falls with a fighting chance."

"I don't savvy that," admitted Broken Hand.

"I'm as good as dead," explained Devlin. "If the Blackfeet don't do it, McKenzie, or Briggs here, will. Redcoat has got to make an example of me, to keep the rest of his men from getting any ideas about cheating the company. I understand that. So I'm going to die. But since I am, I want to die fighting. I aim to ride back to Red Claw, and if I get lucky I'll take him with me when I go to hell."

The others were stunned. For a moment no one spoke. Devlin was talking suicide. Retracing his steps to the falls of the Wind River was certain death. Many of the men who heard him make this extraordinary statement were skeptical. Zach Hannah was one of the few who believed he was sincere. He had a hunch Devlin was resigned to his own death. Somehow Coyote knew his hours were numbered. And he wanted to make amends for the things he had done in his life by going after Red Claw.

Devlin wanted to die a hero.

"I came here to warn you," said Devlin. "Now

that's done, and I want to go back and kill as many of those damned Blackfeet as I can."

Fitzpatrick shook his head. "No. You'll stay here as our guest. If you try to make a run for it, Briggs will stop you. Won't you, Briggs?"

"Dead in his tracks," promised Briggs, and he obviously relished an opportunity to prove *his* sincerity.

"I'll take a few men with me to scout the Blackfeet," said Bridger.

"Good," said Fitz. "Meanwhile, we'll prepare to defend ourselves here."

"How long you reckon we have?" asked Shadmore, to no one in particular. He was just wondering aloud.

Everyone else was wondering the same thing.

Chapter 34

The Teton Basin—or, as many trappers were wont to call it, Pierre's Hole—was a perfect place for rendez-vous. At the headwaters of the Snake River, the valley was thirty miles long and in some places half as wide. It was bare of trees except about the lake and along the river and on the shoulders of the mountains. Where the trees stood, conifers on the slopes and cottonwoods in the valley, there were numerous dense thickets of wild plum, creeper, and willow. Presided over by the magnificent Teton Range, it was a picturesque site. The marsh marigold and paint-brush were blooming in the bottomland, while the asters and columbine decorated the high mountain meadows. The meadowlarks and redwing blackbirds darted across the open ground, while the willow thrush whistled from the thickets and the water ou-zels splashed in the lake, diving sometimes to "stroll" along the bottom.

The Hole's only drawback was its proximity to Blackfoot country, but this was unavoidable. In re-cent years the audacious mountain men had been forced to edge ever closer to the lands of that warlike tribe in their search for brown gold. The only prime beaver country left, after a decade of vigorous trapping, was the northern reaches of the Rockies.

The rendezvous had been going on for more than a fortnight, and already several brigades had departed, having traded their plews and stocked up on supplies.

One such brigade was Milton Sublette's.

In its ranks were the likes of Joe Meek and the Iroquois half-breed, Antoine Godin, as well as several Flathead Indians. Sublette had left the rendezvous that morning. They were destined for the Bitterroot Mountains to the north, in the country of the Flatheads and Nez Percés, having been informed by their Indian allies of several secluded valleys there that contained many beaver, and confident that there at least they would be fairly safe from Blackfoot depredation. As the snows came early in the Bitterroots, Sublette had thought it wise to get an early start, so that the brigade would be afforded ample time for the establishment of its winter camp.

As a result, they were blissfully unaware of what had transpired back at the rendezvous. They did not know that the Blackfeet were coming in force to do battle.

Ten miles up the valley from the rendezvous site, they saw a horde of Blackfeet pouring down out of the hills. Sublette's brigade, thirty-six in number, including several women, were caught out in the open.

A few hundred yards away, just beyond effective rifle range, the Blackfeet stopped.

Milton Sublette calculated that there were at least a hundred fifty warriors. They were done up for war. Brandishing their weapons, they yelled defiance at the trappers. The handful of Flatheads in Sublette's party answered with their own taunts. There was no love lost between the two tribes. These Flatheads were ready to die fighting their enemies. They knew very well that they were sorely outnumbered. They knew there was no chance for them. But that didn't bother them much at all.

It bothered Milton Sublette, though, because his wife, Mountain Lamb, the beautiful Snake girl, was with him.

Meek and Godin rode to the head of the column to confer with their booshway.

"I ain't never seen so many Blackfeet all together in one place," admitted Meek. "And I got to say it ain't a very purty sight."

"They are dressed for war," said Godin, his hawkish features graced with a fierce expression. He sounded like he was eager to give the Blackfeet a good fight. Sublette recalled that Godin's father had been slain by Blackfeet, up Canada way. So the breed's hatred burned every bit as deep as that of the Flatheads when it came to the Blackfoot Nation.

"Then why'd they pull up?" queried Meek. "They could run right over us."

"Count your blessings," said Sublette. He turned and called up one of the Flathead scouts. He spoke to the Indian in the man's own tongue. "Go back to Broken Hand. Tell him to bring all the others and come quick."

The Flathead nodded, wheeled his agile Palouse around, and galloped away, like the devil himself was hot on his heels.

And such was the case, because Sublette grimly

watched several of the Blackfeet take off in pursuit of the Flathead.

Sublette wondered what he should do. Stand his ground? Or make a break for the trees along the river about a quarter mile to the west?

He had no way of knowing that these warriors had come from Crooked Knife's village in response to Red Claw's summons. As luck would have it, the message Red Claw had sent had become garbled, and these braves had not known to proceed to the Wind River falls. Instead, they had headed straight for the Teton Basin, and blundered into Sublette's brigade on their way to the site of the rendezvous.

A single Blackfoot warrior ventured forward alone. An arrow's flight closer to the trappers, he checked his prancing pony and raised a pipe over his head, yelling across the wind-rippled grass.

"He wants a palaver?" queried Meek, wondering if his own ears were deceiving him.

"It's a trick," growled Godin.

"Maybe so," said Sublette. He was inclined to agree with the breed. "I reckon it suddenly occurred to them that we could pick off a third of them before they could close up with us. Reckon he hopes to put us off our guard."

The Blackfoot was a young war chief. Godin didn't know him, but the breed could tell he was a big shot because of the eagle feathers in his topknot and the band of quillwork lying across the scarlet Nor'west blanket that draped one buckskin-clad shoulder. That made this brave an aristocrat of sorts among the Blackfeet, the scion of an important family in his village. His father was no doubt an elder who sat in the council.

Godin rode up on one side of the Blackfoot, while his Flathead accomplice rode up on the other. The half-breed spoke fluent Blackfoot. He stuck out his hand, looked the warrior straight in the eye, and smiled disarmingly.

"You have great courage," said Godin.

The Blackfoot took the breed's hand.

"Shame you have to die young," added Godin, and glanced at the Flathead.

Gloating, the Flathead raised his rifle and fired, point-blank, into the Blackfoot's chest.

"Christ!" muttered Sublette, two hundred yards away. "That crazy breed."

"We're done for now," predicted a laconic Joe Meek.

A howl of surprise and outrage rose up from the horde of Blackfeet.

The Flathead spun his pony around and fled back toward the brigade, hanging off the side of the horse to present the smallest possible target as the Blackfeet started shooting. Dozens of rifles spoke. A cloud of white powder smoke wreathed the warriors. Hot lead sizzled in the air around Godin. Miraculously he was unscathed. The breed uttered a triumphant war whoop as the dead Blackfoot slipped off his horse. The agile Godin leaned way out of his saddle and plucked the quillwork band off the corpse. Then he spat on the dead man. Waving the quillwork band overhead, he screamed an obscenity at the Blackfeet, some of whom were riding toward him now, and then turned his horse and galloped back to the brigade.

In a calm, almost resigned way, Milton Sublette dismounted. He drew his hunting knife and cut the girth of his saddle, pulling the rig off the back of his horse. He got a good grip on the reins before slashing his pony's throat. The horse fell, thrashing a moment as its bright red blood splattered the tall green and golden grass. Sublette put a knee on its neck until the animal lay still in death.

"Reckon that means we're gonna stand and fight it out," observed Joe Meek.

"If we win there'll be plenty of Blackfoot ponies wanderin' loose in this valley," said Sublette. "If we lose, I won't need a ride."

The rest of the trappers hurriedly dismounted. They cut the packs of supplies off their packhorses, and some of them killed their saddle horses, while others let their ponies go. They used the dead horses and the packs for concealment. Sublette walked down the line to where Mountain Lamb was loading extra rifles. There was no fear in her eyes, and he admired her courage.

"I want you to stay down behind those packs yonder," he told her.

"I will fight beside my husband."

"Morning Lamb, if anything happened to you . . ."

"If you die, I die also."

"Listen . . ."

"Shoot now," she said stubbornly. "Talk later."

She raised a rifle, took aim, and fired. The recoil staggered her, but one of the oncoming Blackfeet toppled off his galloping pony.

Godin reached the brigade, executed a running dismount, yanked a pistol from his belt, and shot his pony in the head, all in a matter of seconds. He jumped over the carcass and hit the ground on the other side to draw a bead on another Blackfoot with his rifle and pull the trigger.

All along the line rifles and pistols spoke. Dozens of Blackfeet perished. This withering volley halted the charge. The Blackfeet milled, fifty yards shy of the brigade, returning fire. A trapper fell dead. A Flathead died, too. But a second ragged volley from the brigade put the Blackfeet to flight. They did not stop running until they reached the trees, out of effective rifle range. Godin bounced to his feet and screamed epithets at them, holding aloft the quillwork band. But he could not prod them into another rash headlong charge.

"Now what?" Joe Meek wondered aloud.

"Reckon they'll try something else," said Milton Sublette.

He was right.

After a brief conference most of the Blackfeet dismounted. Horse-holders led the ponies deeper into the forest. Some of the warriors climbed up into trees from which they began to snipe at the brigade. Even though the range was too great for accuracy, the trappers had to concern themselves with the possibility that one of the hostiles might make a lucky shot.

Meanwhile, almost a hundred of the warriors moved in on foot. The grass was waist-high, and when they got within range of the trappers' guns, the Indians sank down out of sight, advancing on hands and knees, popping up to fire, then dropping down out of sight to reload and crawl closer. Every now and then a trapper would plug one as he rose up out of the grass.

Meek was quick to realize that this new strategy of the Blackfeet would succeed. Most of them would reach the brigade alive. A war whoop for a signal, and then they would rise up as one and rush the trappers. With a two-to-one advantage, they would likely win the hand-to-hand combat that would follow.

"I don't like the way this looks," Sublette confessed, as if reading Meek's mind.

Hunkered down behind his pack, Meek tested the wind, wetting a finger and then holding it up.

"I got an idea," he said.

He crawled away, returning a few minutes later with a blanket and a jug of whiskey. He doused the blanket with the panther juice, lit it with a lucifer scratched to life with a thumbnail. Then, dragging the flaming blanket, he ran through the grass parallel to the line held by the brigade behind its makeshift rampart of packs and dead horses. Dried by the hot summer sun, the grass ignited.

Meek covered about fifty yards before a bullet caught him in midstride. Two trappers ventured out to fetch him and carry him back to the line. Milton Sublette ran up to his fallen friend. Meek had been shot in the thigh. He was still conscious.

"I reckon you'll live," said an immensely relieved Sublette.

"Is it working?" mumbled Meek.

Sublette looked around to see the grassfire racing

across the valley, propelled by the wind. The nearest Blackfeet were already up and running for the forest. The trappers picked off a few of them, but the smoke was fast thickening and obscured their vision. Soon a dense black plume was rising into the azure sky, blotting out the sun.

"It's working," he said.

But Joe Meek couldn't hear him. He had passed out.

As Mountain Lamb arrived to tend to the wounded Meek, Milton Sublette stood to survey the field of battle.

The Blackfeet were momentarily stymied. But he knew they wouldn't give up. Before long, the party sent to outflank the brigade would be prowling the woods along the river behind him. It would be hours before help arrived, assuming the Flathead messenger managed to reach the rendezvous site.

Sublette shook his head and stoically checked his weapons, his powder-blackened features grim-set.

He had a hunch it was going to be a long and bloody day.

Chapter 35

It was a long run for the Flathead dispatched by Milton Sublette to get help at the rendezvous site. The three Blackfeet who were after him did not give up. Early on they agreed that their only chance of catching their prey was for one brave to take all three horses, switching from one as it tired to another, and then the third. They made their decisions quickly. Two of the Blackfeet dismounted on the run, having given their reins over to the chosen one.

The strategy worked. The Blackfoot brave was on the last of his horses, having jumped agilely from the back of the second to the third, as they neared the rendezvous site. The Flathead tried to quirt the flagging Palouse beneath him into one last burst of speed. But the horse was bottomed out. It had given all that it had to give.

Off in the distance, on the other side of a wooded spur, the Flathead could see smoke from many fires and knew he was near his goal. Only a little farther. But his foam-flecked horse stumbled. Windbroke and wheezing, it finally went down, its front legs buckling suddenly.

Though he had tried to prepare himself for this

event, the Flathead landed hard. Shaken, he got up slowly. A glance over the shoulder revealed that the Blackfoot was scarcely an arrow's flight away and closing fast.

Seeing his prey unhorsed, the Blackfoot uttered a triumphant cry. Knowing he was near the camp of his enemies, the brave had shoulder-slung his rifle and was now brandishing a tomahawk. A gunshot might bring the mountain men. He would have to kill the Flathead quietly.

The Flathead broke into a run. The lives of his friends in Sublette's brigade depended on him. He refused to give up, though his chances were slim indeed now that he was afoot.

He had lost his rifle in the fall—it lay hidden from view somewhere in the tall grass, and he wasted no time searching for it. Instead, he drew the pistol he carried in his belt. Whirling, he fired at the Blackfoot. The latter was bent low over the neck of his stretched-out horse. The shot went inside.

The Flathead tossed the empty pistol away and kept running. He didn't hold out much hope that the pistol shot would alert the distant camp. There was always a lot of shooting at a rendezvous, most of it done in sport or a drunken spree. It was more likely that no one would give a second thought if they had heard his pistol speak.

The Blackfoot closed quickly. The Flathead felt the earth tremble beneath the thundering hooves of his enemy's horse. He reached for the tomahawk in his belt, even as he said a silent prayer and sent it skyward, alerting his ancestors of his imminent arrival in the next life. If he could just make it around the spur he would be within sight of the camp. Then, even if the Blackfoot killed him, someone would surely see, and the alarm would be raised, and he could die knowing that Sublette's brigade would be rescued. That was all that mattered.

But it was not to be. At the last possible second he whirled, to see the Blackfoot raising his war hatchet for the killing blow.

A rifle shot . . .

The Blackfoot's pony died in midstride, somersaulting, hurling its rider twenty feet. A flailing hoof caught the Flathead a glancing blow to the head. For an instant he feared that the dying horse would fall on top of him. He stumbled out of the way, dropped to hands and knees, stunned, blinded by the blood pouring from the ugly gash at his temple.

The Blackfoot, too, was dazed, but he got up and looked around for his prey.

He did not see the Flathead in the tall grass. But he did see Jubal Wilkes, running straight at him.

The young frontiersman, erstwhile member of Zach Hannah's celebrated, if ill-fated, brigade, was charging out of the woods blanketing the spur. He cast aside his empty rifle as he ran, drawing his own tomahawk.

The Blackfoot let loose with a fearsome war cry and rushed to meet him, swinging his war hatchet at the trapper's skull. Jubal ducked under and planted his tomahawk in the Blackfoot's belly, ripping sideways. The warrior's impetus carried him past Jubal. He died on his feet, his insides spilling out of the gaping hole in his belly.

Bloody tomahawk still in hand, Jubal ran to the Flathead.

"You ride with Sublette," said Wilkes, recognizing the Indian.

The Flathead nodded. He was fighting to stay conscious.

"Blackfeet," he gasped. "Many Blackfeet . . ."

He lost the fight, and passed out.

Jubal Wilkes hoisted the Indian onto a broad shoulder and set out at a ground-eating lope for the nearby rendezvous.

The hue and cry lured Zach Hannah from his lodge. The entire Crow encampment was in a turmoil. Warriors were hastily arming themselves and picking out their ponies as the herd guards drove the cavalcade in. Through this melee came Shadmore at a lope.

"What in the blue blazes is goin' on?" asked the old leatherstocking.

"Blackfeet would be my guess," replied Zach.

Fitzpatrick appeared on a prancing pony.

"Grab your guns, boys," cried Broken Hand. "The Blackfeet have attacked Milton Sublette's brigade some miles up the valley."

"How many Injuns?" asked Shadmore.

Fitz shook his head. "Don't know for sure. Milt sent a Flathead scout back with the word. He's bad hurt. Jube Wilkes saved his bacon and kilt a Blackfoot buck in the process. Must be Red Claw's bunch, though, seein' as how they all met up at the Wind River falls."

Broken Hand moved on. Shadmore went off to

fetch some horses. Zach turned to find Morning Sky, with little Jacob clinging to her leg, standing there.

"I was hoping we'd miss this fight," said Zach. "But it looks like Oregon will have to wait."

Morning Sky nodded bravely. She ducked back into the lodge.

"I want to go with you, Father," said Jacob earnestly. "I'm old enough to fight those durned old Blackfeet."

Zach knelt and put a hand on the boy's shoulder.

"No, son. I want you to stay here and look out for your mother. I'd feel a lot better knowing you're doing that."

Sky emerged from the lodge, bearing his Hawken rifle and cartridge pouch.

"I have to go," said Zach.

"I know."

"I'll be back."

She nodded, rose on tiptoe to kiss him gently, her lips barely brushing his. Then she turned and hastened little Jacob back into the lodge, wanting to be out of her husband's sight before her composure cracked.

Shadmore returned in short order with the horses.

"This doesn't feel right, Shad," said Zach as he mounted up.

"How's that?"

"All of us charging off like this and leaving the camp undefended."

Shadmore shook his head. "Ain't that way atall. Fitz is no fool. He knows he cain't keep the Crows and Nez Percés from goin' after them Blackfeet, but he's got several brigades hangin' back, about sixty, seventy men in all."

Zach scanned the wooded slopes of the foothills with worried eyes. Shadmore could tell that he was torn between going to the aid of his friends and colleagues, and staying here to protect his family in case Fitzpatrick was wrong, and the Indians attacking Sublette's brigade were not the main body of Blackfeet.

Shadmore dismounted.

"What are you doing?" asked Zach.

"I'm stayin' put. What's it look like? I'm a little long in the tooth to go gallivantin' around the countryside lookin' for a ruckus, anyhow. So you go on ahead and plug one of them Blackfoot rascals for me, iffen you get the chance."

"I'll be back soon."

"You're allus sayin' that, scout. Then you go off and disappear for months. Well, you'd better come back this time, Zach Hannah, 'cause you got me lookin' forward to seein' that Oregon country."

Milt Sublette and his brigade were catching hell from both sides.

About forty Blackfoot warriors had slipped into the woods along the river, having circled around to catch the trappers in a crossfire. Meanwhile, those who had fled when confronted by the grass fire conceived by Joe Meek were preparing to charge again.

The fire had burned clear to the wooded slope from whence the Blackfeet had first come. Now it was leaping through the undergrowth beneath the trees, and fingers of flame licked at the trunks of the stately conifers.

The Blackfeet had moved south of the fire and re-mounted. The fire had left scorched stubble where once lush grass had grown. There was now no cover for the Blackfeet—they had to attack on horseback if they wanted to close with their enemies. Seventy strong, they spent some time getting up the nerve, expecting to run into another devastating volley of rifle fire from the hawk-eyed mountain men and their Flathead allies, bracing themselves to endure heavy casualties, but determined to spill the blood of the white men.

They had no way of knowing that Sublette and his men were running perilously low on ammunition.

Seeing the Blackfeet massing for an assault, Milt Sublette figured the end was near. For hours he and his men had been trading lead with the hostiles. All along the line cartridge pouches were nearly empty.

Sublette crawled to where Mountain Lamb was watching over the wounded and still-unconscious Joe Meek. They were sheltered by a pair of laden pack saddles turned up on their ends. Along the way, Sublette paused to confiscate the pistol of a dead trapper. Five of his men were dead, twice that many wounded. Finding the pistol loaded and primed, Sublette moved on.

Reaching his wife and friend, Sublette handed one of the pistols to Mountain Lamb.

"We can't let him fall into their hands," he told her.

Mountain Lamb gave him a long, impassive look.

That remark told her all she needed to know. It was hopeless. They were all going to die.

She touched the butt of the pistol in his belt. "Is that for me?" she asked calmly.

Sublette looked quickly away, his eyes burning with tears. He did not answer.

With bloodcurdling yells, the mounted Blackfeet charged across the fire-blackened ground.

At that moment a hundred trappers led by Fitzpatrick and Zach Hannah, joined by a hundred fifty Crow and Nez Percé braves, appeared on the scene.

The Crows and Nez Percés hurled themselves at the charging Blackfeet. The two Indian forces collided violently in a din of crashing rifles, war cries, and screaming horses. They fought a brief but fierce pitched battle. Outnumbered two-to-one, the Blackfeet were overwhelmed. None were spared. Only a few managed to break out of the melee to take flight, pursued by dozens of their relentless foes.

Meanwhile, Fitzpatrick and the mountain men plunged headlong into the cottonwoods along the river to roust the Blackfeet hidden there.

Zach was with them. A Blackfoot warrior burst out of a willow thicket, wielding a tomahawk, and launched himself at the mounted frontiersman. Zach swung his Hawken down and fired. The warrior's face dissolved in a bloody mist. The impact of the bullet slammed him into the ground.

Another warrior appeared, down at the river's edge. He raised his rifle and fired. The bullet missed Zach by inches. Dropping the empty Hawken, Zach kicked his horse forward and launched himself from the saddle, carrying the Blackfoot into the river. They broke the surface grappling. Zach's knife flashed briefly in the sunlight as they went under again. Only Zach came up a second time. He trudged back to the bank and threw a quick look downriver, to see the corpse of the Blackfoot bob to the surface and roll slowly over.

Retrieving his rifle, Zach reloaded. Only sporadic gunfire reached his ears. The fight was winding down. Catching up his horse, he led it out of the thicket and back to the line Sublette and his colleagues had held all day. Beyond that line, the Crows were busy scavenging the field of battle, taking weapons and scalps from the dead Blackfeet littering the charred ground. Zach spotted the half-breed, Godin, out there lending them a hand in this gory business. The Nez Percés did not partake in this looting and scalp-taking. They quietly gathered their dead.

Fitzpatrick was standing with Milton Sublette. Broken Hand was grinning. Sublette simply looked relieved.

"I thought we were gone beaver for sure," admitted Sublette.

"We whupped 'em good, Zach!" crowed Fitzpatrick.

But Zach was scowling. "This wasn't Red Claw's bunch."

"How do you know?"

"I know!" yelled Zach, furious. "This wasn't the main body. If anything, it was a ruse to get us away from the camp."

He leapt aboard his horse.

"Wait!" said Broken Hand. "I'll get the men together and . . ."

"Hurry!" Zach kicked his horse into a leaping gallop.

Deer Stalker loomed in his path, triumphantly holding a handful of scalps aloft. "A great victory!" exclaimed the Absaroka warrior.

"The fight's just begun!" shouted Zach as he galloped past. "If you want Red Claw's scalp, follow me!"

And he was gone, heading south for the rendezvous site, praying—for Morning Sky's sake, and little Jacob's—that he wasn't too late.

Chapter 36

When Red Claw saw the trappers and their Indian allies pour out of the rendezvous encampment on their way to rescue Milton Sublette's beleaguered brigade, he knew he had been blessed by the spirits and was destined to become a great hero of the Blackfoot Nation.

He was not by nature a cautious man, but in this case he exercised all due caution. Everything—his reputation most of all—depended on success. So he sent a couple of scouts to make sure that the Crows, the Nez Percés, and the mountain men departing the camp in such haste were not going to be coming back anytime soon.

Red Claw was unaware of the battle being waged at the northern end of the valley. He had waited as long as he could at the falls of the Wind River for the warriors from Crooked Knife's village. Over two hundred warriors had joined him at the falls from other villages, but none from Crooked Knife's.

He did not know that Devlin had warned the mountain men. As fate would have it, he and his sixty followers had lost Coyote's trail on the way to the Wind River. Red Claw had assumed that Coyote had done what he always did—run away.

But this bad luck was more than offset by a stroke of good fortune for Red Claw: advancing on Pierre's Hole, he had completely missed Bridger's small scouting party, on its way to the falls to locate the Blackfeet.

The braves Red Claw sent out to shadow Fitzpatrick and Zach Hannah as they raced to rescue Milton Sublette ventured far enough to hear the distant sounds of battle. They reported this to Red Claw, who was quite capable of putting two and two together. The warriors of Crooked Knife's village had bypassed the rendezvous at the falls. Red Claw's only error was in surmising that they had done so intentionally, in hopes of stealing the glory that rightfully belonged to him.

Eager to acquire his just due, Red Claw led his two hundred fifty warriors down into the valley to attack the rendezvous site.

He gave his followers one order.

Spare no one.

They struck without warning.

The first inkling Devlin had that something was wrong was a smattering of rifle fire at the edge of the encampment. He was stretched out on a blanket in the shade of a lean-to. Clad now in borrowed buckskins, his hands were tied with a strip of rawhide. Being bound had long ago ceased to be a novelty for him, having experienced iron shackles while in the Santa Fe jail, then rawhide bindings all the way up to Fort Union as Zach Hannah's prisoner, and again as the prisoner of the Blackfeet after that.

Briggs, the American Fur Company booshway, was sitting cross-legged nearby, smoking a pipe, a rifle laid across his knees. He had curtly refused Devlin a smoke, a meal, and any conversation. Devlin counted himself lucky to have some clothes and a little shade from the hot sun.

When the shooting started, Briggs shot to his feet. Devlin sat up sharply.

"Cut me loose, Briggs."

"Shuddup."

Above the crackle of gunfire Devlin distinctly heard shrill war cries, and his blood ran cold. He clambered to his feet.

"Cut me loose!" he rasped. "The Blackfeet are here, you fool."

Briggs drove the stock of his rifle into Devlin's midsection, then into his face. Devlin fell backward. The lean-to, a buffalo hide stretched on a willow frame and propped up on two stout poles, collapsed on top of him.

"Don't be callin' me a fool," growled Briggs, truculent.

Thundering hoofbeats caused him to turn. A dozen Blackfeet were sweeping toward him. He raised his rifle, aimed, and fired in one quick, smooth motion. A Blackfoot somersaulted over the haunches of his pony. Briggs drew his pistol and shot a second off his horse. Then he brandished a tomahawk and hurled it, burying the hatchet in the chest of a third. He didn't give a thought to turning tail.

He was, after all, a mountain man, and it would be a cold day in hell before he ran from anything.

So he stood his ground—and died, riddled with bullets, as the Blackfoot tide washed over him.

One brave dismounted, drawing a knife. He made quick work of scalping Briggs. Vaulting back aboard his pony, he uttered a piercing yell of triumph and rode on in search of fresh prey, completely unaware that Devlin lay unconscious beneath the collapsed lean-to.

The warrior's shrill cry pierced Devlin's brain. He stirred, crawling out from under the suffocating buffalo hide. Seeing Briggs sprawled on the blood-soaked ground brought him to his senses plenty quick. Using the knife of the dead man, he managed to cut the rawhide on his wrists, gripping the knife between his knees and running the stubborn bindings back and forth across the cutting edge of the blade.

The Blackfoot who had taken Briggs's scalp had not bothered confiscating the mountain man's rifle or pistol. Time enough later for the looting. So Devlin took rifle, shot pouch, pistol, knife. He crouched there for a moment, looking around.

There was sporadic gunfire coming from all directions. The Blackfeet were sweeping through the camp without rhyme or reason, killing anyone in their path, setting fire to some of the tepees and lean-tos. Smoke from the fires drifted across the camp, obscuring Devlin's vision. But he knew that the smoke and the confusion worked in his favor.

A riderless horse loped by. With a running leap he managed to gain its back. Without bridle and reins, he had to use the pony's mane to try to steer the animal in the direction he wanted to go.

His destination was the encampment of the Absaroka Crows. He was confident that there he would find his son and Morning Sky.

Red Claw lost control of his warriors the moment they struck the camp. He kept about thirty of them together and rode into the Crow camp. Old men, women, and children were cut down without mercy. There were few able-bodied warriors left—almost all of them had accompanied Fitzpatrick and Zach Hannah. Every lodge was set ablaze.

Shadmore acted quickly. When the first shots were fired he knew exactly what was happening—and exactly what he had to do. His pony was tied in front of Sky's lodge. He got her and the boy aboard and tried to lead them out of the camp. The Blackfoot attack was coming from the east. The woods along the river lay to the west, across a quarter mile of open ground. The old leatherstocking realized that their only chance lay in reaching the cover of the woods unseen. He realized, too, that their chances were very slim.

He was right about that. An anxious backward glance revealed four Blackfeet galloping after them. Shadmore made a snap decision. He threw the reins to Sky and whacked the horse on the rump with his hat.

"Ride for the timber, gal!" he yelled.

"Shad, no!"

But the pony lunged into a gallop, and Sky realized that for Jacob's sake she had to keep going—had to leave Shadmore behind.

The old leatherstocking grimly raised his rifle and drew a bead on one of the oncoming Blackfeet. A warrior fired at him, and the bullet buzzed past Shad's ear. He did not flinch, squeezed the trigger, and saw one of the warriors fall. Shadmore pulled his pistol. Another Blackfoot got off a shot. The bullet slammed into Shad's leg, almost knocking him down. Somehow he stayed on his feet, waiting until the Indians were closer before discharging the pistol. A second warrior slipped from his horse.

Then the remaining two were upon him. One fired at point-blank range—and missed. The other struck with a tomahawk—and didn't miss. As they galloped on, Shadmore reeled and crumpled.

Reaching the edge of the trees, Sky slid off the horse and handed the reins to little Jacob.

"Run, Jacob!"

"Father said not to leave you!"

"Go!" cried Morning Sky. "Hide!"

She slapped the horse, and it cantered off into the trees. Seeking cover behind a cottonwood, she cocked the pistol she had had the foresight to bring with her. It was the weapon Zach had given her many years ago, the first time he had left her, to accompany the Arikara Campaign.

"Shad," she said softly, seeing that the old leatherstocking had fallen.

When the Blackfeet were nearly upon her she steeled herself and stepped out from behind the tree to fire the pistol, killing one of the Indians. The other warrior executed a running dismount and lunged at her, tomahawk raised, his painted face a snarling rictus of hate. Sky defiantly stood her ground, ready to meet her fate.

Devlin shot the Blackfoot right through the heart.

Stunned, Sky looked up from the corpse at her feet as Coyote steered his horse closer.

He held out a hand.

"Get on behind me, Sky. We've got to make a run for it."

She did not hesitate. But no sooner was she astride the horse than a rifle spoke. The horse jumped, shuddered violently, and then crashed to the ground, shot through the heart.

Devlin jumped clear, and helped Sky to her feet. He looked toward the camp. A solitary warrior was headed straight for them, reloading as he steered his pony with his knees.

It was Red Claw.

"Are you hurt?" Devlin asked Sky.

She shook her head. The fall had stunned her, but nothing was broken.

"Come on." He ran, pulling her along behind him, plunging deeper into the woods.

They reached a small clearing and found little Jacob there, sawing on the reins with all his might to stop the horse beneath him. Devlin picked Sky up and literally threw her on the back of the pony behind the boy.

"Who are you?" asked little Jacob.

Devlin glanced at Sky.

He saw the fear in her eyes. It was not fear of the Blackfeet, or fear of death, but rather of what he would say in response to the boy's query.

Devlin's smile was wistful.

"I'm a friend of your father's," he replied.

The bullet caught him squarely between the shoulder blades. The impact threw him against the startled horse, which jumped sideways. Falling, Devlin clutched blindly at Sky's leg. She reached for his hand. But then his grip loosened in death, and he fell, and an anguished cry escaped Sky's lips.

For the second time in a matter of minutes she saw death bearing down on her and her son.

Ridding himself of his empty rifle, Red Claw flourished his war hatchet as he rode straight at them.

Without warning another rider burst into the clearing. His horse collided with the Blackfoot's broadside. Both horses went down. Both men rolled clear and came up unharmed. The horses got up and trotted off. Charging his adversary, Red Claw brought the hatchet down hard enough to cleave Zach Hannah from scalp to sternum. But Zach's hand closed on the warrior's arm like an iron vise. Surprise flashed across Red Claw's face as he felt the cold steel of Zach's knife. Zach twisted the blade and ripped upward to the rib cage. The tip of the knife pierced Red Claw's heart, and the warrior died instantly. Zach let go of the knife and stepped away, letting the dead man fall.

He turned and caught Morning Sky as she flew into his arms. Holding her tight, he looked bleakly at Devlin's body.

"He saved my life," said Sky.

reloaded the Hawken, and headed for the edge of the woods, leaving the dead to lie as they had fallen.

They found Shadmore propped up against a tree, pale and bloody. It was as far as he had managed to get. Sky's heart sang with joy.

"I thought you were dead!" she cried.

"Dead? Wagh! I ain't ready to cross the river just yet, punkin. Got my heart set on seein' this Oregon country, don't you know."

Zach checked the old leatherstocking's wounds. The Blackfoot tomahawk had broken his collarbone. The bullet was still in his leg, and would have to be cut out. But Shad would live.

A crash of gunfire drew his attention to the rendezvous encampment, a quarter mile away across the tall grass. Fitzpatrick and his mountain men, with the Crow and Nez Percé warriors, had arrived on the scene. Enraged by the sight of their slaughtered friends and families, they swept inexorably through the camp beneath the smoke-blackened sky, driving the Blackfeet before them and showing no mercy. Only a handful of the Blackfeet managed to escape the bloodbath.

Zach Hannah watched the killing from the edge of the woods. His fight was over. And as the bloodred sun sank behind the snow-clad peaks, and cool purple shadows reached for him across the valley's floor, and the sounds of the battle dwindled, he looked west, thinking about the true wonders that lay in store for him and his beyond the high country.

Ⓢ SIGNET

THE OLD WEST COMES ALIVE
IN NOVELS BY PAUL HAWKINS

☐ **THE LEGEND OF BEN TREE** A hero among heroes in a great epic saga of the American West. In the conquered frontier of 1856, Ben Tree is caught between the worlds of the white man and the Indian. He's the last of the mountain men and the first of the gunslingers. (176677—$4.50)

☐ **THE VISION OF BENJAMIN ONE FEATHER** In a great storyteller's glorious saga of the West, a man's quest to make a dream come true leads him to seek the meaning of the vision that comes to him with manhood. (177053—$4.50)

☐ **WHITE MOON TREE** White Moon Tree was far different from either his father or brother.... A rancher and a gambler, ready to stake all on a draw of a card or a gun.... A beautiful orphaned girl asks White Moon Tree to avenge her father's murder at the hands of a savage band ... He took on odds few men would dare in a game of guts and glory. (178289—$4.50)

*Prices slightly higher in Canada

Buy them at your local bookstore or use this convenient coupon for ordering.

PENGUIN USA
P.O. Box 999 — Dept. #17109
Bergenfield, New Jersey 07621

Please send me the books I have checked above.
I am enclosing $_____ (please add $2.00 to cover postage and handling). Send check or money order (no cash or C.O.D.'s) or charge by Mastercard or VISA (with a $15.00 minimum). Prices and numbers are subject to change without notice.

Card #_____ Exp. Date _____
Signature_____
Name_____
Address_____
City _____ State _____ Zip Code _____

For faster service when ordering by credit card call **1-800-253-6476**

Allow a minimum of 4-6 weeks for delivery. This offer is subject to change without notice.

Ⓢ SIGNET

GREAT MILITARY FICTION
BY DON BENDELL

☐ **CHIEF OF SCOUTS** Rich with the passion and adventure of real history, this novel of the U.S. Cavalry brings forth a hero, worthy of the finest military fiction, who had to work above the law to uphold justice.   (176901—$4.50)

☐ **COLT** Christopher Columbus Colt, legendary chief of cavalry scouts, was in for the biggest fight of his life—forced to lead an all-black U.S. Cavalry unit on a suicide mission. And even if the Chief of Scouts could conquer his own doubts, he would still have to reckon with two names that struck fear into the hearts of every frontier man: Victorio and Geronimo, renegade Apache chiefs who led their warriors on a bloody trail.   (178300—$4.50)

☐ **HORSE SOLDIERS** In the embattled Oregon territory, Christopher Columbus Colt was a wanted man. General O.O. "One-Armed" Howard, commanding the U.S. Cavalry, wanted this legendary scout to guide his forces in his campaign to break the power and take the lands of the proud Nez Perce. The tactical genius, Nez Perce Chief Joseph needed Colt as an ally in this last ditch face-off. And only Colt can decide which side to fight on . . .   (177207—$4.99)

*Prices slightly higher in Canada

___

Buy them at your local bookstore or use this convenient coupon for ordering.

PENGUIN USA
P.O. Box 999 — Dept. #17109
Bergenfield, New Jersey 07621

Please send me the books I have checked above.
I am enclosing $_____ (please add $2.00 to cover postage and handling). Send check or money order (no cash or C.O.D.'s) or charge by Mastercard or VISA (with a $15.00 minimum). Prices and numbers are subject to change without notice.

Card #_____ Exp. Date _____
Signature_____
Name_____
Address_____
City _____ State _____ Zip Code _____

For faster service when ordering by credit card call **1-800-253-6476**

Allow a minimum of 4-6 weeks for delivery. This offer is subject to change without notice.

∅ SIGNET   ⬤ ONYX   (0451)

RIVETING AMERICAN SAGAS

☐ **CONQUERING HORSE by Frederick Manfred.** A magnificent saga of the West—
before the white man came. "Offers deep insight into the mind of the Indian ...
as exciting and rewarding and dramatic as the country it describes."—*Chicago
Tribune*
(087399—$4.50)

☐ **FRANKLIN'S CROSSING by Clay Reynolds.** This is the searing and sweeping epic of
America's historic passage west. "Gritty realism on the 1870s Texas frontier ...
expertly crafted, very moving ... this is the way it must have been ... lingers in
the memory long after the last page has been turned."—*Dallas Morning News*
(175549—$5.99)

☐ **CHIEF OF SCOUTS by Don Bendell.** Rich with the passion and adventure of real
history, this novel of the U.S. Cavalry brings forth a hero, worthy of the finest
military fiction, who had to work above the law to uphold justice.
(176901—$4.50)

☐ **HIGH COUNTRY by Jason Manning.** A young man in virgin land. A magnificent
saga live with the courage, challenge, danger, and adventure of the American
past.
(176804—$4.50)

Price slightly higher in Canada

Buy them at your local bookstore or use this convenient coupon for ordering.

PENGUIN USA
P.O. Box 999 – Dept. #17109
Bergenfield, New Jersey 07621

Please send me the books I have checked above.
I am enclosing $_____ (please add $2.00 to cover postage and handling).
Send check or money order (no cash or C.O.D.'s) or charge by Mastercard or
VISA (with a $15.00 minimum). Prices and numbers are subject to change without
notice.

Card # _____ Exp. Date _____
Signature_____
Name_____
Address_____
City _____ State _____ Zip Code _____

For faster service when ordering by credit card call **1-800-253-6476**

Allow a minimum of 4-6 weeks for delivery. This offer is subject to change without notice.